HAVE Mercy

Cover Design by Angela Haddon

Published by Diana Road Books

Edgewater, Colorado

BENNETT SECURITY

6

HANNAH SHIELD

Chapter One

Ruby Whitestone heard the pitter-patter of tiny feet. She set down the bottles of hair color she'd been organizing on the counter.

"Haley? What are you up to?"

There was more running, and then a giggle. Ruby couldn't even be annoyed that her daughter had somehow escaped from the pack and play—again. The girl was a mini-Houdini.

But a salon was no place for an eighteen-month-old to explore. All the hair chemicals and curling irons. The possible dangers gave Ruby hives whenever she had to bring Haley in with her, which happened too often lately.

It was after closing time, and the other stylists were gone, but that just meant fewer eyes keeping watch.

"Where are you, bug?"

Ruby followed the giggles until she spied two little shoes hiding beneath a salon chair. She looked behind it.

"Boo, Mama!" Haley clapped her hands.

Ruby wanted to smile and laugh, because it was freaking adorable, but she didn't want to encourage this game of hide and seek.

The front door opened with a whoosh of street noise. The

salon was located on Ocean Lane, just steps away from the beach, set amidst the hippest commercial block in all of West Oaks.

"Hey, anybody home?" Chase Collins's smooth voice boomed across the salon.

"We're over here," Ruby called out.

"Did somebody escape her pack and play again?"

"You know it." She bent over to pick up her daughter. "Mommy said no, Haley. You have to stay put when we're in the salon. It's not safe." Even though, silently, she praised her daughter for her independent spirit. Ruby wanted to raise a girl who was just as loud and unapologetic as she was.

Haley frowned, and Ruby held her baby tight, closing her eyes for a brief moment as fear settled around her heart. She couldn't lose this precious girl. But her fear had little to do with any of the dangers around her workplace, and everything to do with those text messages on her phone.

We need to talk.

Some of the worst words anyone could say. Especially when they came from your loser, deadbeat ex-boyfriend.

Chase strode toward them in his dark blue police uniform. His hair was buzzed at the sides, slightly longer on top. Ruby had known him for over a year, but she'd seen older pictures of him on his social media. He'd had the exact same haircut back when he'd been a Marine. Chase was reliable that way.

"Got here as soon as I could," he said.

"Thank you so much for this. You're a lifesaver."

"Happy to do it."

Ruby handed over Haley, who immediately grabbed hold of his nose. "Guncle Chay-Chay."

"Hi to you too, princess." His voice sounded nasally.

"Don't call her princess. You're setting up the expectation that a man will swoop in to save her."

"Like I'm doing for you right now?"

Ruby scoffed. "Hardly. I appreciate the babysitting. But I'm no princess."

Chase smirked. Haley's laughter turned to delighted shrieks as he tickled her stomach.

"Shouldn't she want a significant other who treats her like a princess?" Chase asked. "Who spoils her and takes care of her?"

"You mean, who tries to control her?"

Chase shook his head. "Not what I said. Is somebody grumpy today?"

"No, just not in the mood for you to poke at me. You're worse than Devon." Her older brother, who happened to be Chase's best friend.

"Why? Something wrong?" His ice-blue eyes were studying her, head tilted. Of course, he'd picked up on her anxiety. Chase was obnoxiously perceptive sometimes.

"Nope. I just have a thing, and Mrs. Murtree was sick again." She looked past his shoulder and saw her after-hours appointment arriving. "I'm meeting with Lana to go over things for the wedding. *Such* a demanding client."

Lana Marchetti came through the door, followed by Aurora Bennett.

"Haley's here!" Aurora squealed, dashing over to give the baby a kiss.

"Hey, I'm here too," Chase said.

"Hi, Chase. Didn't mean to leave you out." Aurora kissed his cheek.

There were lots of hugs and more kisses as they all greeted one another.

"Lana, Ruby said you're being a total Bridezilla." Chase winked.

"Well, it's supposed to be *my day*." Lana poised one hand on her hip and pouted, which was all the more ridiculous because she was one of the most no-nonsense women Ruby had ever met. Lana worked in the West Oaks District Attorney's Office prosecuting criminals.

Aurora huffed, making a lock of blond hair fly away from her forehead. "I wish you *would* be more opinionated about this event. It's not easy to plan a wedding when the bride's too busy working to make any decisions."

Lana wrapped an arm around Aurora. "I trust you. You're the best event planner I know."

"I'm the *only* event planner you know. Everybody else is a lawyer or a cop or a bodyguard."

"Or a stylist," Ruby chimed in. She grabbed the diaper bag and handed it to Chase. "I should be home by eight. Can you make sure she's had dinner and some storytime? And don't let her trick you into more than one Jell-O cup. It's gross, but she loves that stuff. Mom gave her the kind with artificial coloring last week, and she barfed green."

"The usual. I got it."

Ruby knew he did. Chase was an unofficial part of the Whitestone family. A fixture in Haley's life, and in Ruby's. But this was the over-protective mom in her talking.

"Have fun with Gunkle Chay-Chay. Be wise." She liked telling her daughter to be wise, instead of being "good." Being good didn't protect a girl from getting stepped all over and abandoned. Neither did being "bad," as Ruby could tell from personal experience. She wished she'd been wiser. About so many damned things.

Haley and Chase both waved as he walked out the door. Ruby watched them get into Chase's truck, which already had a spare car seat inside it.

There goes my heart, she thought.

"Speaking of weddings," Lana said. "When are you going to marry that one?"

"Who, Chase?" Ruby made a face, and Aurora groaned.

"We're not supposed to tease her about Chase anymore, L," Aurora said. "They're just friends."

"Right. And Max and I were just 'friends' before we got together."

Time for a subject change. Ruby walked over to her chair and pointed at it. "Sit down, Bridezilla. We have work to do."

In about a month, Lana would marry Max Bennett, the

owner of Bennett Security. They'd been in love but apart for a million years or something, so their engagement had been relatively short. Ruby was doing the hair and makeup for both the bride and Aurora—her brother Devon's girlfriend—who'd be the maid of honor.

In the past, Aurora and Devon had both pestered Ruby about her closeness with Chase. But she truly felt nothing for him but friendship. And a hell of a lot of gratitude for being an honorary uncle to her daughter.

Chase was a wonderful guy, even if he pulled the annoying big brother routine on her sometimes. She could always count on him to step up. But when it came to attraction, he wasn't Ruby's type. He was a muscular jock. A Prince Charming who'd make some princess happy one day.

Ruby tended to go for messier, rougher, tattooed guys. Unpredictable guys. Because she had a rebellious streak like that. A streak the rest of her family didn't even know about, which went along with the trail of star tattoos on her hip. Straight-laced guys didn't do it for her.

Especially not military guys. Or cops. And Chase was both.

"Did you bring the veil?"

Lana nodded, holding up a bag.

They spent the next hour planning out Lana and Aurora's hair and makeup for the big day.

These were some of the people Ruby loved most in the world. As she set the veil on Lana's head, laughing and joking with her friends, Ruby wished she could tell them what was going on.

But Mickey was her mess. Her problem. She was going to fix it.

I'm Haley's father, he'd texted. *I have rights.*

Like hell he did.

If that asswipe thought he could waltz into their lives after abandoning them when Ruby was pregnant, he had another thing coming.

RUBY PARKED her car in front of the apartment building, double-checking the address against the one in Mickey's last text.

She pushed out a breath. This would be the first time seeing him in almost two years. Not since she'd told him she was pregnant. And if she'd had her way, she'd have gone a whole lot longer without seeing his face.

Mickey Waverley lived in Los Angeles, but he'd rented this apartment in West Oaks. *To prove I'm serious*, he'd said in his text.

After a quick check of her makeup in the rearview mirror, she got out of the car. It was stupid how much care she'd taken when she'd dressed that morning. Ruby had worn a deep purple, off-the-shoulder top and straight-legged jeans. Earrings made of tiny strips of wood dangled to either side of her neck, a gift she'd bought herself from a fair for local artisans.

But she wanted to prove to Mickey that she was doing great without him. She'd never asked for money, though his family was swimming in it. Never asked for a damn thing.

Mickey wanted some sort of custody of Haley. He'd claimed he was sorry for being absent from Haley's life and wanted to make up for it. But with his family's money, he could hire the best lawyers. How was Ruby ever going to compete with that?

Her brother had already nearly worked himself into the ground trying to provide for Ruby and their mother. She couldn't let him do that again. She was proud of being a single mom, and she was strong enough to make it on her own.

But what if joint custody wasn't enough for Mickey?

What if he tried to take Haley away?

Her sandals thudded on the pavement as she walked toward the building. Her heart hammered her ribcage, and she rubbed her chest. *Calm down*, she told herself. If she didn't, she was going to hyperventilate.

A moving truck was parked by the curb, and someone had propped open the building's front door. It was a nice place, with a renovated lobby and mail room. Lots of potted plants. She could smell the ocean, which was just a few blocks away. Only the best for Mickey. The cocky asshole.

Once, she'd thought his confidence was sexy. It was maybe the single thing in the world Mickey had in common with Chase.

Not that she thought of *Chase* as sexy. Ew. That would've been weird.

All this stress was scrambling her brain. Ruby shook off that train of thought.

One of the elevators was blocked off for the movers, so Ruby took the other to the fourth floor.

The elevator dinged, and Ruby stepped out. She passed an open doorway and saw the movers unwrapping plastic from somebody's couch.

The apartment numbers were counting up, which meant Mickey's place would be at the end of the hall. Her anger grew with every step.

How dare he think he could reappear now, after all she'd had to sacrifice to get this far on her own? Leaving all her friends, moving out of LA. Moving in with her mom. Thank goodness Ruby had her own place now, but that was only because she'd kicked ass building up a loyal clientele at the salon.

Her fists clenched. *I am not letting him take Haley away from me.*

She spotted his door. Number 429. It was cracked open, like he was eager to see her. Like he couldn't wait for this little *chat.* Defiant words sprang to Ruby's tongue. She was going to tell him exactly where he could shove his—

There was a grunt inside the apartment. A crash and a heavy thud.

What the hell?

"Mickey?" Her fingers reached out and pushed on the door. It swung open.

Ruby gasped.

Mickey was on the ground, his blond hair plastered to his forehead, arm outstretched as he crawled toward the doorway.

There was a trail of blood behind him on the wooden floor.

His eyes lifted. His hand reached for her, fingers red. Blood poured from his throat. His mouth opened like he was trying to speak, but nothing came out.

Mickey. Oh my god.

Ruby wasn't sure if she'd said that aloud, or just in her head. She rushed forward and knelt. Mickey's hand landed on her wrist. His eyes pleaded.

"It's okay. Hold on." Quickly, she turned him over, trying to push her hands over the wounds, but there was too much. Just too much. "I'll—I'll get something to stop the bleeding. It's going to be okay."

Ruby looked around for a kitchen. She needed a towel. There was a doorway to the right, and she started toward it.

Then a chill of terror ran through her body.

There was someone in that room, hiding behind the open door.

An eye, watching her through the crack.

Oh, god. No. Get out. Get out.

Ruby's pulse rushed in her ears. Her feet turned and took her out of the apartment. She wanted to scream and run, but it was like her brain wasn't fully attached to the rest of her anymore.

It was like being inside of a nightmare. Totally surreal.

She reached the apartment with the movers and walked inside, shutting the door behind her. Ruby set the lock and fixed the chain into place.

"Please. I need help." Her voice sounded strange. Far calmer than she felt.

A tall guy in a T-shirt and shorts looked over, then did a double take. "Shit! What happened?"

"Mickey's hurt. Call 911. The police." The guy was just staring at her, so she said it again. "Call the police."

"Okay. Okay." He got out his phone and dialed. But he didn't take his eyes off her.

Ruby looked down, trying to see what he was seeing.

Her hands were covered in red. Red on the knees of her jeans.

She felt her eyes roll back, and everything turned dark, and she was falling.

Chapter Two

"Where did Haley go?"

This was one of her favorite games. Run and hide from Uncle Chase. Especially when he'd only been looking at his phone for like *half a second* and then, boom—she took off and made him look negligent.

"Is Haley in the kitchen?" Chase glanced behind the island. "Mama's going to be home any minute." It was after eight already.

He heard a giggle and followed it to the hall closet. Haley was crouched down under the shelf.

And the smell hit him. *Dang*. His eyes watered, but he held back any comments. Didn't want to make the kid self-conscious about bodily functions. "Let's get that diaper changed." Haley tried to wriggle out of his grasp, but he held onto her. "Nope, some things just gotta be done."

There was a knock at the apartment's front door. Was that Ruby? Did she forget her keys?

Holding the stinky toddler under his arm, Chase went over and opened it.

But it wasn't Ruby. It was Devon, her older brother and Chase's bestie. "Hey, Aurora said you were here with my niece."

Chase stepped aside to let his friend in, then shut the door. "Perfect timing. She's got a present for you." He held up Haley, and Devon gagged.

"Dude, no fu—freaking way. You're the babysitter."

"But you're blood. Her shit shouldn't smell as bad to you."

"Don't say 'shit.' She's going to repeat it."

"You're the one repeating it."

Devon and Aurora lived a few floors up from Ruby. Chase had his own place a couple miles away, but he found himself in this apartment building so often he wondered if he should just move here to join the party.

Chase and Devon had met last year at a local boxing gym. They'd become fast friends, bonding over their shared military background and the close ties of Devon's family to the police community. Devon was now a bodyguard for Bennett Security, and Chase had helped out—unofficially—on multiple situations for that company.

A few times, his friend had even hinted that Chase should quit the force and come to the private sector. But Chase loved his job. He had his eye on the next detective exams, which were coming in a couple months.

Devon pulled back Haley's diaper and peeked inside. His eyes bulged, and he gagged again. "I swear, it's getting worse as she gets older. How does Ruby do this every day?"

"So much for that Army Ranger toughness you're always going on about," Chase said. "Should've been a Marine like me."

"Exactly. You should be great at shoveling sh—crap."

"Fine, dude." Chase rolled his eyes. "God forbid you ever have a kid."

Devon got a weird look on his face. "I'll change the effing diaper." He grabbed Haley around the middle, holding her at arm's length on his way to the changing table.

Chase was going to ask about that look on Devon's face. But then his mind went back to what Devon had said a couple of minutes ago. "Wait, Aurora told you I was with Haley? I thought she was doing some wedding hair thing with Ruby."

"Yeah, she was. But she'd already made it home when I got there." Diaper velcro ripped open, and Devon made a sound of disgust. "Aurora's working on wedding stuff, calling vendors and basically freaking out about every little detail being perfect. Because it's Max and Lana, you know? They're like her parents in some ways."

"Right," Chase said in a monotone. But he wasn't even listening. His brain was still focused on Ruby.

She'd said she'd be home before eight. It wasn't like her to be late. A few minutes was one thing, but now it was 8:15.

He took out his phone and called her. No answer.

Chase went into Haley's room, where Devon had replaced the diaper and was vigorously rubbing his hands with a wet wipe.

"Ruby's late," Chase said. "Did she say anything to you about where she was going tonight?"

"Nope. She doesn't like explaining herself."

"I'm worried."

Devon set Haley by her toys on the floor. "Ruby doesn't want our worries, man. I've learned that the hard way. She used to listen to angsty indie rock in her room when we were kids and always got pissy when I went in there. Only Kellen knew how to talk to her the right way."

Kellen had been Devon's twin. A cop like Chase, but for the LAPD. Kellen had died over two years ago now, and though Chase had never met him, he knew he would've liked the guy.

"And when I tried to cover expenses so she could stay home with Haley," Devon went on, "Ruby hated that, too. She doesn't like people hovering."

"I'm still worried. She's never late."

Devon shrugged. "Maybe she's got a hookup."

"A hookup?" Chase wrinkled his nose. He didn't like the sound of that. "If she had a date, wouldn't she plan to be out later than eight o'clock?"

"Seriously? I doubt Ruby would allow herself an entire

evening for a date. Even if she deserves it. I can't remember the last time she's talked about a guy."

Relief loosened the tension in Chase's shoulders, and then he felt guilty. Ruby did deserve a guy. Someone who'd treat her right, take care of her.

They watched Haley grab a board book and sit down to open it.

"Ruby's not the only one who could use a hookup." Devon elbowed him. "When's the last time you got out there? Every time I turn around, you're subbing in as a babysitter. If it wasn't Ruby we were talking about, I'd think you were trying to impress her."

Chase felt a surge of alarm. Devon was getting a little too close to the truth. "I remember when it was me bugging *you* about being a monk. I don't think you appreciated that."

"Exactly why I'm returning the favor."

"I hook up plenty. I just don't kiss and tell."

Actually, he hadn't been with anyone in months. And he knew why.

Chase had his eye on someone. A certain hair dresser with an infectious laugh, an edgy sense of style. Long, dark curls and stormy blue-gray eyes. A whole lot of personality wrapped in a sexy small frame.

He'd been having these feelings for a while, and he had zero desire to hook up with anyone else. Which sucked because that certain someone clearly had no interest in him. Not as anything more than a friend.

But Devon was right. Chase was in dire need of a new prospect, a one-night distraction, *something*. He loved sex, craved it, and this situation was getting sad. His dick was so fucking needy even his hand was asking for space.

It's not you, man. It's me. Carpal tunnel is imminent.

Would Devon be upset if he knew? Maybe not. Devon had slept with his boss's sister, after all, and he knew better than to pull the over-protective brother card. But that didn't help matters.

If Devon knew about this unrequited obsession, he'd feel sorry for Chase. And he'd tell Aurora because he told her everything. And pretty soon, everybody in West Oaks would know how pathetic Chase was.

Ruby would find out.

What if she thought he was kind to her daughter because of some ulterior motive? Devon had just been joking about him trying to use Haley to impress her. But would Ruby see it that way? Chase didn't want to cheapen the very real affection he felt for that little girl.

No matter what happened, he'd keep on being Haley's honorary uncle, regardless of any romantic inclinations he might feel for her mom.

So he just had to get over it. Maybe getting laid again would help…maybe. Even if the thought of going out sounded like a chore.

As the minutes ticked by, Chase tried not to worry about Ruby. But his eye kept drifting to his watch. He called her number again, but now it wasn't ringing at all. It had been turned off.

Where was she?

Finally, Devon started to worry too. They called Aurora and Lana and were considering driving over to the hair salon to look.

Then Chase's phone rang. He answered without even checking the screen. "Ruby?"

"Chase, it's Shelby."

Madison Shelborne. She was on patrol with Chase at West Oaks PD. One of his closest friends on the force.

He could tell from her voice something was up. "What is it?"

"Ruby Whitestone's down here at the station."

Chase's hand went to his forehead. Devon was watching him closely, holding Haley against his side.

"Is she hurt?" Chase asked.

Devon's eyes bugged.

"I don't think so. She's safe." Shelby was keeping her voice down, like she didn't want to be overheard. "But something's going on. They say she witnessed an attack."

His heart had leaped into his throat, choking him.

"What happened?" Devon whispered. He'd been trying to listen in.

Chase held up his hand. He couldn't concentrate with Devon talking at him, too. "An attack?" he asked Shelby. "Where was this? When?"

"I don't know the details. Just that it happened in an apartment building on the northwest side of town. And they've been holding her in an interview room for a while. A long while."

"Whoa. Wait a second. Are you saying they're considering Ruby a *suspect*?" Chase's mind was spinning.

"I'm not saying anything. I shouldn't be talking to you about this at all. But maybe you should get down here and find out for yourself."

"Yeah. Thanks, Shelby." He ended the call, feeling like he was in a daze.

Devon grabbed his arm. "What the hell is happening? Are they accusing Ruby of something?"

"I don't know." Chase remembered how Ruby had seemed anxious earlier. She'd brushed off his questions, but what if she'd been planning to meet up with someone? What if something bad had happened? The asshole might've tried to hurt her…and she'd defended herself…

Chase saw too much shit in his job. Too much darkness. His mind was going to all sorts of awful places.

He wiped a hand over his face. "I gotta get to the station and find out what's going on."

"Then I'm coming with you. I'll ask Aurora to come down here to stay with Haley."

Chase didn't see how Devon could help, but he wasn't going to say no. He had a really bad feeling about this. "Okay. Let's go."

Chapter Three

Ruby sat in an interview room, shivering and rubbing her arms. She didn't even know how long she'd been in here. Hours? It felt like days.

The room was quiet except for the clicking of a pipe or some kind of machinery. Ruby was alone here with her thoughts.

Was Mickey at the hospital right now? Could he have survived his injuries? Could she have done something more to help him?

Before she'd found him on that apartment floor, Ruby had wished him off the face of the earth. But she'd never wanted something like that to happen. *Never.*

She took a sip of the water bottle they'd left for her, but she didn't really want it. She only wanted her daughter. Wanted to go home.

Why the heck was this taking so long?

This wasn't the first time she'd seen a room like this at a police station. Her dad and Kellen had both been LAPD officers.

They would've been shocked to find her on this side of the door.

Ruby imagined her brother's wry grin. *I dunno*, Kellen would've said. *You always had a flair for the dramatic. Remember that black lipstick phase you had in high school? Or that flash mob you organized with the other theater kids at lunch?*

Ruby snickered at the memories, though they also made her heart hurt.

Finally, the door opened, and she gasped with relief.

A woman in a pantsuit walked in. Her hair was braided into cornrows, some piled into a bun on top of her head, while the rest hung down her back.

"I'm sorry for the delay, Ms. Whitestone. I'm Detective Angela Murphy. Can I get you a drink? Something to eat?"

Ruby sat up straighter. "No. I just want to get this over with and get home to my daughter. Is Mickey at the hospital? Is he alive?"

"We're waiting on word." The detective took the seat on the other side of the table. "Keep in mind this interview is being recorded and can be used later."

"I understand." Ruby glanced up, not sure of where the camera was located. "What did you want to know?"

"Before we chat, I have to make sure you understand your legal rights." The detective pulled a piece of paper from her file folder. "You're under no obligation to talk to me. You can have an attorney present, if you want, and if you can't afford one, we'll appoint one. But that would kick this interview until the morning. Most lawyers aren't on call this late at night."

"What time is it? I don't even know."

After passing out in front of the movers, she'd woken up with paramedics around her. Patrol officers had brought her down to the station, where they'd taken pictures of her. They'd asked her to remove her clothes and had given her new ones, which she was wearing now. They'd taken her phone too, though she'd declined to give them her passcode when they'd asked.

Murphy held up her watch. "It's almost eleven."

Eleven? Had Chase put Haley to bed? He was probably worried sick. "Is there a way I could call my friend Chase Collins? He's with my daughter."

"Chase Collins?" Murphy asked. "The patrol officer?"

"Yes. I need to tell him where I am. And make sure they're okay."

"That'll have to be later. First, could you review your rights on this form and sign to acknowledge you're aware of them?"

Ruby signed the document. Detective Murphy tucked away the paper, then folded her hands in her lap. "Can you tell me how you know Mr. Waverley?"

Ruby sighed. "That's a long story."

"But it's important. Faster we get through this, the faster you can head home."

She gripped the skin between her eyes. "Okay. I'll try. I met him in Los Angeles. He's a mixed martial arts fighter. MMA." The first time she'd seen Mickey, he'd been in the practice ring, pummeling another guy in the face.

If the detective was surprised, she didn't show it. "Professional?"

"Not exactly. He doesn't fight with any official league." Though he'd made plenty of money at it. "He's the father of my daughter. But before today, I hadn't seen him since I was pregnant. Two years ago at least."

"Why did you go see him today?"

"I already explained that to the patrol officers who responded to the scene. Is this really necessary?"

Detective Murphy smiled patiently. "The more we go back and forth, the longer this will take."

She pushed out a breath. "Mickey told me where and when he wanted to meet. I did what he asked, but only because he left me with no other choice."

"Why didn't you have a choice?"

"Because he said he'd hire lawyers. Haul me into court over custody. I thought talking it through would be better. I arrived at the address he'd given me. And then, when I got upstairs…" She shook her head, remembering him on the floor. "I tried to help him. I tried to stop the bleeding."

"Even though he wanted to interfere with your life?"

Ruby's eyes narrowed. "Of course. I'd have done the same for anyone."

"But wouldn't it have been easier for you if Mickey were gone? Didn't you want him gone? I would've, in your place."

"*What*?" In some ways, it was true. But a creeping feeling had wound through Ruby's insides. "Why would you say that?"

Detective Murphy crossed her arms, sitting back in her seat. "No one would blame you for trying to protect your child."

"Protect her *how*?"

The other woman just stared back at her.

Ruby pressed her palms flat against the table. She'd thought this night couldn't get any more surreal, but she'd been wrong. "Do you think *I* did this? I hurt Mickey? That's insane."

The detective just waited.

This couldn't be real. Couldn't possibly be happening. Ruby almost laughed at the idea. And then she got really pissed.

"There was someone else in the apartment." She punctuated each word by tapping the tabletop with her finger. "Someone watching us from the other room. The attacker could've gone after me too. That's why I freaked out and ran."

"But *did* you run? The other witnesses said you were calm. They didn't even hear you scream."

"I was upset. I was *shocked*." One of the movers must've seen the killer leave the apartment. Or another tenant had seen. Or a camera.

"You didn't answer my question from before," Detective Murphy said. "Wouldn't it have been easier for you if Mickey Waverley were gone?"

"I…"

"Ruby?" The detective leaned forward, elbows on the table. "Didn't you want Mickey gone?"

A laugh snuck out of her chest. "This is ridiculous. You're twisting everything around."

Ruby's eye caught on the file folder on the table. The rights Detective Murphy had read to her.

Her eyes sank closed, frustrated by her own naivete. But she just hadn't been able to believe that they'd see her as a suspect. That she was being interrogated right now.

I could've told you that, Kellen's voice said in her head.

Quiet, big brother. You're as annoying as Devon.

She had to get out of here. Had to go out and find witnesses or camera footage showing the real culprit. Whatever she needed to do to prove she *hadn't done this*.

"I want to talk to a lawyer," Ruby said.

Detective Murphy stood. "Then this interview is terminated." She grabbed the folder. Glanced at her watch. Turned to go. "You'll need to wait."

"I thought you said a lawyer couldn't get here tonight."

"That's correct."

"But you can't just leave me here again."

Murphy opened the door. It slammed closed behind her.

Ruby cursed.

She'd tried to cooperate like a good girl, and where had that gotten her? This was exactly why she'd told Haley to be wise instead.

At least she'd asked for a lawyer. But that didn't seem to be working either. Not if they'd make her stay in this room all night.

She got up and paced.

This was bad. *Really* bad.

She just hoped it wouldn't get any worse.

Chapter Four

Chase rushed into the station with Devon right behind him. The place was crackling with energy, personnel murmuring tensely, the scent of coffee bitter in the air.

That was how it always felt when something big had happened. Big, like a homicide investigation.

The officer manning the reception desk stood up. "Collins? What're you doing?"

"We're holding someone named Ruby Whitestone. She's my friend. Who's questioning her?"

"I'll see what I can find out. But you know you can't just—"

Chase pushed past him, heading toward the interview rooms. Half a dozen of his colleagues—his *friends*—stared as he passed, but no one said a word.

Detective Murphy had just stepped into the hall, closing a door behind her.

"Is Ruby in there?"

"Officer Collins, I didn't authorize anyone to call you yet. Who was it?"

"Nobody. I had a hunch. Where is Ruby?"

Murphy's glare moved to Devon, who'd crowded in behind Chase. "Who's this?"

"I'm Ruby's brother. Devon Whitestone. We want to know what's going on. Please."

Murphy crossed her arms. "I recognize your name. You're with Bennett Security, right? You were involved in that mess last year with Max Bennett's younger sister. Multiple fatalities, property damage. Chaos over half the town."

"That's right."

The detective's upper lip curled. "And if I remember correctly, Officer Collins was involved, too."

"I was off duty, and I called for backup. I didn't violate any regulations."

She let that subject go. "If you'd been slightly more patient, an officer would've called you both in. We need to talk to all of Ruby's friends and family."

"Why?" Chase barked, though he already knew.

This was standard investigative procedure. Call in all possible witnesses and family members of the victim. Or of the *suspect.*

Detective Murphy pointed at an interview room. "Collins, inside. Now. Whitestone, you wait in the next room."

Chase shared a glance with Devon. They had little choice but to do as the detective said. Even though he wanted to shout and demand answers.

Chase went into the interview room, and Murphy shut the door. He realized he was still half in uniform. He had on his blue pants, but he'd taken off his shirt at Ruby's place. He wore the white tank he'd had on underneath. Despite the thin fabric, he felt himself sweating.

Chase took off his baseball cap and ran a hand through the short bristles of his hair. "If you were going to call me in, why didn't you notify me sooner?"

"Because I already knew Ms. Whitestone's connection to Bennett Security, and I guessed her brother was going to be a pain in the ass. But I didn't expect it from *you.*" Murphy pointed at a chair. "Sit down."

"No. Tell me what happened."

"Collins, *sit down.*"

He complied, chair legs scraping on the floor.

"Here's the situation. A man named Michael Waverley was assaulted."

"Assaulted how? Is he dead?"

The detective continued on without answering his questions. "Ruby Whitestone was at the scene. We're trying to piece together what happened. I understand you may have some information?"

Murphy was playing games with him. Chase felt it. "I don't know anything. That's why I'm upset."

"Did you know Ruby was going to meet with Mr. Waverley?"

Nausea swirled in Chase's stomach, thinking that some lowlife had hurt her or tricked her. "I've never heard that name until tonight. Who is he?"

Detective Murphy's mental gears were working. He could see it in her eyes. She was deciding how much to give him.

"Michael Waverley is the father of Ms. Whitestone's daughter."

"Haley's *dad*?"

"Ruby didn't tell you she was meeting with her child's father?"

"No," Chase sputtered. "I didn't even know he was in the picture. At all."

"But she said you're a friend of hers. Why wouldn't she have told you?"

"I don't…I don't know."

Honestly, it kinda hurt that Ruby hadn't told him. She didn't trust him enough to share that?

"Are you more than a friend? Are you Ms. Whitestone's boyfriend?"

"Just a friend," Chase said tightly.

Why would her ex be contacting her at all? Unless…he wanted to make up for abandoning them. That sent another jolt of anxiety through Chase. But Ruby certainly wasn't the type to forgive. She wouldn't have wanted that deadbeat to be a part of Haley's life.

The detective had said the guy had been assaulted.

Had Ruby done it?

Was Ruby going to be *arrested*?

"Has Ms. Whitestone ever mentioned her child's father to you?"

"A few times. Not much."

"Did she dislike him?"

Uh, the loser who left her after she got pregnant? You think?

"I'm not a mind reader."

"Did she seem nervous about the meeting today?" the detective asked. "Angry?"

Those questions confirmed Chase's worst fears. Immediately, he shut down his facial expression. "I'm not sure."

Detective Murphy squinted at him. She leaned over the table, her voice dropping to a dangerous whisper. "Officer, I'd advise you to be honest with me. Detective exams are coming up. I know you put in your name."

Cold fury raced through his insides. "And?"

"If you value your job, and any possible promotions, you'll tell me whatever you know."

"I don't know anything."

And if he did? No fucking way he'd do anything to hurt Ruby. He wasn't going to outright lie, but he wasn't going to say a word of substance until he knew what was really going on.

"Can I talk to her?" he asked, even though he knew what the answer would be.

"Watch yourself, Officer Collins. You impede this investigation? You'll be out on your ass faster than you can say *accessory*."

"We'll see what the union rep thinks about that."

The detective left the room, slamming the door on her way out.

Fuuuuck.

She hadn't told him he could leave, but he got up anyway. Chase pounded on the door until another officer came to let him out. He charged down the hall, catching the eye of Officer Shelborne on the way.

Shelby. The friend who'd called to tell him Ruby was here.

Chase walked into the breakroom, and Shelby followed.

The place was deserted, smelling of burned popcorn. They found a quiet corner to bow their heads together.

"You okay?" Shelby asked. "This is messed up."

"No kidding. Thank you for calling."

She nodded. "I met Ruby at your birthday last year. When we all went out for beers? Minute I heard on the radio what was going on, I knew you'd want a heads-up."

"What can you tell me?" Chase whispered. "Who responded to the scene?"

Her mouth twitched. "Um, Perez and Lansing."

They were okay. "What about the vic? How bad was he injured?"

"Dead when paramedics arrived. Multiple stab wounds, sounds like. Really bloody. Crime of passion type stuff. Detectives are walking the scene as we speak."

So they were talking murder. Holy… Ruby couldn't have. Could she?

"She just asked for her lawyer, right before you got here," Shelby continued. "They're doing the arrest warrant and the booking paperwork."

"Shit. *Shit.*" He closed his eyes, reeling.

She was going to spend the night in jail. Maybe even longer.

He'd seen Ruby just a few hours ago. *Why didn't she tell me? If I'd been with her when she went to meet her ex…*

But it was way too late for thoughts like that.

"Then I'd better find her a lawyer, because she probably doesn't qualify for a PD." The income limits for getting a public defender were very low, and Ruby had done well for herself as a stylist. She worked so hard. He knew what that job meant to her. "And I need to make sure she gets bail and can pay it. And…"

Shelby grabbed Chase's arm. "Hey, stop and think for a second. Her brother's here, right? Maybe you should take a step back. Let her family handle it. There's a lot at stake right now, not just for her but for you."

"You think I don't know?"

She sighed, hands on the hips of her uniform. "I can't keep feeding you info. You know that, right?"

"I know." Even talking to him right now would get Shelborne in hot water if Murphy found out. As a possible witness, Chase was supposed to be staying as far from the investigation as possible. It went without saying.

But he refused to believe he couldn't be a good friend to Ruby and a good cop at the same time.

"I appreciate what you've done. And if I can ever pay you back, I will."

Shelby nodded, backing away. "Good luck, man." She spun on her boot heel and left the room.

Chapter Five

Ruby and the other inmates filed into the courtroom. The chains binding her wrists and ankles jangled as she walked. She was wearing a green cotton top and pants that said *West Oaks County Corrections*.

"Keep moving down," one of the guards said. "All the way to the end."

Ruby reached her chair and sat. There were eight other jail inmates besides her. They'd all spent the night in the county lockup. Not that Ruby had slept. Or eaten. The thought of breakfast had almost made her vomit.

It could've been worse, though. She'd survived plenty of shitty moments in her life, and she could survive this. Just so long as she got to go home to Haley.

In the meantime, Ruby was determined to keep her spirits up. She'd even made a friend.

Destiny nudged her. "Hey, check out the eye candy that just walked in. Usually, the view isn't anywhere near so nice at these things."

Ruby followed her new friend's gaze.

Devon, Chase, and another man were sitting in the front row

of the audience. The three of them definitely stuck out in the room. And they were all staring at Ruby with cautious smiles.

"My brother and his friends," Ruby whispered.

Destiny whistled quietly. "Lucky girl. Well, except for the murder charge. That part stinks."

"Yeah, there's that."

Last night, Ruby and Destiny had been arrested around the same time, so the police had transported them to the jail together and placed them in the same cell. After fingerprinting, a strip search, and their lovely wardrobe change, of course.

In the cell, Ruby had occupied herself by French-braiding her own hair. It was like meditation, a way to force her mind quiet. And she'd desperately needed a way to channel her terror and frustration.

Then Destiny had spoken up. *Could you fix my hair too?* They'd ended up chatting most of the night.

Destiny was twenty-six, the same age as Ruby. She'd been arrested for prostitution. She wasn't the kind of person Ruby would ever have met outside these walls. But they'd found they had things in common. A love for bubble gum ice cream, a fondness for black and white movies. Destiny was struggling to raise a younger sister after their parents had died.

Ruby had told her about Haley. That had been cause enough to smile, even in that bleak jail cell. Her memories of Haley's silly antics and hugs.

In the audience, Chase lifted his hand to Ruby. He looked even more exhausted than she felt. Instead of his police uniform, he'd worn a button-down white shirt that was a little too tight on his arms.

"All rise," the bailiff said, and the judge walked in.

"Now they'll call us up one at a time," Destiny whispered. "That's when we talk to the lawyers."

The first case was called, and Ruby caught Chase's eye again. *Haley?* she asked silently, moving her mouth to make the word clear.

Chase nodded, and she exhaled. Haley was okay. Of course she was. He wouldn't be here otherwise.

Destiny's boney shoulder nudged hers. "He has a thing for you."

"Chase? Um, *no*."

"Keeps on staring. Poor guy's pining away for you over there. And you know what? He looks familiar."

Ruby's head turned sharply. "*Familiar*?"

Destiny cackled, and a guard shushed them. "Not like that. Not a john. He's a cop, right? I've seen him around. He's one of the kind ones."

"Yeah. He is."

"But I'll bet he's got a wild streak."

"Hardly. Chase is a sweetheart, but he's a straight arrow like my brother."

"I can usually spot the naughty ones who want to get really freaky. Sometimes, it's the types you'd least expect."

Ruby closed her mouth as she giggled.

It was bizarre to laugh right now, when her hands and feet were cuffed and chained. But it felt really good. Rebellious. Like she and Destiny had found a tiny bright spot together in this sea of darkness.

Chase's eyebrows lifted in a question.

"People versus Ruby Whitestone," someone called, along with her case number.

Immediately, Ruby sobered.

The bailiff escorted her to a table in the center of the room.

A woman with an expensive suit already sat there. She put her hand on Ruby's shoulder and leaned in. "Ruby, I'm Jane Simon. Your lawyer. I apologize for not getting here earlier this morning to meet you, but I had another commitment. Are you well?"

She'd spoken so fast that it took Ruby a second to catch up.

"Um, yeah. I don't really know what's going on. Are you a public defender?"

Jane smiled. "Nope. Noah Vandermeer hired me."

"Who?"

"A friend of yours. But we can discuss that later. After your advisement." She pressed a button on the microphone on the table. "We're ready to proceed, your honor."

"What's the People's position on bond?" the judge asked.

The man at the opposite table spoke. The prosecutor, Ruby assumed. "Your honor, Ms. Whitestone is charged with second-degree murder."

Ruby felt these words like a punch to the gut, even though she'd expected them.

The prosecutor continued. "Given the serious and violent nature of the crime, Ms. Whitestone is a flight risk. We would ask for a significant cash bond, if any."

"My client has never been arrested before," Jane said. "She comes from a family of LAPD officers, two of whom gave their lives serving their community. Ruby also has an eighteen-month-old daughter. She doesn't pose any danger."

"No danger? Seventeen stab wounds doesn't sound like a danger?"

Seventeen? Chills ran through Ruby's insides. Her chains rustled as she shifted in the chair.

The judge sighed. "Enough. You'll address me, counsel, not each other. Let me hear from the defense."

Jane regarded the prosecutor calmly. "Accusations are not proof, your honor. I've presented evidence of the People's shoddy investigations in prior cases. Ms. Whitestone deserves a chance to defend herself adequately."

"Bail is granted," the judge said. "I set bond at one million dollars, cash only, no collateral."

Then Jane was standing up and smiling. The whole exchange had happened in a matter of minutes, and the bailiff was already gesturing Ruby back to her seat.

Jane walked alongside her. "This is great news. You'll be out in no time. After the advisements are finished, you'll return to the jail, and they'll process the bond payment and then your release." She squeezed Ruby's shoulder.

"But..."

A million dollars cash? A *million*?

How in the world was she supposed to pay that?

A FEW HOURS LATER, Ruby found herself walking out the door of the jail with Destiny alongside her. Destiny had been granted release as well, on personal recognizance rather than bond.

A million dollars in bail. Somebody had paid it. She couldn't imagine who would have that kind of money.

It was hot and sunny outside, and immediately Ruby started to sweat.

"You have a way better welcoming party than I do," Destiny said. "All I have to look forward to is the bus."

Chase, Devon, and their friend were waiting in the parking lot.

Devon practically leaped across the street. He pulled her into a hug. "Thank god you're out of there. Can't imagine what you've been dealing with."

"I survived. Maybe I'm a little tougher than you thought?"

"You're tougher than most of my army buddies. Male or female."

"I probably smell worse, too."

"That, I can't argue with."

Ruby looked over her brother's shoulder and found Chase right there, his ethereal blue eyes fixed on her.

"Hey," Chase said softly. "You all right?"

She was surprised to find herself blinking back tears. "I'm hanging in. And really grateful for all the help. All *your* help. Where's Haley?"

"With mom and Aurora," Devon said, releasing her. "We'll take you home to see her. But first, this is Noah. He works at Bennett Security with me. He's a captain of our bodyguard team."

This was the third man who'd been with them in the audience. Ruby hadn't met many of Devon's co-workers. She'd been too busy the last year with Haley and her own responsibilities.

Noah stuck out his hand, a disarming smile on his face. "I'm surprised we've never met. It's about time. Though a barbecue or a holiday party would've been more fun than this."

"Yeah, this venue sucks." So this was the Noah Vandermeer her lawyer had mentioned. The pieces kept falling into place. "You're paying for my lawyer. Did you cover my bail, too?"

Noah exchanged a glance with Chase and Devon. "We're a family at Bennett Security. We stick together. And I owed Chase a pretty big favor, so when he called me last night…"

"But a *million dollars*? In *cash*?"

"Ruby," Devon murmured, "don't worry about that right now."

"How can I not?"

Noah shrugged. "I'm lucky enough to have a banker who acts quickly. Couldn't imagine a better use for it than helping out a friend."

He still had his hand out. She hugged him instead. "Thank you. I don't know how to ever repay you—literally—but thank you."

"Just show up to your court dates, and they'll give the money back. No big deal."

"That, I can do."

Suddenly, Ruby remembered Destiny. She'd been so swept up in seeing her brother and Chase.

After scanning the street, she spotted Destiny at a bus shelter down the block. "Do any of you have money? Well, *more* money."

"How much?" Chase asked.

"Not a million dollars. But whatever cash you have. For another friend. I think she could use some help too."

"You already made a friend in there?" Devon asked. "Why am I not surprised?"

"I'm a hair stylist. Talking to people is my superpower."

Chase opened his wallet first and handed her the bills from inside. Devon and Noah did the same.

Ruby ran over to the bus shelter. Destiny looked up as she approached. "Hey, my brother can give you a ride wherever you're going." Ruby pumped her eyebrows. "I'll even introduce you."

"Tempting offer. But I'm good with the bus."

"Will you at least take this?" Ruby held out the bundle of cash. "Thanks for keeping me company last night."

Destiny's lips pressed together. "You kept me company, too. And you fixed my hair. No payment necessary."

"Please. I want you to have this."

Her eyes hardened. "But I don't want your charity."

"It's not charity if it's between friends. That's what I'm telling myself right now, because my brother's friend put up my bail. I just want to pay it forward." Ruby would add this money to the tab of everything else she owed her friends.

Destiny hesitated, then took the bundle. "Fine. If it makes you happy."

"Can I give you a hug goodbye? If it's not too much to ask. Sorry, I'm a hugger."

"Then don't apologize for it. Just be whatever you are." Destiny stood up and embraced her.

"Maybe I'll see you around?" Ruby asked.

"Probably won't. Unless your brother's single?"

"Afraid not."

"Too bad. If that changes, feel free to track me down."

"Chase is single."

"I bet, but that man's all yours." Destiny winked. "Take care of yourself."

"You too."

The bus pulled up, and Ruby watched her friend mount the steps.

~

NOAH LEFT in his own car to head wherever he was going. Devon drove Ruby and Chase to her apartment.

She took shotgun. The car pulled onto the road, and Ruby turned around. Chase was frowning with his hands clasped in his lap. "You look tired," she said.

Chase perked up, his smile returning. He hadn't shaved, and the shadow across his chin made him look rougher than usual. Not like such a perfect Prince Charming. His eyes were red at the edges.

"I'm just glad you're free. We're going to sort all this out."

"But helping the defendant in a murder case? Can't be a good look for you at the station."

A wrinkle appeared at his forehead. "I don't care what anyone else thinks." The rumble in his voice hinted that Ruby's case might've caused him trouble already. She really hoped not.

Chase was just the type of guy to swoop in to a girl's rescue, consequences for himself be damned.

But is he a freak in the sheets, like Destiny said?

It felt good to smile. But she was not going to imagine Chase having sex. Some lines just couldn't be crossed.

"Well, I appreciate you calling in Noah and his big bank account," Ruby joked. "Glad *somebody* was thinking on their feet." She poked her brother in the ribs.

"Hey! I've had my hands full keeping Mom from storming the West Oaks County Jail."

"Ugh." Ruby's head fell back against the seat. Their mom didn't handle stress all that well. Megan Whitestone had lost both her husband and her son, which had toughened her, but she also had a quick trigger finger as a result. Their mom could go from zero to freak out in less than a second where her family was concerned.

Ruby hoped her mother had calmed down by now, because she really didn't need that anxious energy. Ruby was struggling to keep herself together as it was.

"Everybody's at your place waiting for you," Devon said. "Mom, Aurora, Haley. Lana stopped by, but it's a little awkward for her, given her position in the DA's office."

"Yeah. I get it." Lana worked with the prosecutor who'd gone against Ruby in court that morning.

I've been charged with murder.

Those words were only beginning to sink in.

I've been charged with Mickey's murder.

Ruby felt Chase watching her. She turned toward the back seat again.

She'd just realized she hadn't hugged Chase that day. She'd hugged everyone else—Noah, Devon, even Destiny. But not Chase. Made her feel like a crappy friend.

"What is it?" The tenderness in his voice made a lump gather in her throat.

"Everything," she whispered. "Just…everything."

He put a hand on the seat by her shoulder, though he didn't touch her. Then Ruby put her hand on top of his. Chase turned his wrist so his palm was against hers.

His fingers were warm. Strong. His callouses created gentle friction with her skin, and she shivered at the sensation. Somehow, it was better than a hug.

The contact was almost…intimate.

Which seemed strange since only their palms were touching, but that was the word that popped into Ruby's mind.

She startled when Devon drove over a pothole. Ruby pulled her hand away. "Thank you again, Chase. Really. For all you've done."

He nodded. "Want to swing by a drive-through on the way? You're probably starving. Unless you filled up on jail food?"

"Oh, you know it. I asked for their recipes." She forced the smile back onto her face. "I need to get home first. No delays. I want to hug Haley, eat a giant cheeseburger, and take a shower. In that order."

And she was going to keep on smiling and joking and laughing through it all. No way was she letting her daughter see her fall apart.

Chapter Six

Chase carried an armload of fast food bags to the kitchen counter. "Who wants a regular cheeseburger, and who wants animal style?"

Haley was the first to come running. She collided with Chase's legs, wrapping her little arms around him and looking up.

"Fies," she said.

Ruby walked into the kitchen. "I told her fries were coming."

After they'd gotten to Ruby's apartment, Chase had volunteered to run out for food. While he was gone, Ruby must've combed out the braid in her hair, leaving soft waves.

Chase hadn't thought she looked bad even after a night in jail, but now she looked much more like herself. In other words, gorgeous.

"Here you go, princess." Chase handed a couple fries to Haley, who grabbed them in her fist.

Ruby grumbled at the term of endearment. She stopped when he held out the bag with her order.

"I got you a double-double animal style, and two orders of fries. As requested."

"And I'll love you forever for it. Even if you're forcing archaic gender roles onto my kid." Ruby winked as she took the bag. "But let us never speak of this again, because this is enough food for three people, and I'm going to scarf down every bite."

"I'm not judging." He leaned his hip against the counter. "How's it going?" he murmured.

He knew that Ruby was probably putting on a brave face for the rest of them, her daughter especially, even if she did a convincing job of it. But he'd seen the cracks in her facade in the car on the way home. She was struggling. Anybody would be.

"My mom is calming down," Ruby said. "Food is exactly what we need. Maybe everyone will take a nap instead of asking me questions I don't want to answer."

"I can run interference for you."

"I appreciate the offer, Prince Charming, but I need to fight my own battles when I can."

Chase shrugged. "But if you need backup, let me know."

Aurora and Devon came into the kitchen, followed by Megan—Devon and Ruby's mom—whose eyes were bloodshot and swollen from crying. They gathered around the table, paper bags and wrappers crinkling as they ate.

Damn, comfort food was a real thing. All the carbs and salt and fat warmed Chase's stomach.

Ruby was sitting next to him. He knocked his knee against hers. "Good burger?"

"Hmmm." She mumbled something, and he was pretty sure she'd said, *Better than sex.*

Which was a depressing thought. But accurate for him as well, given his lack of action in a very long time.

That made him wonder how long it had been for Ruby. Only thing better than comfort food was an orgasm.

Not like she'll let you help her with that, dumbass.

She'd once commented that she could never fall for a cop after losing both her dad and brother. She hadn't said it to Chase directly, and he doubted she'd been thinking of him at all. But that fact just made the sting all the worse.

"Ruby, you need to talk to us," her mom said. "What I've been hearing so far just doesn't make sense."

Ruby didn't look up from the remains of her lunch. "And what's that?"

"Just what Devon and Chase shared. That your…" Megan glanced over at Haley, who was busy playing with a box she'd found. "Your ex was murdered? And you were there?"

Ruby almost never spoke about her ex, at least not to Chase's knowledge. He figured that if her brother had known the guy's identity, Devon would've paid him a visit and had some strong words for the asshole.

"His name was Michael Waverley. Mickey." She rubbed her hand over her face. "I met him when we still lived in LA. It wasn't that serious, and it was right after Kellen died. I wasn't being very careful."

Across the table, Devon's shoulders stiffened, and his head bowed. Kellen had been killed responding to a mass shooter. Devon had been in the army then. Chase knew how guilty his friend had been that he couldn't make it home when his family had needed him.

"By the time I gave birth to Haley, Mickey was already way out of the picture. Devon had just gotten back home, and we were about to move to West Oaks for him to start at Bennett Security. I didn't tell Mickey where I was going, and he didn't ask. He had my number, though. He could've called."

"Why did Mickey contact you again, after all this time?" Megan asked.

Ruby looked up at her mom. "He wanted to see Haley. To share custody, or maybe get primary custody. I don't know."

Devon's hands splayed on the table. "Why didn't you tell us he'd contacted you? Why would you go there alone?"

Exactly what Chase had been wondering.

"Dev, I can't get into all of it now. I just can't. I'm so fucking tired."

Megan cringed, but held back her usual plea for better language.

Chase brushed Ruby's hand with his pinky under the table. She entwined her fingers with his.

"But there are going to be a lot more questions like this," Devon said. "You need to think about how you'll answer. You did good asking for a lawyer last night, and they can't force you to testify, but if your story doesn't make sense—"

"Oh my god, *I know*," Ruby yelled.

Haley turned around at her mom's outburst, and everyone froze.

"Mama?"

"Sorry, baby," she whispered back. "I'm okay. Everything's okay."

Chase could feel her coming apart beside him. But she held onto his hand, and nothing in the world could've made him let her go.

Aurora was the first to speak again. "Ruby, no matter what happened, we will stand by you. Whatever took place yesterday, it's in the past, and you did what you had to do. You don't have to answer any questions you don't want to answer."

Chase nodded. So did Devon.

But Ruby glared at them. "Wait. You guys don't actually think I did it, do you? You think I'm capable of killing someone?"

Again, silence.

Megan shrugged. "Well, honey, if some jerk threatened to take one of *my* kids, I'd open a can of whoop-ass, too."

Aurora snickered first. Then Chase smiled, and Ruby laughed as her brother did.

"Glad to know you're all willing to stand by me, even if I'm a killer." Ruby rolled her eyes. "But I didn't do it. I'm telling you the truth." She sounded completely confident, if annoyed.

Half the tension in Chase's muscles loosened. He hadn't really thought she'd done it, but…jeez, it was good to know.

Then a new thought dawned on him, obvious though it was.

"That means the real killer is out there," Chase said.

"Exactly. And he saw me."

Aurora gasped. "Then you need a bodyguard. Like how Devon was guarding me after I witnessed that murder last year."

"And you were *so* eager for him to protect you?" Ruby reminded her.

"After I realized the danger, then yeah, I was all for it!" Aurora bumped her shoulder against Devon's. "Especially after I realized how cute he was."

"Let's not get ahead of ourselves." Chase's stomach lurched, thinking of one of Devon's fellow bodyguards watching after Ruby that way. Maybe if it was Noah or Tanner or another guy with a serious girlfriend…

"I agree." Ruby got up from the table and scooped up Haley, who whimpered and reached for her toy, still wanting to play. "Before you all start planning out my entire life for me, I'm going to take a nap with my kid. I'm exhausted, and that makes me grumpy."

"No gumpy," Haley said.

Ruby bounced her daughter on her hip. "That's right. No grumpy allowed."

Haley pointed at Chase. "No gumpy, Chay-Chay!"

"Hey, I didn't say a word!"

Ruby grinned at him, and his heart squeezed.

God, he loved them. Why did love have to hurt so fucking much?

DEVON WALKED Chase out to his car. Now that Ruby was back with her daughter and in safe hands, Chase was ready to head home and crash. He'd been lucky not to have work today, but he did in the morning.

That was going to suck.

"I spoke to Max," Devon said, "and Bennett Security is going to help Ruby's defense attorney with her investigation."

"That's great news."

"Thank you for everything, man. Especially for calling Noah. That didn't even occur to me. My mind was all over the place last night."

"Happy I could help."

"I'm going to keep an eye on things here whenever I'm around," Devon said, "but I was hoping you could do the same when you can."

"Yeah. I'll stop by every day. But think about it. Whoever really killed Mickey, they'll *want* Ruby to take the fall. Whether it was a coincidence that she showed up then, or some kind of plan, the real killer has no reason to go after her so long as the police think she's responsible."

"Shit. So if we clear her name, then she's in greater danger?"

Chase frowned. "Maybe. But she didn't see the killer's face. She can't identify them."

Devon shook his head. "Just keep an eye out for her, will you?"

"We both will."

"You've always been there for my family whenever I've asked. That means a lot."

About a year ago, when Devon had been protecting Aurora from a crime syndicate, Chase had stepped in to keep the rest of Devon's family safe. Chase and Ruby had been acquaintances before, but those stressful days had bonded them together.

Afterward, Devon had asked some pointed questions about why Chase and Ruby were suddenly so close. Chase had told him the truth. That they were friends and nothing more.

Of course, Chase hadn't shared that he'd *wanted* more.

He hadn't fallen in love with Ruby right then. His feelings had taken longer to develop, to cement in his soul. To start feeling like a weight he was carrying around. A weight he wished he could set down, though that didn't seem to be happening.

Devon gripped Chase's shoulder. "We might've lost Kellen, but Ruby still has two brothers in her corner."

Chase ignored the sting of guilt in his chest. He didn't want to be Ruby's brother, but he also didn't want to explain his reasons. He settled on letting that comment go.

"I'll look out for her," Chase said. Because that was what really mattered. "Always."

Chapter Seven

"Come on, bug. Time to head home." Ruby paid Mrs. Murtree her daily rate, picked up the diaper bag, and set Haley on her hip.

Haley blew the babysitter a kiss on the way out.

"She was a sweetheart, as always. Have a good night."

Mrs. Murtree didn't have any clue about Ruby's arrest. The woman only ever seemed to watch the Lifetime Channel, and Ruby wasn't about to inform her.

But she had the feeling her other neighbors would find out soon, if they didn't know already. There'd been some uncomfortable stares in the elevator.

The far worse thing? She'd lost her job at the salon.

She'd gotten the call the day after her release from jail. The owner of the salon—very apologetically—had let her know that they couldn't have a stylist who was out on bail awaiting trial for murder.

Yeah, Ruby had wanted to say. *No shit.* But she'd been polite instead.

She understood. Of course she understood. Even though it was awful. The whole "presumed innocent" thing was clearly just a suggestion. And she figured she'd made such assumptions herself in the past.

Ruby unlocked her apartment and carried Haley inside. The place was a mess. Usually, she took pride in keeping it tidy, even if it meant staying up late or waking up early to clean. Ruby wasn't about to judge somebody else for their appearance or the messiness of their living room, but she knew a calm, organized environment helped keep her mind calm as well.

Lately, she hadn't been able to manage it.

Her mom and Aurora had been coming by with groceries and craft projects, and Devon and Chase had been popping up nearly every day. Even Lana had stopped in with hugs and cookies and moral support, though they'd avoided discussing Ruby's case given Lana's job at the DA's office.

But at the moment, just keeping her smile for Haley was taking all the effort she had.

Hopefully, her clients would come back to her once this whole disaster blew over. And if they didn't? She'd figure out something else.

That was how Ruby had dealt with the unexpected and tragic in her life. Losing her dad, her brother, getting knocked up… No matter how awful it had seemed in the moment, no matter how badly a new development had screwed up her plans, she'd known it was possible to come out better in the end. It was all about looking for the opportunities amidst the mess. The rainbow between the clouds.

She set down her daughter, and the toddler immediately made a beeline for the set of wooden blocks Chase had bought her last month. Her Uncle Chase spoiled her, but it was probably just enough.

Ruby sat beside Haley and kissed her head. Haley wiggled away, not wanting to get distracted from building her tower. "You're the best remedy of all, bug. You know that? Because you're perfect, and I love you."

"Luvoo, Mama."

"Luvoo." Ruby sighed, wiping her eyes.

Someone knocked at the door. She checked the peephole and saw Chase juggling takeout bags.

Ruby opened up, and Chase came inside. "Dinner delivery."

"You don't have to do that."

"I know I don't." He went into the kitchen. Chase had on a pair of workout shorts and a sleeveless tee, a backward baseball cap on his head. Every inch the jock.

"Devon must've told you to check up on me. It's not necessary."

Chase didn't respond to that. Instead, he unpacked boxes of food on her kitchen counter. "I wasn't sure if you'd be in a Pad Thai or a Panang curry mood, so I got both."

"Considering how much I've been eating? Definitely both. I've gained five pounds in the last two days."

"You don't look any different."

"Did you just check me out? Seriously?"

"What? I looked. That's not the same as checking you out."

"If you say so." She was just giving him crap because any minute he'd give it right back. She'd missed this banter with him. She couldn't stand the way everyone had been treating her like she was breakable lately.

Ruby got out plates and utensils. "How was work?"

He shrugged. "Fine."

"You could share a few details. Let me live vicariously."

"Sorry. I guess I'm a boring guy."

"You're reliable. But boring? I don't think so."

"I guarantee you've called me boring at least twenty times in the past."

"You were counting? Jeez, then I was right. You *are* boring."

He grinned at her. "Or maybe I'm just really good at hiding my wild side."

Ruby remembered what Destiny had said about him after their night in jail. *I can usually spot the naughty ones who want to get really freaky.* It made Ruby wonder, just a little…what was Chase into?

The wondering lasted for half a second before she cracked up at herself.

"What are you laughing about?"

"Well…" She started laughing even harder. "Remember that friend I made in jail? Destiny?"

"The prostitute?"

"Don't make that face. Don't do the stereotypical cop thing and make assumptions."

"I'm not. I remember her. She helped you."

"We helped each other." Ruby set the plates out on the table and opened the takeout containers, sticking a serving spoon into each. "Well, Destiny thought you looked like the type who…" She snickered.

Chase opened a cabinet and reached for a glass. "Who what?"

"Likes to get freaky in bed."

Chase fumbled the glass, barely catching it before it reached the granite counter. The tips of his ears were crimson.

Ruby crowed. "Oh my god, it's true!"

"I plead the fifth."

"It *is*." She braced her hands on the counter top and hopped up to sit on it. "What do you like to do? Dress up in costumes? Like, a doctor/nurse situation? I'm dying of curiosity."

He pulled off his ball cap and ran a hand over his short hair. "I'm not discussing this with you."

"Because it's *true*." She studied him. "Teacher/student? No… prison guard/inmate! With chains and everything."

Then Ruby realized what she'd just said, and she felt her own skin flushing. She might as well have said cop/suspect. And who here would fit those descriptions?

The doorbell buzzed, saving her. "I'd better see who's at the door."

"Great idea. You do that."

Ruby opened the door, her smile vanishing as she looked at the two women on the other side.

They were official looking, dressed professionally, holding a briefcase and a folder. This wasn't a friendly social call. And they weren't neighbors asking nosy questions.

"Ms. Ruby Whitestone?" the first one said. "My colleague and I are with West Oaks County Child Protective Services."

Ruby's stomach fell straight to the floor.

She felt Chase right behind her. "What's this about?" he asked.

"We're here to check on the welfare of Haley Whitestone. Given Ms. Whitestone's recent arrest and the circumstances surrounding it?"

Ruby struggled to keep her composure. "But I didn't do anything. I'm innocent."

Chase pushed in front of her. "Let me handle this."

No freaking way, she wanted to argue. But she hung back, waiting to see what would happen.

"We need to ensure Haley is in a safe environment," the woman said. "That's our job, and we have the legal authority to do it."

"Haley *is* safe," Chase snapped. "She's with Ruby."

"And who are you?"

Ruby was shocked by the words that came out of his mouth. "Officer Chase Collins, West Oaks PD. I'm her boyfriend."

Boyfriend? Ruby poked Chase in the back, but he ignored her.

The woman glanced at her colleague, who made a note on her phone. "Do you live here, Officer Collins?"

"I'm here right now, aren't I?"

Shit. What was Chase doing?

The CPS officers insisted on coming inside, so Ruby and Chase stepped out of the way. Haley had toddled over to see what was going on, and now she grabbed Ruby's legs, hiding her face.

Chase crossed his arms. "Ruby's mom and her brother are here a lot, too. They live nearby. Haley is well cared for. She's loved. Ruby is a great mom, and she's going to be found innocent because she didn't do anything."

The CPS officers looked around for a while. They spoke to

Ruby and then tried chatting with Haley. Finally, after more questions and notes, they left.

Ruby watched through the peephole until the two women were gone. Then she spun around.

"What the hell, Chase? What was that? You're my *boyfriend*?"

"I just wanted to defend you."

"You assumed my word wouldn't be trusted, but yours would simply because of your job title?"

"That's how the world is. You know that."

Ruby threw up her hands. "Now what? Those people think you live here."

"Then let them think it. What's the harm?"

"They're going to say I'm a liar when they figure it out."

"I didn't actually claim to live here. How the hell do they know I'm *not* your boyfriend? Just because they've never seen us making out? Pretty sure that's not a requirement."

She didn't want to talk about this anymore.

They sat and ate dinner in silence. Chase got Haley to try some of the spicy curry. "Hey, she likes it. Adventurous eater over here."

This was obviously an attempt to get back into Ruby's good graces. And of course, it was working.

"You like spicy, don't you, bug?" Ruby said.

Haley giggled, smearing yellow curry on her high chair.

They cleaned Haley up, put her to bed, and went back to the kitchen. Chase didn't mention going home, and Ruby didn't either. She wanted him here. Even though she was annoyed at what he'd done, she also appreciated it.

Ruby hated that anyone would see her as incapable. As not enough. She had infinite love for her little girl. But it was hard being on her own sometimes. Really, really hard.

"Since you're my boyfriend, maybe you could help with the dishes?"

He smirked. "I could do that. Yeah."

After they'd finished, she opened the fridge. "You want a beer?"

"You having one?"

"Yes."

"Then sure, I'll have one."

They sat down on the couch together. The apartment was quiet except for the white noise from Haley's baby monitor.

"I feel like there's so much coming at me, all at once." Ruby could barely even process this feeling. It was terrifying. Like her entire life was spinning apart in slow motion. "I want to protect Haley. That's what I've tried to do since I got pregnant, but…" Ruby pulled at the label on her beer. "I've never felt until now like I'm failing."

He turned to her, bending his leg on the cushion. "Hey, you're not failing. You're the same person you've always been. The same mom."

"But I lost my job. I'll have to move back in with my mother. In a couple months, my health insurance will end. And I could *still lose Haley*. What if I'm found guilty at the trial?"

"That won't happen."

"But it could, Chase. You know it could."

He set his beer on the coffee table and put his arm around her. Ruby closed her eyes, resting her head on his shoulder. He smelled nice, like forest-scented deodorant. Masculine.

"No matter what, your mom and Devon and Aurora will be there for Haley. And I will, too."

"But that's no guarantee. None of you are her parent or her guardian." Ruby laughed bitterly. "I am so proud to be a single mom. But sometimes, it really sucks."

She knew there wasn't anything Chase could do to fix this. But it had felt good to vent a bit. Ruby started to drift toward sleep, feeling relaxed despite all the chaos in her life right now.

"I could marry you."

"Huh?" She blinked her eyes. "I was falling asleep. It sounded like you said something about marrying me."

"I did."

Ruby hit his chest with the back of her hand. "Shush."

"I'm serious."

She sat up and looked at him. His pale eyes looked back, and he clearly wasn't kidding.

Chapter Eight

What the hell am I doing? Chase asked himself.

He'd just asked the woman he loved to marry him. The woman who didn't love him back. Who didn't see him as anything more than a friend, which was embarrassingly clear from the way she'd been kidding around about his sex preferences.

But still, he said it again. "Seriously. We should get married."

"This isn't funny."

"I'm not joking."

"I just… *No.*"

She got up from the couch, and he followed her into the kitchen. "Think about it. This could work. If we got married, you'd have my health insurance. I'm a cop, and that could help with defending your right to custody if CPS becomes an issue. And I could file the paperwork to adopt Haley, in case anything happens to you—which it won't—but, you know, in case."

Ruby whirled around, her expression pure shock. "You would do that? Adopt her?"

"Yeah." The more he spoke, the surer he was.

This could help them. This could protect Ruby and Haley both. These two people that he loved. "I mean," he said, "if you'd want me to adopt her. It's a big deal. I know that. Not just for me, but for you. It's giving up some of your rights, and you'd never take that lightly. You know I'd never try to undermine you in any way."

Ruby just stared at him.

"Why?" she asked.

"What do you mean, why?"

"You're not human, Chase. Nobody is this selfless."

Fuck, you're right. I'm not that selfless. I'm in love with you. I want to do freaky things to you.

But really? He expected nothing from her. Not when it came to loving him back or absolutely anything else.

"It's what I said. So I can help you. And help Haley."

"Do you even realize what you're saying?" Ruby threw her hands up as she paced. "You'd marry a woman who's been arrested for murder? What are your bosses going to think? And everyone down at the station?"

"I don't care about anyone else. I care about you and Haley and Devon and this family." *The only real one I have.*

"This is bizarre. My life has officially gone sideways." Ruby sat at the kitchen table, fingers tapping on the surface.

Chase walked around the room, trying to find the words he needed. Because he *did* know why he wanted to do this.

It wasn't about his attraction to Ruby. It went much deeper. To the scarred parts of him he didn't like for anyone to see.

"My mom left when I was eight. My younger sister was six."

Ruby looked over at him. "You have a sister?"

"I don't like talking about my family." He rested his back against the wall, hands in his shorts pockets. Chase had never told this story to anyone. Not even Devon. He'd always deflected questions about his childhood when anybody asked.

"Our mom got tired of putting up with our dad, so she packed up a few suitcases one day while we were at school and he was at work. Drove away. I got home and found her side of the closet empty, drawers cleaned out. She was just gone."

It had been a long time, and it didn't affect him so much anymore. But it still wasn't easy to discuss.

"I'm so sorry."

"It is what it is."

His mom had often seemed distant, and Chase had wondered what he could do to make her happier. After she'd left, he'd felt like it was his fault, until he'd realized it was really his father's. But his mom's love for her kids hadn't been strong enough to overcome her hatred for her husband.

"Was your dad abusive?"

"Not physically. Just an all-around asshole." Nothing had been good enough. Growing up, Chase hadn't heard his father utter a single kind word to his mom. "Maybe she thought she wouldn't have been able to keep us. Or didn't know how she'd manage on her own." He shrugged. "We got a few birthday cards from her. A few calls over the years. That was it."

His sister preferred to act like Chase and their dad didn't exist. She'd moved to Florida. Maybe that made it all easier for her to bear.

Chase still spoke to their father about once a month, even though his dad only ever made him feel like crap.

When he'd made corporal in the Marines, his father had asked why he wasn't a staff sergeant yet. The day he'd graduated from the police academy, his dad had asked why he didn't do something "impressive" like joining the FBI. No matter what he did, his dad thought he should've been better.

So no, his dad wasn't abusive. But he had a way of chipping at your soul until you doubted you were worth anything at all.

"You deserved better." Ruby got up and reached for his hand.

"Maybe so. But that's why I want to help. Because you would do anything for Haley. This is what family is supposed to do."

Ruby looked thoughtful. Her expression didn't give anything away.

"It wouldn't be forever," he said, because he was realistic. Someday, she'd want to marry someone she actually loved. Of course she would. "Just until you've cleared your name and you're confident about keeping custody of Haley."

"Is this even…is it possible it could work? A fake marriage?"

"It wouldn't be fake."

Her eyebrows shot up.

"I mean, as far as you and I were concerned, it wouldn't be the real thing. We're friends and nothing about that would change. I wouldn't expect…"

Ruby snorted. "Good to clear *that* up."

Chase felt his skin heating. "I don't need to ask women to marry me just to get laid."

"So that wasn't some weird come-on?"

"If I was coming onto you, you'd know."

"Oh, would I? Is there a role-play scenario involved? Whips and chains?"

He held his breath until she cracked up.

"Your ears are so red right now."

Chase shook his head. He went back to the coffee table and grabbed his beer. Sipped it.

Most of the time, he was pretty open about sex. About what he wanted.

Chase bet he could make Ruby enjoy the experience a *lot.*

But Ruby wasn't just some woman. With her, everything was different. *He* was different. He felt like he always had his heart on his sleeve, ready to get crushed. How could she not see it?

God, he was glad she didn't see it.

Because this offer wasn't about his feelings. If she said yes, his feelings were going to get buried way down deep.

"We'd have to live together," she said.

"Probably. If we want to make it look right." He shrugged, sitting in the chair next to hers. "The world's not fair, Ruby. But we have to exist in it. I want to give you every possible chance to come out okay from this."

"And Devon didn't put you up to it?"

"Devon? No. God, no." Taking care of his sister probably hadn't included marrying her. "He might be pissed."

"Then that's a slight vote in favor of this plan. I don't need big brothers calling the shots for me." She eyed him, conveying her meaning.

"I don't see myself as your big brother." *Believe me.* "It's up to you. Just think about it. The offer stands, and I'm not going anywhere."

They were both quiet for a minute. Ruby sat beside him. "No one's ever asked me to marry him before."

Chase took a swig of his beer. "Hope the next proposal you get is better. This one was lame. I didn't even have a ring."

"It wasn't *that* bad. You meant well."

Ouch. "I'll take that as a no?"

"You said I could think about it. And I plan to."

To Chase's surprise, Ruby rested her head on his shoulder again. Second time in one night.

As friends, they had sometimes talked for hours. He'd held her daughter, changed dirty diapers. Shared meals. But before her arrest, they'd never been touchy-feely like this.

In some ways, it had been better not crossing that line. Because having her this close, smelling her coconut-vanilla shampoo, set off an unbearable ache in his center.

"Thank you," she said softly. "For offering."

"Any time." They sat there in silence as Chase drank his beer, feeling like an idiot. A hopeless, lovesick fool. But he also didn't want to be anywhere else in the world than right here.

Chapter Nine

Ruby parked in front of her lawyer's office. It was in a stucco building on the outskirts of West Oaks, set amidst suburban neighborhoods and chain stores.

The assistant smiled as Ruby walked in. "Hi, how can I help you?"

"I'm here to see Ms. Simon."

"Of course. You must be Ms. Whitestone. Jane's waiting for you. First door on the right."

Ruby had worn a dress with an asymmetrical hemline, and she'd styled her hair and makeup. It made her feel like her normal self again. Like her entire world hadn't turned inside out in the last week.

Jane's door was open, and she stood when she saw Ruby. "Thanks for coming." She came around the desk and wrapped Ruby in a hug, like they were old friends and hadn't just met the one time.

"Sit down, sit down. Tell me how you are." Jane took a leather chair and gestured for Ruby to take the one next to her.

Everything about Jane's office, her energy, her expression—it relaxed Ruby. She didn't even think before responding.

"It's been tough."

She'd already called Jane about the CPS visit yesterday. Jane had referred her to a family lawyer, who was going to help advise her. Because of Ruby's murder charge, CPS was going to open a court case to consider Haley's best interests. Ruby would have to respond to all kinds of requests for information and questions about her parenting.

There were so many worries, so many uncertainties. She'd barely slept last night.

Especially after Chase's bonkers offer of marriage. That truly showed what a mess she was in. Chase was normally so level-headed and reasonable. If he was willing to go to such extremes, then her situation had to be desperate. Right?

"Where's your little girl today?" Jane asked.

"With a neighbor who looks after her. I don't really need day care anymore since I've lost my job." Jane already knew about that, too. "But my neighbor needs the money. And it was useful today."

"Indeed. You and I have a lot of work to do."

Ruby nodded. "I want to figure out how to pay you. I know that Noah Vandermeer is taking care of it for now, but I don't feel right about that."

"Why not? Wouldn't you help a friend in need?"

"Of course. I just..."

"You don't like being the one in need?"

Ruby laughed sadly. "Exactly. I like to be the one dispensing sage advice. Not the one needing it."

"I get that. Believe me."

Jane crossed her legs. Now that they weren't in a courtroom surrounded by prosecutors and prisoners, Ruby studied the woman more closely. Jane was older than her, maybe mid-thirties. Great skin and an expert hair cut. No wedding ring. A warm smile.

She wasn't what Ruby had expected, but then again, Ruby had never known any defense lawyers before.

"How did Noah find you?" Ruby asked. "I didn't have a chance to ask him."

"He went to Lana Marchetti for a recommendation, and she gave Noah my name."

"Really?"

"Sure. Lana and I have been close since she joined the West Oaks DA's Office. We clash in the courtroom, but we can set that aside and go out for drinks. You're surprised she'd hang with a defense attorney?"

"No, it's not that. I just know she's staying as far away from my case as possible. I've seen her, and we've texted. But we haven't spoken about what's happening except in really vague terms."

"Lana's recused herself, and she's letting the other DAs do their job. But I know she wishes she could do more as your friend. You have a lot of family and friends who love you. That's clear."

She was more right than she even knew. "One of them asked me to marry him last night."

Jane sat forward. "Hold on. What? I thought you didn't have a boyfriend."

"I don't! It was Chase. My friend who's a cop with West Oaks PD. He just wants to do something. He probably feels powerless, like I do."

She wasn't marrying Chase. She'd just have to come up with some other magical idea, because that one? It was too bizarre. He was... *Chase.*

"I promise, we are not powerless." Jane reached over to squeeze her hand. "You've got Bennett Security in your corner, for one. Which is some serious firepower, from what I've heard."

"My brother works for them."

Jane nodded. "Max Bennett has called me, too, letting me know we have their full resources. I intend to take them up on that. But even more importantly? You've got *me.* It might sound cocky to say it, but I'm kind of a badass in the courtroom." She winked. "Sucks for the DA's office that Lana can't go up against me in this case. I don't think anyone else can handle what I'm going to be bringing."

Ruby laughed. "Glad to hear it."

"I intend to press every advantage we have. Maybe even your not-boyfriend Chase at West Oaks PD. But in the end, you and I are in charge of this case, and we're going to be an epic team. We'll put up a hell of a fight."

She reached over to her desk and flipped through a file folder. "I've received the police report and the prosecutor's initial discovery. The murder weapon was missing from the scene, as were the cash and credit cards from Mickey's wallet. The prosecutor will claim you stashed those somewhere, trying to make it look like a robbery. But the police took you into custody at Mickey's apartment building, so they'll have a hard time convincing the jury."

Ruby nodded. "Exactly. I had no time to hide anything."

"The police chose not to search your home apartment. They believe you attacked Mickey in a fit of rage at the murder scene. But we can argue they decided on one suspect and one theory, and ignored anything to the contrary. For example, the autopsy report showed bruising all over Mickey's body, some of it old."

"That would make sense. He was an MMA fighter."

"Exactly. But some of the contusions were fresh. I'll bet my expert will testify that a woman with small fists, like you, probably couldn't have made them. There was also bruising and bleeding inside his nose, as if the attacker grabbed him by his nostrils. A very aggressive, threatening kind of move. I want to find out if the coroner swabbed for foreign DNA from the individual's fingers."

Ruby suppressed a shudder. She was glad Jane didn't pull out the autopsy report or photos. It was hard to even think about Mickey's injuries, much less see them again. Those images were already haunting her memories.

"And don't even get me started on their comments about

your demeanor. You were in shock. People who've just experienced trauma behave in unpredictable ways. It's normal not to scream or cry until later. Even to appear calm. I'll hire an expert to explain that to the jury."

The more Jane spoke, the more relief Ruby felt.

"The judge set your first appearance for next week," the lawyer explained. "You'll be with me in the courtroom. The first appearance will be pretty boring, but it's a step in the process. Later, we'll enter your plea of not guilty. If the prosecutor decides to make an offer, we can discuss it." Jane held up a hand. "I know you don't intend to plead guilty, but let's just wait and keep all options on the table. This will take time, Ruby. There will be a lot of waiting. It will be hard, but I can tell you're a fighter, and I'll be with you all along the way."

"Thank you. I really appreciate this."

"You can call me anytime." Jane grabbed a piece of paper and jotted down a number. "You have my office line, but this is my personal cell. I'm here for you. Oh—and I almost forgot. We got a call yesterday. Someone named Tag Bailor who claimed to be an old friend of yours. He must've seen in the news that I'm representing you."

"He was a friend, yeah. But I haven't spoken to him in a couple of years."

Tag had been Mickey's best friend, but he hadn't approved of the way Mickey had treated her. Tag had tried to contact her after she'd gotten pregnant, offering his help.

"He said he believes you're innocent and has info to share with you, but wasn't sure if you wanted to hear from him."

"I don't mind."

"Would you like me to call him back right now?" Jane picked up her phone.

Ruby was relieved that Tag was on her side, but couldn't imagine what else he would have to say to her. More than that, Tag's name brought up uncomfortable feelings. She liked Jane, but she didn't want to spill every raw detail of her life to the woman.

"No, I can call him myself. Thanks."

"You shouldn't tell him anything about the case, all right?" Jane added Tag's number to the paper she'd given Ruby. "If he's willing to chat about Mickey, I'll follow up with him more formally. You have a lot of friends on your side, but I'll never say no to more."

Chapter Ten

Chase stepped out into the ring. He shuffled his feet and hit his gloves together, loosening up.

"How's vice treating you?" he asked his opponent, though it came out slightly garbled through his mouthpiece.

"Raided a nightclub the other day. Girls' dresses were so short their asses were hanging out."

A couple of people on the sidelines laughed.

Chase rolled his eyes. How had he gotten stuck sparring with this douchebag today?

A lot of West Oaks cops belonged to this gym, which was about a mile from West Oaks PD headquarters. Chase got along with most everyone in his department. But there'd been extra tension lately.

Especially with certain people who liked to run their mouths.

Chase missed the days when Devon had worked out here all the time. Now, Devon was too busy with his job and Aurora to come by the gym much. He did his training with the other bodyguards at Bennett Security headquarters.

"I hear there's been a lot of action in major crimes," the vice cop said.

"There's usually something going on."

They circled one another. Jabbed. Blocked. Chase bounced on his toes.

"Yeah," his opponent said. "But that murder? Guy got stabbed seventeen times? That was messed up."

"Can't talk about it."

"Because you know the girl who did it?"

Chase tensed. The vice cop took advantage, landing a punch to Chase's lower torso. He grunted, taking the blow.

"Where'd you hear that?" Chase asked.

His opponent shrugged. "Just something that's been going around."

Everybody had heard about his refusal to answer Detective Murphy's questions. It didn't help matters that most of the department hated Ruby's attorney, Jane Simon.

Chase had hoped that things would settle after the initial excitement had worn off. But every day, somebody else decided to bring up the subject. Like they were testing him. Waiting for him to slip up.

Waiting for him to reveal he wasn't on the same side.

"Surprised me though," the vice cop said. "That you'd stick up for a murder suspect."

"Let's just fight. You talk too much."

They traded blows. Bobbed and weaved. His opponent grunted when Chase landed a hook.

The vice cop got a vicious glint in his eye. "She your girlfriend or something? This Ruby Whitestone chick?"

"No. But she's a friend."

"Yeah, I'll bet you know her *real* well." He tried a jab. Chase blocked it, then followed up with two body shots. The guy rolled his neck as he breathed, like he was trying to shake it off.

They took a break, grabbing water.

The vice cop wiped a towel over his face. "Better be careful, though. She'll probably knife you in your sleep."

"Watch your mouth." Chase took a step toward him. People on the sidelines were whispering.

He knew he should stop talking. Probably should get out of here. But his opponent wouldn't fucking quit.

"They found her with the vic's blood all over her hands."

"Wrong place at the wrong time."

"That's what they all say, right before they demand a lawyer. We don't arrest innocent people. You know that. So you'd better find someplace else to get your dick wet, because your girl's going down. She'll be some prison guard's bitch in a few months."

Chase threw off his glove and slammed his fist into the guy's face. The vice cop went sprawling on the mat.

Chase wasn't thinking. Wasn't breathing. His arm pistoned back to hit the guy again.

"Hey!" Someone ran into the ring, pulling Chase away. "That's enough, Collins. Stop."

Chase shook the guy off. "I'm done. I'm going."

The vice cop was moaning, putting on a show. Wasn't like he'd gotten knocked out. Nose was barely bleeding.

Shit. What did I do?

He was already on thin ice at work, and was this going to help? No. It was not. He grabbed his gear and shoved it into his bag.

"Chase."

Shelby was running after him. Chase pushed through the exit.

The sun was bright today, making him squint. Palm trees waved in the late afternoon breeze.

"Hold up."

"Leave me alone, Shelby. It's probably better for you if you're not seen talking to me, anyway."

"Don't act like you're some martyr. Plenty of people around here have your back and aren't afraid to show it."

"Yeah? Like who?"

"Don't I count?"

He sighed, shaking his head. "Sorry. You've helped Ruby and me both as much as you could. I appreciate that." He ran a hand through his sweaty hair. "But I don't want you to get penalized for it."

"I'm your friend. I'm worried about you."

Another patrol officer pushed out of the gym exit, eying them as he walked into the parking lot.

"Let's go over there." Shelby nodded at a shady spot. "I don't want a sunburn." She was a pale blond with light skin. But they both knew she really wanted to move this conversation away from being overheard.

Chase tossed his gear bag at his feet and sat on the grass.

Shelby had been in his class at the academy. She was tough and beautiful and didn't take shit from anyone. In other words, exactly Chase's type. He'd even had a slight crush on her at first, but she'd shot him down when he'd asked her out.

Now, they were close friends and always had each other's backs. They were both in major crimes, with dreams of making detective together. Hopefully, someday soon. If everything didn't go to shit.

"Are you okay?" she asked.

"What do you think? One of the people I care about most has been charged with murder. CPS is threatening to take her kid away."

"That sucks. You think that could happen?"

"I don't know. They saw how well Haley is cared for. But it's fucked up that they even could."

"It's their job. We see neglected kids all the time. I've called CPS on people, and so have you. This is the process."

"But now it's Ruby." He knew how hypocritical that was. Yet it was true. She didn't deserve any of this.

"You said she's a friend, but it seems like she's more than that."

Chase's insides burned. "I asked her to marry me."

"Jesus. Are you for real right now? You're serious?"

"As a punch to the head. But it gets worse. I'm in love with her. Even though I keep trying not to be."

Shelby groaned. "Chase. No."

"She doesn't feel that way about me, and she doesn't know my real feelings either. But if I can help her, I will."

"Ruby was arrested for murder a week ago. If you suddenly marry her, how's that going to look for you?"

"Why would anyone assume it's not genuine?"

"I'm not saying they'll suspect. Dude, the problem is they'll think you're a head case."

"Because I love someone, and she happens to be in trouble? Because I won't abandon her?"

"No, because you choose to make a wild, grand gesture that's basically a 'fuck you' to our entire department!"

He refused to view it that way. He could be loyal to Ruby and still be a good cop, and someday a good detective.

"There are plenty of people who support you," she said, "but if you do this? Marry her? They're not going to understand. Don't do something stupid that'll tank your career."

Chase was afraid his career could be tanking already. If he didn't fix things now, he might not get the chance later.

But compared to Ruby or Haley's wellbeing? He wasn't sure he cared.

Chapter Eleven

Ruby drove down the freeway, tapping her fingers and singing along to the radio. She'd decided to make the drive into LA instead of calling Tag. Maybe he wouldn't be at work today, and this trip would be wasted. But it felt good to be out. To be doing *something*, even if it was just reconnecting with someone from her old life.

In the last week since her arrest, her apartment had started to feel claustrophobic. Haley brought her joy every single day, but Ruby needed a little time to herself, too. A drive, even through Los Angeles traffic, was a welcome change of scenery.

The sign for Bailor Fitness appeared, and with it a flood of memories.

She pulled into the parking garage. Tag's place was in an office park, unassuming on the outside. But for a short, vivid period of her life, this place had been like home.

The parking spots on the main level were full, so she parked one floor below and took the stairs up.

When Ruby stepped through the glass doors, familiar smells assailed her. Sweat and leather, cleaning spray and coffee. Somewhere, a smoothie machine whirred. Metal plates clanked in the background as club members lifted weights.

She'd first come to Bailor Fitness with a friend. They'd known MMA fighters trained here. But Ruby hadn't known that the kinds of fights they participated in were strictly private, invite only. She definitely hadn't expected to fall in love with this world.

The irony had seemed so fitting before it all went wrong. The cop's daughter, the cop's sister, caught up in an underground fighting ring.

The funny thing was, Devon and Chase were members of a boxing gym now. A cop hangout. But they had no idea about Ruby's ties to a very different group of fighters on the other side of the law.

"Oh hell, look who it is." Tag Bailor looked good as always, tall, lean, spiky black hair. His beard was thicker and his tan was darker. Wrinkles appeared around his eyes as he smiled. He stood behind the front desk, along with a woman.

"Ruby. Hey."

"Oh my gosh, Nora? I didn't recognize you at first. How are you?"

"Not bad. Sorry for your troubles."

"Thanks."

Nora Rodgers had been a fighter for as long as Ruby had known her, but she'd put on even more muscle. Nora's arms were cut, and she'd styled her hair into a faux hawk. Her pink lipstick and trendy workout clothes added a contrasting touch.

Tag came around the desk to give Ruby a hug. "Even prettier than I remembered. Especially given the shit that's been stirred up lately. I can't even believe…" He shook his head. "Come into my office so we can talk. Nora, handle the desk?"

"Sure thing, T."

Tag moved slowly, limping as they went down the hall. In his office, he moved a box of protein powder from a chair and set it on the floor.

Ruby took the seat. "Your office is still a mess, I see."

He laughed, leaning his weight against his desk. "Yeah, that hasn't changed. But shit, so much else has." His expression slid into a frown. "I'm really sorry, Ruby. About all that happened."

"It's been pretty messed up. Never been arrested before. Eye-opening experience."

"Not just that. I know you couldn't have done what they say. But I mean all that happened with Mickey when you got pregnant. I wish I could've done more for you."

"You tried. I didn't want anyone's help, especially not anyone connected with Mickey." *Don't talk about the case*, Jane had said. But how could she sit here and not offer condolences? "This must be hard for you. I'm truly sorry for your loss. Mickey was your best friend."

He nodded. "Mick wasn't perfect, but I still loved him. He didn't deserve what he got. But neither did you."

"I was a different person back then." She shrugged. "Was Mickey still on the circuit?" Ruby asked. Still fighting, she meant.

"I'd been telling Mick for a while that he should get out of it."

"I told him the same after what happened to you."

Ruby swallowed down bile as she thought of the night Tag had been injured. He'd gone down, but the ref hadn't called the fight. His opponent, a brute named Conrad Decker, had kept kicking him. Hurting him. The audience had just roared, eager for blood.

Tag had ended up in the hospital, bones broken all over his body. Arms shattered, knee almost destroyed. Her stomach twisted as she pictured it.

Decker had gone way too far. Should've been arrested. But the fights Tag and Mickey had fought in? They weren't the kinds to welcome police.

"But you know Mickey," Tag said. "He wouldn't listen. He loved the thrill of it too much." Tag glanced around the office like he might somehow find his old friend here. "Lately, I thought he might be getting tired of it. But he was in deep. I was always afraid it would catch up with him."

Ruby blinked, her mind turning over what he'd just said. "What do you mean?"

"The people who run things, they never cared about us. Just

about the money." Tag shrugged. "And you know how Mickey had a way of finding trouble."

She sat forward in her chair. "Do you think the fights could be related to Mickey's murder? That he pissed somebody off, and they went after him?"

"I don't know anything for sure, Ruby. I left that shit behind, and so has most everyone else who trains here. Things have changed since you left LA. You should stay away from the circuit. That whole life. It's bad news."

Ruby scoffed. "I've been charged with Mickey's murder. It's not like I'm safe if I just crawl under a rock and hide away from the world."

Tag screwed up his lips.

She cringed. "I don't mean that's what you're doing."

Ruby couldn't blame Tag for avoiding the people responsible for nearly killing him. She didn't know who ran the fighting ring, but she'd heard rumors. Chase and Devon would be scandalized if they ever knew what she'd really been into.

But she was a mother now. She wasn't that reckless girl anymore.

Tag made his way behind his desk and sat down. "Look, there's a reason I needed to talk to you, and it wasn't just to commiserate. It's Mickey's family. I spoke to his brother and his mom. Did you ever meet them?"

"No. Never." As far as Ruby was aware, they hadn't known she or Haley even existed.

Tag exhaled. "So, they're wrecked, as you can imagine. I tried to tell them the police are wrong about you, but they wouldn't listen. They're hiring a fancy lawyer from some big firm. They want Haley."

She rocketed up from her seat. "No."

It was bad enough to have CPS questioning her fitness as a mother. But now this?

How many lawyers was she going to need?

"I'm sorry," Tag said. "I wanted to warn you so it wasn't a total—"

The door to the office burst open, and a blond woman stormed inside.

"This is her? The bitch who killed Mickey?"

"Oh, shit," Tag muttered.

The blond strode over, pulled back her arm, and slapped Ruby across the face. Ruby gasped, hand going to her stinging cheek. She was too shocked to respond.

Then Nora raced in. "Cami!"

"Get her out of here," Tag said, pointing at the door.

Nora grabbed Cami around the middle. "I'm not going until that bitch confesses what she did!" Cami kicked her legs, screaming obscenities, but she clearly was no fighter. Nora hauled her out of the office.

Tag cursed. "She's Mickey's girlfriend. I'm sorry."

"It's fine. I should go anyway." Ruby's eyes were watering. But that slap didn't even rank with the other crap she'd had to deal with. "Thanks for the information."

"Are you okay?"

"I'll survive." Just like she'd been doing, and just like she'd keep on doing. There was no other choice.

RUBY LEFT the gym and ducked into a bathroom. She glanced around first, making sure no one else was inside. Anyone at the club would probably use the restrooms there.

Her cheek was bright red where Cami had slapped her. A few tears leaked from Ruby's eyes, and she brushed them away.

So Mickey had a new girlfriend. It shouldn't have been a surprise. Ruby wondered how long he and Cami had been together. Had he hooked up with Cami right after Ruby left LA?

Not like any of that mattered.

She splashed cold water over her face. Breathed deeply.

Earlier, driving out here had felt like an adventure, but now she just wanted to be home. Maybe Chase would come by again for dinner.

I could marry you.

Why was she even thinking about that? Chase was probably regretting that he'd asked because it was ridiculous. They couldn't get married.

Right?

Unless…

No. She couldn't be considering this.

Ruby had never thought about marrying Mickey until she'd taken that pregnancy test. She'd been infatuated with him, but love? She'd been stupid, but not stupid enough for that.

Ruby took the stairs down a level to where she'd parked and walked across the garage. The heels of her shoes echoed against all the concrete. This level was even quieter than it had been earlier, just a handful of cars parked here and there across the space.

Another car started, headlights flaring, and she jumped. Her nerves were on edge, but who could blame her after her week?

Ruby hugged her purse to her side, walking faster. She wished she'd parked closer to the stairs, but she hadn't been thinking of that earlier.

Footsteps echoed somewhere behind her.

Ruby glanced back quickly. But there wasn't anyone there.

She turned and screamed just as someone darted in front of her. The other person reared back, hands up, staring.

It was Nora.

"Whoa, Ruby! You okay?"

"Yeah, I…never mind. You startled me."

"Can't blame you. Sorry about what happened in there. I tried to head Cami off, but that girl's quick. Like a sneaky little rodent."

"I've dealt with worse. She's lucky I didn't slap her back."

"No doubt." Nora nodded her head to the side. "I was just heading home. Do you need a walk to your car?"

"That would be good. It's right over there."

They walked in silence for a moment.

"Hey," Nora said, "I heard you were there the day it happened. You…found him." She cleared her throat.

"I did. It was terrible."

"Did he seem like, you know, like he was in pain?"

Ruby pushed away the images. She couldn't deal with that right now. "Pain never bothered him. You know how he was."

Nora laughed, though it seemed like she wanted to cry instead. "Yeah. That's true."

Ruby hadn't realized Nora had been that close to Mickey. But they'd been on the circuit together, and violence was an awful way to lose anyone. "I didn't get the chance to ask how you've been," Ruby said.

"I'm all right. Not that much has changed for me since I last saw you."

"Really? Tag made it sound like the gym has gone straight. Nobody there is on the circuit anymore."

"I wouldn't say that."

"Wait, are *you* still fighting?" Ruby asked.

Nora bit her lip. "The money's good. I love Tag, but he pays minimum wage. You know the cost of living in LA."

"Tag thinks it's dangerous. He thought Mickey could've been in trouble. Have you heard anything like that?"

Nora's brows pinched together. "Trouble? Mickey?"

Ruby nodded. "Anything at all?"

She shrugged and averted her eyes. "No. I haven't. Sorry."

Nora was lying. Or at the very least, she was acting like someone with things to hide.

But anyone participating in those underground fights had plenty to hide.

"If you think of anything that might help my case, anything about Mickey, will you give me a call?"

Nora hesitated.

"Please?"

She sighed. "Yeah. Sure. Give me your number." Nora took out her phone and typed in Ruby's contact. "If I think of anything, I'll give you a call."

Ruby nodded and said goodbye. She got into her car and drove away, thinking about everything Tag had said.

She had to figure out what she was going to do to keep her daughter. And to save herself.

Chapter Twelve

Chase had just gotten home, nursing his sore knuckles with an ice pack, when his phone rang.

"Ruby? Hey, what's up?"

"I'm heading back from LA. Could you pick up Haley from Mrs. Murtree? Wait for me to get home?" She sounded anxious.

"What were you doing in LA? Is something wrong?"

"When is something *not* wrong lately? Just wait for me. Will you?"

Like he was going to say no.

Fifteen minutes later, he was unlocking Ruby's apartment with the spare key she'd given him. Haley ran between his legs and inside, nearly making him lose his balance. "Hey, slow down there."

"No!" she shouted.

Had she reached that stage already? If he remembered correctly from growing up with a younger sister, this would last until Haley was about eighteen.

The toddler ran around the apartment, and Chase lumbered after her growling like a bear, until they knocked over a basket of laundry. Towels and baby clothes scattered over the rug, along with a few silky scraps of fabric that might've been Ruby's underwear.

"You're going to get me in trouble. Come help me with these before your mama gets home."

"No!"

Chase laughed, shaking his head. He grabbed a towel from the floor. And wouldn't you know it, Ruby opened the door and hurried into the apartment.

"I know this looks bad, but I promise I'm—" He stopped talking when he saw the anxiety on Ruby's face. Chase set the towel aside.

"Did you mean it?" Ruby asked.

"Mean what?" His brain wasn't keeping up.

"Getting married. Did you mean it?"

Lightning zapped to his nerve endings. Excitement, terror, a roller coaster of emotions. "Uh…yeah. Absolutely."

"Okay."

"Wait. Are you saying yes?"

The door to the hallway was still open. Chase went over to close it. Haley came out of her room, and Ruby kneeled to hug the baby.

He really couldn't tell if this conversation was making Ruby feel better or worse.

"Let's back up," he said. "What happened today?"

"A lot. Too much."

Ruby carried Haley into the living room and sat on the couch. Chase followed, sitting on the coffee table so he could face them. Haley squirmed in her lap, but Ruby didn't let her go.

"What happened?" Chase reached out and rested his hands on Ruby's knees.

"I saw Jane. And she's great. I'm so thankful to have her. I'm thankful to have so many people looking out for me. Especially you."

Her dark eyes were so vulnerable. A pang hit him in his chest.

"Jane said a friend of Mickey's was trying to contact me. This guy named Tag. I went to see him in LA, and he told me Mickey's family hired a fancy lawyer. They want to take Haley away from me. Because they think I…" Ruby glanced down at her little girl. "You know what they think I did."

Killed Haley's father.

"That's why I called you. I just needed to know Haley was okay. That she was safe."

"Did you think she wouldn't be?"

"It was an instinctual fear, okay? I felt like my baby was being threatened. And while Mrs. Murtree is sweet, the lady's a toothpick."

"And I'm not?"

Ruby gave him a sardonic look. "You have a few muscles, I guess."

"I didn't realize you'd noticed."

"I notice things about you."

"Oh yeah?"

"Like how you try to distract me when I'm worried. Which I don't need you to do."

"Uh oh, Haley. Your mom's grumpy."

Haley patted her cheek. "No gumpy."

"I know, I know." Ruby took a heavy breath. "Anyway, on my way back to West Oaks, I called Jane, and she conferenced in that family lawyer who's been consulting with me. I asked if Mickey's family could really do that, and the lawyer said the court considers a bunch of factors when it comes to custody. They want to keep a child with people she loves and knows. But if I…I wasn't around, and it was a battle between Mom and Devon on one side, and Mickey's family on the other? It's really hard to say what the court would do."

Chase could feel Ruby's agony, the terror of not knowing. Like it was inside his own heart and under his skin.

"But then, I asked what would happen if Haley had a stepdad." Ruby bit her lip. "A police officer with good standing in the community."

He could hardly breathe with how much he wanted to shield them, protect them. "Yeah?"

"The lawyer said it would make a big difference. Both with CPS, and with the court when it comes to custody."

"Then we have to do it." There was no question in Chase's mind. But she still seemed to be hesitating.

"I need you to be sure. I'm asking you for so much."

He tilted his head. "If I remember correctly, I'm the one who asked you."

"And it's just like you to offer everything you have to someone else without thinking."

"And it's just like *you* to be too proud to accept."

Her foot knocked against his leg, and a smile ghosted over her lips. "Ever since I got pregnant, I hated the idea of being a burden on my mom or Devon. I've wanted to provide for Haley on my own. To prove I didn't need Mickey, didn't need his money or anyone else's. I've worked hard to get to this point, where I had my own place, was standing on my own feet."

"I know you have."

"But this time, I might not be…" She blinked rapidly, her voice breaking. "I might not be enough. Mickey's family—and plenty of other people—think I did something terrible. If the worst happens, I have to make sure Haley's safe. No matter what."

"That's what I want, too."

I love you, he thought. *More than you will ever know.*

Because he wasn't going to let her know. This wasn't about his feelings or his needs. It was about Haley. It was about giving Ruby some peace of mind and a fighting chance to get through this unscathed.

Chase held out his hand, palm up. "Let me do this for you."

It was Haley who reached back. "Chay-Chay." Her little arms stretched toward him.

Ruby let her go, and Chase kissed Haley's head before setting her down. "You want to go play?" he asked. The little girl nodded and toddled off.

"Oh my god." Ruby's eyes squeezed shut, and tears cascaded down her cheeks. "I can't believe we're really doing this."

"I can think of worse ideas. Like…anchovies and chocolate ice cream."

"Ew. That's disgusting."

Chase slid down to the floor in front of her, going onto his knees. Ruby's eyes widened. He'd thought kneeling might lighten the mood, like this wasn't deadly serious. But his heart didn't think it was funny.

This felt like flying through the clouds and crashing to the earth at the exact same time.

"Ruby Whitestone, will you marry me?"

"Okay," she whispered. She slid her hand into his. Their fingers wound together. He needed a ring. He needed…holy shit, a lot of things.

His wife. She was going to be his wife.

BUT FIRST, they had to tell her family.

Ruby called Devon and Aurora and asked them to come down to her apartment. They readily agreed, probably thinking this was just a casual meetup like they often had.

Devon grinned when he saw Chase was there. "Hey, man. How's it going?"

Chase couldn't even manage a response.

Guess what, Dev? I'm marrying your sister.

This was going to be a slightly awkward conversation.

Aurora was cooing over Haley. "Look at these cheeks! Even chunkier than a few days ago. She's the cutest little chipmunk."

"Can everyone come into the living room?" Ruby asked. "Chase and I have some news."

Devon sat on the couch. "Is this about your case?"

"Sort of."

Ruby had washed her face. Any trace of redness was gone from her eyes, and Chase wondered if she'd used some magic eyedrops or something. Ruby looked totally confident and put together, like she was her old self. Not facing a murder charge and about to marry his ass.

Chase, by contrast, felt like he'd just jumped into the middle of the ocean and had no idea how to swim.

Aurora joined Devon on the couch. Haley had coopted Aurora's phone and was playing with it on the floor.

Chase and Ruby stood in front of them, and she surprised him by taking his hand. "Chase and I are getting married."

Aurora's plucked eyebrows slowly rose. Devon tilted his head, as if he hadn't heard. "I'm sorry. What was that?"

Chase cleared his throat. "I asked Ruby to marry me, and she said yes."

"Oh," Aurora said in a tiny voice. "Wow."

Devon fixed Chase with an intense gaze. "Can somebody please start talking some sense? Because I feel like I stepped into a fucking parallel universe."

Chase nodded toward Haley. "Dude, chill on the f-bombs."

"*Dude*, explain why you asked my sister to marry you!"

"My ex's family wants to challenge my custody of Haley, and Child Protective Services has already been sniffing around. If Chase is Haley's stepdad, it'll carry a lot of weight with the court."

"It'll mean I can put her and Haley on my health insurance, too," Chase added.

Devon was shaking his head. "I could've added you to my health insurance if you'd asked. I'm sure that Max would—"

Ruby groaned in exasperation. "You aren't listening. It's already decided. Chase offered, and I said yes."

"When?" Aurora asked. "When is this happening?"

"As soon as we can, I think." Chase looked at Ruby. They hadn't even talked about timing.

"You'll need a marriage license." Aurora took her phone back from Haley, who whined until Aurora handed her a toy train instead. "It says on the West Oaks County website that there's no waiting period, no blood tests required. They're open tomorrow morning for walk-ins. The clerk can perform the ceremony, if you really want to make this as quick as possible."

"Why are you helping?" Devon cried.

"Because they've clearly thought this through, and I'm an event planner. This is what I do."

Devon jumped up from the couch. "I need to talk to Chase."

"Devon," Ruby and Aurora both said, in the same warning tone.

"I'm going to talk to my *best friend*."

They went into Haley's bedroom, which still smelled like baby powder and milk, even though she was getting older. Chase was careful not to step on the toys she'd left scattered on the floor.

"You're *marrying* Ruby?" Devon whispered. "Are things really that dire?"

"Yeah, Dev. It's bad. Like Ruby just said."

"But does it have to be you?" Devon asked. "What about… Noah?"

Chase took a step back. "*Noah*? Why him? Because he's richer than I am and has a fancy house in the hills?" Did Devon not think Chase was good enough? "Noah's billionaire girlfriend might have a problem with it. Sorry he's not available."

"That isn't what I meant. You're…" Devon waved his hands around. "You're like Ruby's brother. And now you're going to marry her? It's creepy."

"I'm like *your* brother. I never said I viewed Ruby as my sister."

Devon's gaze turned steely. "Are you trying to confess something?"

"*No*. Jeez. Ruby and I are friends and nothing more. That's all we'll ever be. But you can't seriously be pulling this over-protective older brother shit. Really? You? With your history?"

He groaned, dropping his head into his hands. "I *know* that. I've been on the other side of it with Max. I'm in no place to judge."

Max was both Devon's boss and Aurora's older brother, and

there'd been some tension when Devon and Aurora had gotten together.

"There's nothing to judge," Chase said. "I care about Ruby. I care about Haley. I'm just doing my part to protect them."

"And I'm so grateful, man. I'm doing a shit job of showing it. My head's a mess over this. I can hardly think. And there's other stuff going on…"

"Like what?"

Devon shook his head. "I'll tell you another time. Not now."

"Is it bad?"

Devon's expression was still heavy, but the corner of his mouth curved. He glanced around Haley's room. "Not bad at all. But it's a lot. I'll share when I can, okay? I promise. Sorry I'm being an asshole."

"You're not. Come here." Chase hugged him, and Devon returned it. But this wasn't their usual slap-on-the-back kind of embrace. It felt like Devon was holding on for dear life.

"You asked me to look out for Ruby a year ago," Chase said, "and you asked me again the other day. That's what I'm doing."

"You're right." Devon let go of him, blinking rapidly.

"You say all the time that we're brothers. This is just brothers-in-law."

"Brothers-in-law." Devon said the word like he was trying it out. "Yeah. I can deal with that."

"Someday, it'll be Max. I've got to be better than that, right?"

Devon barked a laugh. "You have no idea."

"He did ask you to be his best man, though."

"Yeah. Still trying to figure *that* one out. Maybe Lana made him do it."

Chapter Thirteen

The clerk stamped a form. "You're lucky we're not busy today. Might've been hard for the little one to wait in a long line."

"Yep, lucky," Ruby repeated.

They were sitting in the county clerk's office, about one minute from getting married, and Ruby still didn't believe this was happening.

"Mama," Haley said. "Fower." She handed Ruby the pink flower she'd just plucked from her hair.

"Thank you, bug. But those are supposed to stay in your braids." She kissed her daughter's nose.

Haley reached for the back of her head, grabbing another one. A white daisy. "Chay-Chay."

He smiled and accepted it. "Haley wants me to look pretty too. Why didn't you braid *my* hair, Ruby?"

"I will for your next wedding."

Ruby had dressed herself and Haley in floral prints. It had seemed like the right choice for a wedding. Chase was wearing slim khaki pants and a light blue button-down that matched his eyes.

That morning had been chaotic. Finding out what paperwork they needed, applying online for the marriage license, and sorting out other logistics, which Aurora had helped with. Chase had a day off work today already, so that hadn't been an issue. But in some ways, Ruby had felt like they were rushing so that nothing else could happen first. As if this marriage was her one hope, and the next terrible thing was waiting just around the corner.

"All right, just need your signatures here and here."

Ruby was glad she had her daughter to hold on to because her hands were shaking. Her signature came out messy on the license.

Chase signed next.

"And the witness?"

Ruby's mom stepped forward. They'd only been allowed to bring a single person, so Devon and Aurora were waiting outside.

The clerk beamed at them. "You're a beautiful couple. A beautiful *family*, I should say."

"They *are* beautiful," Megan said emphatically. Ruby's mother had been battling tears all morning. "And very strong and loyal and…" She sniffled, waving a hand in front of her face. "I'm sorry. It's just overwhelming."

Ruby looked over at Chase and found him smiling back.

"Chay-Chay." Haley held out a sprig of baby's breath to him. "Fower."

"Thank you, princess." He took it and stuck it behind his ear.

We're doing this for Haley, Ruby told herself.

Shit. We're doing this.

"Do you have the rings?" the clerk asked.

"Oh. Yes. Hold on." Chase patted his pockets. "Here." He pulled out two silver rings, one large, one small. Both simple. Ruby didn't even know where he'd gotten them.

"All right," the clerk said with a smile. "Time for the vows."

Ruby handed Haley to her mother. They'd agreed not to use traditional ones, since this was hardly a traditional marriage. But all the romantic stuff she'd found online hadn't been right either.

Ruby read the notes she'd jotted in the car on the way. "I

promise to be your partner. To accept you and…care for you the best way I can. To be honest and loyal for as long as we're together."

She felt a tug inside her chest to be saying these things—because she meant them. And that was big and scary. Making these kinds of vows, even to a friend. *Especially* to a friend.

Then it was Chase's turn. "I promise to protect and care for you and Haley, as long as you need me, no matter what comes our way." The tips of his ears had turned red.

Ruby realized she'd been staring at him when the clerk said, "Ruby? Do you take Chase to be your spouse?"

"Oh. Yes, I do."

He slid her ring over her finger.

"Chase, do you take Ruby to be your spouse?"

"I do."

Hands shaking, Ruby pushed his ring over his knuckle.

"Congratulations. You're married."

They were holding hands. Ruby looked into his eyes.

For the first time in her life, she had no words. None.

AFTERWARD, they went to Megan's house for lunch. Aurora had organized a get-together, which she'd promised wasn't a party. Ruby didn't exactly feel like celebrating. But when they walked inside, Aurora had set out enough food that it *looked* like a party.

Max and Lana were here too. Lana squeezed Ruby's shoulder. "Aurora told us the news. Is it okay we came?"

"Of course. I'm glad you did."

"I want to say congrats, but I'm not sure if that's right."

"You mean, they don't make a greeting card for marriages of convenience when the bride's awaiting trial?"

Lana cringed. "The store was out."

"We're here for you," Max said. "I've got our research team working hard on your case."

"Thanks."

Maybe it would've been easier if Ruby had written the words on her forehead. *Thank you.* She owed all of them so much.

Chase, Max, and Devon congregated together in the kitchen, digging into the food. Haley toddled over to stand in the middle of them, demanding the men's attention. Ruby's mom and Aurora were mixing up punch.

Ruby wondered if anyone would notice if she slipped out the back door. Or maybe went to hide in the bathroom.

Forty-two minutes in—Ruby had been watching the clock—Aurora grabbed a glass and tapped it with a fork. "Thanks for coming today to show your support. Ruby knows we all love her, and we all know she loves us back. No need to say it again right at this moment. I have the feeling Ruby's sick of the spotlight."

No kidding, she thought.

"Devon and I want to share a little announcement of our own. If it's okay with you, Ruby?"

She waved for them to continue. "The less attention on me, the better. Go for it."

"Chase?"

He nodded.

Aurora's face beamed. "We've been keeping this quiet, but everyone's together today, and mostly? I just can't keep this in." She rested a hand on her flat stomach. Devon put his arm around her, smiling. "Haley's going to have a cousin in about seven months."

Ruby felt her entire body go still. Lana and Megan both gasped.

"You got her *pregnant*?" Max turned a scowl toward Devon, who was very conspicuously not glancing in Max's direction.

"Of course it was Devon," Aurora snapped. "Who else?"

There was a lot more hugging and exclaiming. Haley was jumping around, enjoying the excited energy.

It was all just a little too much.

Ruby watched them for a while, and when nobody was looking, she snuck through the back door and went around the side of the house.

She hadn't bothered to put on her shoes, and the grass poked between her toes. She rested her head against the brick wall, closing her eyes.

A few minutes later, she heard the soft rustle of footsteps in the grass. "Can I join you?" Chase asked.

"Sure. Just wishing I had a cigarette."

"You don't smoke."

"I quit when I got pregnant. It was part of my whole rebellious, bad-girl persona before I was a mom." She glanced over. "Never tell Devon."

"We're married now. We're legally required to keep each other's secrets." Chase leaned against the brick wall next to her. "You okay? I didn't know if Aurora's announcement…if it brought up things for you."

"Because I got pregnant at the age she is now, but I didn't have anyone like Devon to care about me?" Ruby's throat felt thick, and her nose burned. "Nah. I wasn't thinking that at all."

But she felt like she'd been rubbed with sandpaper today, and everything that touched her was too intense. Even that little glimpse of happiness.

"My mistake. I'll go if you'd rather be alone."

She felt his eyes on her. But unlike everyone else at the moment, Ruby didn't mind Chase's presence. "You can stay."

"You look beautiful. I don't think I said that earlier."

"Everyone inside is pretending this is a normal, happy day. You don't have to do it too." Her fingers itched for that cigarette. Her eyes stung, and that lump in her throat just kept getting bigger.

"What makes you think I'm pretending?"

Exhaustion washed over her. Despair over everything that had happened, even though she was determined to keep smiling. For some reason, with Chase, she couldn't manage it.

"I don't want to feel like this."

"Like what?"

"Like I'm not myself anymore."

"Do you want to get out of here?"

"No. I'm not running away." But she needed something, and all she could see was him.

Ruby pushed away from the wall, wrapped her arms around him, and rested her cheek on his shoulder.

Chase was tense at first, but then his arms closed around her like he was ready to hold her up. She shut her eyes. Breathed in his forest-scented deodorant.

"Today, we hugged every other person inside the house except each other." Ruby looked up at him. "Why is that? Do I smell weird?"

He smirked. "You don't smell weird. If you want to hug more, we can."

"*So* accommodating of you. Mr. Selfless."

"You sound annoyed. Did I say the wrong thing?"

Everything in her head came spilling out. "You've been my friend for a while now, one of my *best* friends, someone I could count on. But I gave you my friendship back. And now, what do I have to give you? I'm just…" She averted her gaze, blinking back tears again. Damn it. "We're doing this for Haley, and I know how much you care about her. But I feel like I'm this black hole, and I'm taking from everyone. Especially you."

Ruby pushed back from him. Even right now, she was taking comfort from him and didn't know how she'd ever repay it.

A wrinkle appeared between his eyebrows. "You've given me a lot. You make me laugh and think about things I wouldn't have otherwise. You make me see the world differently. None of that's changed. I do love Haley, but I also care about you."

"But I don't want your pity. *Ever.*"

"And you won't get it. Honestly, I'm in awe of you. Always have been." He'd said this so matter-of-factly that it didn't sound patronizing. She almost believed him.

"You're in awe of me? Is that why you don't like to hug me? I'm intimidating?"

"You figured out my secret. But I hear you got married to a total idiot, so obviously you can't be *that* awesome." He leaned in and whispered, "Now's when you say, 'Shut up, Chase, I'm still awesome.' Come on, say it."

"I'm not saying it."

"Not even for me? Mr. Selfless? You won't give me this tiny thing?"

"Fine. I'm awesome."

"Not bad, but try it again without the eye roll."

"You're a bossy husband, you know that?" They both laughed, and Ruby felt a little more like herself again.

"Your bossy husband thinks you need another hug." Chase pulled her closer again. His eyes locked onto hers.

Suddenly there was this strange feeling in her center. Like she couldn't get enough air. She still wanted something, *needed* it, and didn't know what it was.

It definitely was not a cigarette.

"You didn't kiss me after the ceremony," Ruby said.

"You *wanted* me to kiss you?"

"Not really."

He barked a laugh. "Okay. Thanks for letting me know? I guess."

"But now, I kind of do."

"Do what?"

"Want you to kiss me."

His eyes darkened. "Oh."

"Not like it would mean anything. I just want to do it once. To see what it's like. Because otherwise, I'll be wondering."

He made a face. "That makes perfect sense."

"Doesn't it? We're married. It seems strange if we've never even kissed."

"Just this once, huh?"

"Yep. One and done."

"Then I'd better make it good." His voice had dropped low, and there was this swooping feeling in Ruby's stomach that took her completely by surprise, and suddenly his hand was in her hair.

He dipped his head and pressed his soft lips to hers.

The kiss lingered, but he didn't push, didn't try to deepen it. Instead his lips moved to her chin, pressing small, gentle kisses along her jaw. Chase used the hand in her hair to angle her head back. He kissed where her chin met her neck, and Ruby heard a small whimper. Had she made that noise?

Chase let go of her. It took Ruby a moment to remember where she was. Her blood was rushing, yet she also felt a stillness at her center. Like she was completely steady for maybe the first time since the day that Mickey died. Maybe even before.

"How'd I do?" Chase asked.

"I'm pretty sure that was more than one kiss. But I'll let it slide."

He rolled his eyes, turning around to head back to the house. She smiled, watching him go.

The kiss—kisses—had been nice. She definitely hadn't hated it, which was weird. But if a girl couldn't get a decent kiss on her wedding day, when could she?

Chapter Fourteen

Chase set down his suitcase on the hallway carpet. Then he barred his arm across the door to block her from going inside. "Hold on."

"What? Why?"

"I want to do something." Chase unlocked the door to Ruby's apartment, but he didn't let her in.

"You're strange. But okay. Sure."

Ruby was carrying a sleeping Haley. All the flowers were gone from their hair, and Ruby had unbraided hers. Soft, dark curls fell around her face and spilled across her shoulders.

Chase put one arm around Ruby's waist, the other at her knees, lifting her. She yelped, holding tight to her daughter.

"What are you *doing*? You're going to wake her!"

"You're my bride. I'm carrying you over the threshold."

"Such a cliche. I hate cliches."

"It's not a cliche, it's a ritual."

Ruby grumbled under her breath, and he thought he caught the words *Prince Charming*.

"You got a kiss, this is what I want," he said.

"Because the kiss did nothing for you at all."

"Nope. That was just for you." He walked them to the living room.

"Can you put us down now?"

Chase set them gently on the couch. "See? Haley's still asleep. I'm smooth, aren't I?"

"*So* smooth." Ruby shook her head, but she was hiding a smile. "I'm going to take her to her crib. You can put your things in my room."

"I figured I should keep my suitcase out here." There'd be less awkward maneuvering that way.

But Ruby didn't answer. She'd already gone into Haley's. He went back to close the front door and lock it.

Chase's house only had one bedroom, so it had made far more sense for them to stay at Ruby's. But it only just occurred to him that he'd be sleeping on that tiny loveseat in the living room for the next several months.

According to her lawyer, the trial could happen within six months, or the process could take a lot longer. Especially if Ruby—his throat clenched at this thought—was convicted and had to appeal.

Could he fit an air mattress in here? He wished he'd brought a sleeping bag.

Chase went back to the hall for his suitcase. He'd packed it that morning before he'd left his house. His place was a rental from his cousin, so he had some time to decide whether to keep it. But it all depended on how long this arrangement with Ruby lasted.

She'd been quiet the rest of the party and during the ride to her building. Chase knew that today had been overwhelming for her. In some ways, it had been for him too. But he wasn't the one facing a murder charge or afraid of losing a kid.

The being-in-love-with-her part was confusing, and he'd already resolved to get over that nonsense. But Ruby had spent most of the last two years taking care of other people. Her mom, Haley, even Devon in some ways. Now, she deserved to have somebody looking out for her. Chase was honored to be the one to do it.

He just wished Ruby could see that for herself.

Her head popped out of Haley's room. "She wants you to give her a kiss goodnight."

"I'd love to."

After they'd put Haley down, they both went back to the living room. Ruby saw his suitcase sitting there. "Wasn't there room in my closet?"

"I thought I should keep my stuff here."

"But it's no trouble." She grabbed his suitcase and wheeled it into her bedroom. Chase heard a drawer slide open.

He followed and found Ruby bent over her dresser, taking out piles of clothes. "I'll make some space."

A bunch of lacy things landed on top of the dresser, and Chase quickly averted his gaze.

The room smelled like Ruby, coconut and vanilla. Her bed was covered in blue and white throw pillows, a white quilt, and a furry blanket.

"But if I'm sleeping in the living room…"

"Why would you sleep there? I want you in my bed."

Desire shot straight down his spine and into his dick.

Ruby dissolved into giggles, hand covering her face. "Okay, that came out really wrong. But we're a team, right? It doesn't have to be weird."

"It doesn't *have* to be." *But it will be.* He subtly adjusted his pants.

That was a queen-sized bed at most. He was going to take up more than half of it.

And his nonstop erection was pretty much going to take up the other half.

It had taken all of his control not to get hard when he'd kissed her during the party earlier. Sharing a bed with her? He'd be lucky if he didn't have a wet dream like he was a sex-starved teenager.

"I'll keep my hands to myself," Ruby said. "Promise. Let's get you unpacked."

"It's really not necessary."

She whirled around to face him, and her mouth had pressed into a hard line. "It's necessary for *me*."

That vulnerability was back in her eyes, the same thing he'd seen just briefly that afternoon.

"This is my home, and Haley's home, but I need you to feel like it's yours too. I want you to be comfortable, and that tiny couch out there isn't going to do it, so don't bullshit me."

"Fine, I agree the couch won't be that comfortable. But…" He gestured at her bed. "This might not be, either."

"You carried me over the threshold because we're married, and it's weird, and we might as well laugh about it. Right? Neither of us knows how to do this, but we're doing it anyway. So let me make a place for you here. Let me give that to you."

"Okay," he said softly. She wanted to feel like she was giving something back, not just taking. "I'll sleep here."

"If you want, *I* can sleep on the couch. I'm way more likely to fit. Or I could share Haley's room if I rearrange her furniture or something."

"No." He rested his hand on Ruby's shoulder. "You're right. I'll be here for a while, so this will work. We'll make it work. Thank you."

She exhaled, nodding.

He grabbed his suitcase and unpacked. His uniform pieces went on hangers in the closet, along with the lockbox for his gun, which he stowed on a high shelf.

He couldn't help staring at his dark blue clothes next to Ruby's small, richly colored ones. Hard to believe how much life could change in just a couple of days. But if he were ever in trouble, he'd want Ruby in his corner. Chase had no doubt about that.

~

AFTER WORK THE NEXT DAY, Chase came home to music playing. "Hey girls, I'm home."

"We're in the kitchen."

He stopped by the bedroom to lock up his gun, then went to join them. He'd already changed out of his uniform in the locker room at the station, which he did when he wasn't in a rush.

An upbeat song played from Ruby's phone, probably some indie singer-songwriter he'd never heard of, because that was the kind of music she liked. Ruby's hips swayed as she stirred a pot on the stove. Haley was dancing frantically, waving a spatula in the air.

It was possibly the cutest thing he'd ever seen.

"This looks like fun. Just an average night at the Whitestone residence?"

"Whitestone-Collins now." Ruby smiled at him, and he felt a tug behind his belly button.

The night before, Chase had stayed up later than he usually would, scrolling his phone. Then he'd taken a shower and jerked off, which he figured he'd be doing a lot over the next several months. Like, twice a day.

By the time he'd gotten to bed, Ruby had already been asleep with the lights off. Her back had moved with her even breathing.

So damn beautiful.

Which he was going to stop noticing…now.

"Can I help with dinner?"

"Nope, I've got it. Just pasta." Ruby switched off the stove and carried the pot to the sink to drain. "I did a lot of thinking today while you were gone."

Chase leaned against the counter. "Sounds like your day was more productive than mine."

He hadn't told anyone at work about their marriage, except for adding Ruby and Haley to his health insurance with HR. He figured the change in his marital status would stay confidential for the time being. But eventually, word would get out. Chase would deal with that when it happened.

It had been hard enough ignoring the feelings that were tapping insistently with every beat of his pulse.

Not to mention the morning wood that had greeted him when he woke. Luckily, he and Ruby had slept with their backs to one another, several inches of space separating them. He hoped he hadn't snored, but she hadn't complained.

The pot clanked as Ruby set it on the counter. "I decided I'm not going to let this beat me. No feeling sorry for myself. I'm going to be the kickass woman I know I am."

"Right on." He was proud of her, though he wouldn't say that. She didn't need him to.

"I hope you're aware how lucky you are."

He felt himself grinning. "Am I?"

"It's going to be a nonstop slumber party around here. Popsicles after naptime. Dance parties. Taco Tuesday *and* Thursday."

"No effing way."

"Way. Everyone else out in the world is going to wish they married me first because they're missing out on all the amazingness."

"Damn, I should've married you sooner."

"You should've."

Haley jumped up and down, banging her spatula on a cabinet.

Chase couldn't resist. He grabbed Ruby, spun her around, and planted a kiss on her head.

"What was that for?" she asked, laughing.

"For being you. For letting me be on your team."

"I'm glad you're on my team."

His arm was still around her waist, and she was still gripping his shoulders. A new song came on, and Haley dashed around the living room, but in the kitchen everything seemed to have stopped. Chase looked down at Ruby's stormy blue-gray eyes. Her eyelashes lowered, her gaze going soft, though it didn't waver from his.

"I should get the munchkin some dinner before she gets too riled up." Ruby's voice sounded husky.

"You mean, *we* should. Don't leave me out of the fun."

"Wouldn't dream of it."

That night, they both got into bed, and Ruby switched off the lamp on her nightstand. He heard her shifting around against her pillow, though it was too dark to see much more than her profile.

"Jane and I have a meeting with Bennett Security tomorrow," she said.

"Did you want me to come?"

"Don't you have work?"

"Yeah, but I could figure something out."

For several minutes she didn't say anything, and Chase wondered if she'd fallen asleep. Then she spoke.

"I thought you were supposed to stay away from the investigation."

"I am."

"Going to a meeting with my lawyer doesn't sound like staying out of it."

He sighed, rubbing a hand over his face. "Ruby, what do you want me to do here? You're my friend. My *wife*. I want to do whatever I can."

"But you've done enough. What's going to happen when your sergeant finds out you married me? Or the other patrol officers and detectives?"

Shit's going to hit the fan. "It'll be fine."

The mattress moved like she was sitting up. "Let my lawyer and Bennett Security handle my case. You focus on your job. Promise me you won't get involved. Don't be Mr. Selfless."

His teeth dug into the tip of his tongue.

"Chase, promise me."

"All right. I promise." Even though he really wasn't happy about it.

Chapter Fifteen

Ruby had been to Bennett Security headquarters before, but never as a client. She followed her lawyer to the reception desk. "Jane Simon and Ruby Whitestone, here to see Max Bennett," the lawyer said.

The receptionist nodded. "I'll let Mr. Bennett know you're here."

They took a seat on one of the leather couches. Past the lobby, employees bustled around the vast workspace. Computer screens covered one wall, and huge windows took up another, showing a panoramic view of the ocean.

"Fancy digs," Jane muttered. "I've heard plenty about Max Bennett over the years, but I never imagined he'd be the investigator on one of my cases. It's lucky you have connections. There's no way we could've afforded these guys otherwise, even with Mr. Vandermeer's generous retainer fee."

"No kidding. Not on my hairdresser's salary." Which she no longer had anyway. This company usually catered to the wealthiest of West Oaks, and while Max volunteered his resources often for the government, Ruby doubted he'd ever done so for a criminal defendant before.

The receptionist lifted her chin. "Mr. Bennett will be down in a few minutes. Could I offer you something to drink?"

"Coffee, please," Jane said.

Ruby nodded. "Same. Thanks."

She hadn't slept well the night before. Chase had been snoring, and his long arms and big body had been taking up more than his share of the bed.

At one point, his fingers had brushed her thigh, and she'd practically leaped off the mattress in surprise. But the rest of her body's reaction had made no sense at all. Her nipples had hardened, and blood had coursed through her.

She'd been almost…turned on.

Maybe it had been that kiss on their wedding day. And it had been far too long since she'd had a man in her bed. Her body was getting confused.

Chase had a penis. So what?

Oh god. I'm thinking about Chase's penis.

"Any updates from your husband on the investigation?"

Ruby coughed. "Um, no. I asked Chase to stay away from my case. I don't want him in trouble at work."

"Chase is a big boy. He's done a lot to help you already."

"Exactly. I don't want him doing more."

They'd been discussing the adoption petition with the family lawyer, who'd advised that the court wouldn't consider it yet anyway. Not with the open case filed by CPS. But just the fact that Chase was willing to adopt Haley as his own? It was huge. Ruby didn't want to give up any of her parental rights, but she was blown away that Chase would offer to take on that kind of responsibility.

Devon and Aurora had also offered to adopt Haley if it really came down to it, but Ruby hoped all these hypothetical plans would never be necessary.

In the meantime, CPS had issued a safety order that required Ruby to have "supervision" when she was with Haley. Chase was supposed to be in the house whenever he was off duty, and

Aurora, Devon, or Megan were supposed to come by the apartment every day to check up on things. Ruby chafed at the interference. But at least Haley would stay with her. That part was a relief.

The receptionist brought their coffees to a small table, along with sugar and cream. Ruby sipped hers black while Jane added multiple packets.

"I don't want anything to happen to Chase's career because of me," Ruby said.

"If he was all that concerned about his career, he wouldn't have married you in the first place." Jane tilted her head sardonically. "I would say this is none of my business, but when it comes to my clients, I consider *everything* my business. Are you sure Chase is just a friend?"

"We're close, but not like that."

"You're protective of him."

She almost laughed. "As a friend. And even if I were attracted to him, which I'm not, there's no way I could end up with a cop." Jane knew about how Ruby's brother and father had died. They'd had some long, personal conversations on the phone. Jane had been true to her word—she really did answer any time Ruby called. "I want Chase in my life, and in Haley's life. But…"

She tried to think of how to explain it. With most anyone else, Ruby wouldn't have tried. She didn't want anyone to take it as disrespect for the vocation her dad and brother had given their lives serving.

"It's like a mental block," the lawyer supplied, as if she'd plucked the right words out of Ruby's head. "Or perhaps an emotional one. You've been hurt so badly that your heart won't risk it again. Loving someone that much when you know you could lose him in the same way."

"Yes. That's it."

"I'm sorry you went through that." Jane reached for her hand. "I couldn't end up with a cop either, but for totally different reasons. Mostly the fact that every cop I've ever met can't stand me. I'm on one side, they're on the other." Then she leaned in and lowered her voice to a whisper. "Too bad that antagonism just makes them sexier. I'm the type of person who thrives off confrontation, and the way they scowl at me? Mmm. I've had some *really* dirty fantasies that take place in courtrooms."

Ruby snorted a laugh. "Can we be friends after this is over? I like you."

"We're already friends." Jane squeezed her hand. "I like you too. Wish I'd met you another way. But some of my best friendships have been forged under pressure."

They both looked over as a woman in black combat boots strode across the workroom, heading straight for them. Her strawberry-blond hair was cut into a bob, and she wore a pair of chunky pink glasses.

"Ruby? I'm Sylvie Trousseau." She was petite, with defined biceps showing beneath her T-shirt. "Devon is one of my best friends here at work. I'm so glad to finally meet you, except for the circumstances of course."

"I've been getting that a lot. Glad to finally meet you, too." Devon had mentioned his co-worker plenty of times. Sylvie was Bennett Security's resident computer expert, and she was second only to Max in the company. She'd helped Devon when Aurora had been in danger last year. "Sylvie, this is Jane Simon. My lawyer."

"Grab your coffees and let's head to the conference room. Noah's already there, and Max is on his way down."

"Not my brother?"

Sylvie looked over her shoulder as they walked into a hallway. "I thought you might prefer Devon keep some distance from this one. Was I right?"

"Hell, yes. I've got plenty of other people looking out for me. I get Devon's opinions enough as it is."

The conference room had a view of a small park. Palm trees waved across the blue sky. Ruby and Jane greeted Noah warmly.

Max shut the door and took a seat at the head of the table. "How's married life treating you?"

Ruby felt Noah's curious glance. "I was wondering that, too. Can't believe Chase didn't send me an invite."

How could she even answer? "It's weird as shit. But also, not that bad."

Everyone laughed, and Sylvie reached over to swat Max's arm. "And what about the other big news, boss? You're going to be an uncle."

Max's eyes glittered menacingly. "Let's get focused on why we're here, shall we? Supporting a member of the Bennett Security family."

"That's all Sylvie was talking about, right?" Noah said innocently. "The ever-expanding Bennett Security fam."

"I'm thrilled to be an uncle," Max deadpanned. "Don't I look excited?"

Noah gave Max a lopsided grin, and a dimple sunk into his cheek. "Sylvie, you want to do the honors?"

Sylvie opened the laptop in front of her.

But Jane held up a hand. "Before we start, I just want to clarify where we stand. Nothing we say leaves this room. Any and all results of your investigation on behalf of Ruby's case are confidential work product, and therefore protected from disclosure unless I say otherwise. Got it?" They all nodded. "Perfect. Please continue."

"I've been working on background," Sylvie said. "Putting together all I can find on potential avenues for our investigation. Based, of course, on the info and documents Jane provided to us, as well as Ruby's statements."

Ruby sat and listened as Sylvie reviewed what they knew about the murder itself, most of which Jane had already told her. No eyewitnesses had seen anyone else leaving the scene of Mickey's murder, and no cameras had caught the person on video. The camera in the building's lobby had been pointing at the mailroom. Apparently they had issues with packages getting stolen. But they'd had no cameras on the actual doors in and out.

"I'm going to interview each of the movers and the neighbors Ruby saw at the apartment building that day," Jane said.

"Max, if you want to send someone along with me, that could be helpful."

"Already planning on being there for any witness interviews myself. Just let me know the when and where. And I assume you have forensics experts you typically use?"

Jane smiled. "I do. Not my first rodeo. Though my first with Bennett Security riding along."

"And we intend to pull our weight, but don't hesitate to let me know when I'm screwing up. Lana certainly does, and I know she's a friend of yours." He nodded for Sylvie to continue.

"Thanks, boss. I've been putting together a profile of Mickey Waverley. Who he was, who might have wished him harm." She punched a button, and a picture of Mickey appeared on the big screen on the wall. It was a posed publicity shot of him wearing a hoodie and a dark scowl.

Ruby sat forward. "That's from when he was trying to make it as a pro MMA fighter." Before she'd met him. He'd had a framed copy of this poster on his bedroom wall.

Sylvie was nodding. "Mickey grew up in West LA. His parents were both in the entertainment industry. Mom was an agent before she retired, and dad was a movie producer. Mickey went to the University of Southern California for a couple of years before dropping out to pursue MMA. After that point, I found no official employment. Almost no social presence."

Ruby hadn't known all these specifics, but this account fit. "That's when Mickey joined the circuit."

When she'd met him at Tag's club, Mickey had already failed in the professional mixed martial arts world. But you never would've guessed from his cocky charisma, his trash talk, his loud laughter carrying across the gym floor.

Mickey had seemed like a guy who knew exactly what he wanted and was used to getting it.

From the first day they'd met, he'd made it clear that he wanted Ruby.

She hadn't given in right away. But after seeing that first fight, the thrill of the danger and the secretiveness… It had all been insanely hot. Mickey hadn't cared what anybody thought, or so she'd assumed.

As she'd gotten closer to him, she'd seen how jealous he could be of the other fighters. He hadn't been possessive of her, but several times he'd withdrawn for days over a lost fight and shown up with a fancy new car or Rolex. She'd seen other hints about his family and his past. Nannies, private schools, trips all over the world.

It had turned out that Mickey was rebelling, just like her. But he'd been acting out of boredom and resentment instead of the pain of loss.

"The circuit?" Jane asked.

"Underground fights. They took place a couple times a month," Ruby explained, "always at a shifting location so they'd stay off the radar of the police. Invite only. A text would go out a day before with the next time and place. Usually private property, but sometimes an abandoned warehouse or factory."

Sylvie chimed in. "I've spoken discreetly with some of our contacts at LAPD. They've known about this underground fighting circuit for a while. But they haven't been able to shut them down."

Jane lifted an eyebrow. "And LAPD was willing to talk to you?"

"I didn't mention Ruby's or Mickey's names. Or yours."

Jane huffed a laugh. "So that explains why they were so helpful."

"Is organized crime involved?" Max asked.

"Not exactly," Sylvie said. "LAPD believes it's a man named Adrian Peele."

She tapped the keyboard, and the big screen switched to a photo of an older man in a well-tailored business suit. Everything about Peele conveyed money, from the flashy watch on his wrist to the thick hair that was probably an expensive weave.

"Peele started out as a collateral lender to the rich and famous of LA," Sylvie said. "That's a fancy way of saying pawn broker, and he had no scruples. If you wanted to fence a stolen

Van Gogh or Basquiat, he was your guy. He's an MMA fan, it seems, and built up a large enough fortune to start this circuit. The fights draw high rollers who gamble millions and flock to see no-holds-barred aggression."

Max crossed his arms. "Perhaps Mickey gambled on fights. Got in over his head."

Jane pointed at Max. "I like where you're going with this. If Mickey owed this Adrian Peele money? Plenty of people have been murdered for less. His death wasn't execution-style, though. A knife suggests anger. Passion."

Noah rested an elbow on the table. "What about defensive wounds? I didn't see any mention of that in the autopsy report. If he was a fighter, why didn't Mickey fight back?"

Jane tapped her fingers against her mouth as she thought. "I've wondered the same thing."

The image of Mickey crawling toward the apartment door, reaching out with a bloody hand, flashed through Ruby's memory.

Mickey had chosen the thrill of fighting over Ruby and their child. Yet in the end, he'd wanted something different. He'd wanted to be a part of Haley's life. Could that change of heart have led to his death?

Maybe he'd finally wanted to stop fighting, but it had been too late.

Chapter Sixteen

After his shift, Chase was on his way out of the station when Shelby stopped him. "Hey, can we talk?"

Chase hiked the strap of his bag onto his shoulder. "Sure. I was going to head to the gym. What's up?"

She nodded her head at the exit. "In private?"

Shit. The news had gotten out sooner than he'd expected. He wondered who else knew.

They jogged down the steps onto the street. People were bustling up and down Ocean Lane. He and Shelby kept going until they'd crossed the street, heading for the beach. Kids ran around in the sand, probably just out of school for the day.

"So you heard?" he asked.

Shelby gave him the side-eye. "Heard what?"

Now he was confused. "What did you want to talk about?"

"Nuh-uh. Your turn first. What did you *think* I was talking about?"

Chase was hesitating, but he knew his friend. Shelby wasn't going to let him deflect. "Ruby and I got married over the weekend."

"Aw, hell." Shelby's face pinched. "I hope I never fall in love, because it turns otherwise reasonable people into complete idiots."

"I don't need the lecture. What did you want to tell me?"

She glanced around, though no other officers were anywhere in sight. "I heard some guys talking about the Mickey Waverley investigation. Apparently, a tip got called in. Owner of a shop a few blocks away from Waverley's apartment saw somebody suspicious running down an alley around the time of the murder. But nobody's followed up."

"*What?* Why the hell not?"

"Beats me. But I looked up the tip report, which I probably shouldn't have done, because I wasn't assigned to it. And now I'm telling you about it, which I *really* shouldn't be doing. Because you're our main suspect's husband, apparently."

"But you're doing it anyway. I'm grateful."

"I thought we'd go find out what this potential witness saw. *Not* because Ruby's close to you, but because it's the right thing. 'Cause I'm honorable like that, even when it would be smarter to stay out of it." She was shaking her head. "You and I have that in common, I guess."

"I can go. You don't need to come along."

"No, I've got your back. Can't have you going around being reckless all by yourself."

SHELBY LOOKED up at the sign. "This is the place."

It was called Cakes 'N' More, a storefront at one end of a strip mall. Chase and Shelby walked inside, bell tinkling.

They wound through the displays of icing and plastic tools that looked more like they belonged in a hardware store. A gray-haired woman was struggling to carry a cardboard box from a back room out to the register.

"Can I help you with that?" Chase took the box and set it on the counter.

"Thank you. My grandson is usually here in the afternoons

to handle inventory, but I am completely out of meringue powder, and I don't want to be the cause of a riot in the streets."

Chase laughed. "I don't even know what meringue powder is. What about you, Shelby?"

"I watch the Food Network."

"There you go," said the woman. "Now you see my predicament." She picked up a pair of scissors and sliced open the tape. "Are you two here about that murder nearby?"

Chase lifted an eyebrow, glancing at his friend. "You guessed it. I'm Officer Collins. This is Officer Shelborne. Were you the one who called in the tip?"

"Indeed. I'm Phyllis. Pleasure to meet you. I was starting to think no one would ever come."

"Sorry about the delay." Shelby took out a notepad. "Could you tell us what you saw the day of the murder?"

"Well, sure. But didn't you already arrest the killer?"

Chase's shoulders tightened. He reached into the box and picked up one of the plastic containers. "Where do you want these?"

"Oh, that shelf over there. Thank you. That's very kind."

He started unloading the box.

"Why don't you tell us what you saw," Shelby prompted again.

Phyllis leaned against the counter. Chase stacked the plastic jars on the shelf, though he was listening closely.

"The first thing I noticed was the sirens. I was in the back room, getting a special order together for an online customer. Well, I heard the sirens, looked up, noticed movement in the window overlooking the alley. There was a man running past. I thought right away that he could be running from the sirens, so I should've been scared. But it was the strangest thing. I couldn't pull my eyes away from that window, even though he could've looked over and seen me."

"Did he?" Shelby asked.

"I don't believe so, no."

Shelby tapped her pen against the pad. "What did the man look like?"

"Tall. Muscular, like your partner there."

Shelby wasn't his partner, but he didn't bother to correct her.

Phyllis glanced over Chase from head to foot. "But this guy was even bigger. Like one of those wrestlers on TV. Huge shoulders, shaved head. He seemed, I don't know, mean."

Chase lined up another jar of powder, his heart rate picking up. "What makes you say that?"

"Just an impression. The way he frowned. He seemed agitated, and was looking all around like he was afraid of being followed. And he had something balled up in his hands. Tossed it in a trash can on his way past."

Chase cursed under his breath. "And nobody came to ask you about this? Or searched the alley?" Unbelievable.

"Not until you." But Phyllis was smiling. "You're lucky I watch a lot of police shows. I went outside and grabbed that bag of trash right out of the can. It smelled terrible, so I wrapped it up, but it's still in the back room. It could be evidence, isn't it? I'd love to get rid of it, but I was afraid to in case somebody finally came looking."

Hope had inflated in his chest. He'd heard the murder weapon had been missing from the scene. Could it be in that trash bag?

"We can take a look," Shelby said.

The three of them took the bag out into the alley. Phyllis provided a pair of rubber gloves, and Shelby put them on. "You take pictures with my phone," Shelby murmured to Chase. "Better if you don't touch anything. You were never here."

"Shouldn't we just take the whole thing back to the station? Make forensics sort through it?"

"A bag of trash that's been marinating for over a week and may or may not have anything useful? No, Chase. I don't think I'm going to bring that in. Not unless we have something to show for it."

But his pulse was racing. This could be big. It could be evidence that would help win Ruby's case.

Chase took pictures of the outside of the bag. Shelby unwrapped the outer plastic, then split the bag along the side. She spread the contents onto a flattened cardboard box.

Discarded food wrappers. A few baggies holding dog waste. An issue of the LA Times, which Chase photographed for the date. It all reeked, though nowhere near as bad as most major crime scenes.

"What's that?" he asked, pointing. "Right there."

Phyllis squatted near the ground. "I see it too."

Shelby picked up a wad of fabric. It looked like a small, dirty towel.

"Is there blood on it?" Chase asked.

"I can't tell." Shelby went to fetch a plastic bag from her car and came back to store the towel inside.

To his disappointment, nothing else in the trash bag seemed remotely interesting or unusual. No murder weapon.

Finally, they were done taking Phyllis's statement and headed back to the car. "I'm going to take this in to the station and get it into evidence," Shelby said. "I'll talk to Detective Murphy about how I found it. She's going to be pissed that I did this on my own, but I'll deal with it."

"On your own?" Chase said. "What about me? I'm going down there with you. I want to know why the hell nobody followed up on the tip before."

"Which is exactly why you'd better stay away. You're too close to this."

Chase grumbled, but he knew Shelby was right.

If he went down to the station and confronted Murphy about why she'd ignored this tip, he'd lose his shit. And that wouldn't help anyone. Not Ruby, and certainly not him.

~

CHASE WALKED IN THE DOOR. Ruby was setting dinner plates on the table.

"Are you okay?" she asked.

"Why wouldn't I be?"

"Your eyes are funny."

Haley toddled over to him, and he picked her up, planting a kiss on her hair. "I'm better than okay. Maybe."

"What does that mean?"

"I don't know for sure yet." He set Haley down, then went into the bedroom to change.

Ruby followed him, waiting outside the door. "That's mysterious."

"Not trying to be." Chase emerged a minute later, gun put away. He'd taken off his uniform shirt but still wore the pants and his undershirt. He was too excited and needed to get this out. "Shelby and I may have found another suspect."

"Another suspect? In Mickey's—" Ruby glanced at Haley, who was clinging to her legs and asking to be picked up. "Want to watch some Coco Melon, bug?"

Once Haley was in front of the TV, singing with the characters on the video, Ruby grabbed Chase's arm and pulled him into the kitchen. "Tell me."

Chase explained what he and Shelby had found. Ruby's frown only deepened as she listened.

She was quiet for far too long after he finished.

"What?" he asked.

"You promised me you were going to stay out of the investigation."

He blinked at her. "That was before Shelby told me about the witness tip. What was I supposed to do? Ignore it?"

"No, you should've given the information to Jane. She and Bennett Security are handling my case. You're just going to get yourself into trouble at work."

Chase cocked his hip. Ruby was mad at him? Seriously? "I can worry about work myself."

"Not if you're too busy running around trying to save me."

He sputtered a laugh. "And that's a bad thing?"

"It's bad when you're putting your career at risk. When you *promised* me."

"Ruby, you're facing a murder charge. I'm trying to help you. To protect you."

"So you're allowed to protect me, but I'm not allowed to protect *you*?"

He opened and closed his mouth like a fish. Haley's video switched to another kids' song.

Shit. He hadn't expected this. And he didn't want to admit that she maybe had a point. A very small one.

Ruby crossed her arms, glaring up at him. "You've already given up too much for me."

That again. He shrugged. "If I want to run around being a hero, that's my problem."

"I'm not some princess you're keeping in a tower. I have a say."

"And I don't? I should just leave it to Bennett Security?" His skin flushed. Shelby had told him earlier not to come to the station with her. Now Ruby was chewing him out like he was an asshole for caring about her. "Maybe you should've married Noah Vandermeer instead of me. Since *Bennett Security* is running the show."

"*What*? What are you even talking about? Are you jealous that Noah's helping me?"

"*Jealous*? Why would I be jealous?"

"Then this is some territorial guy thing. Because I'm your wife, suddenly you have to be in control of everything."

"That's ridiculous."

"You know, maybe I *should* have married someone else. Then you wouldn't be such a pain in the ass about trying to rescue me. You're not my Prince Charming."

His jaw clenched, the muscle working. "Never claimed to be."

"But you constantly seem to be auditioning for the role."

"Then I'll be a narcissistic jerk from now on. Happy?"

"Very. Can we eat dinner now please?"

"Nobody's stopping you."

"Perfect."

"*Great.*" Chase sat heavily in his seat, grabbed his fork, and speared a piece of shrimp.

They'd just had their first real fight. Not just of their marriage, but of their friendship. Chase knew he should apologize. But then Ruby would just get pissed at him again. She'd probably say he was being too nice. Because that was a crime, apparently.

Whatever he was, it was too much of the wrong thing. And clearly not what she wanted.

Chapter Seventeen

Ruby followed Chase into his bungalow.

"I can't believe I've never been to your place before," she said.

He switched on the light in the living room. "I guess I've always gone to see you guys." He'd spoken all of this in a monotone. Like he hadn't wanted to respond, but felt obligated.

They hadn't made up yet after their fight.

Today was Sunday, and Haley was spending the afternoon with Ruby's mom. Chase had needed to come to his house for a few belongings, and Ruby had volunteered to go. Partly because she'd been eager for an excuse to get out of the apartment, and partly because she was sick of this awkwardness between them.

It had been days since their argument. But aside from pleasantries at meal times and talking about Haley, she and Chase had barely spoken.

All the while, she'd been waiting for *something* to happen in her case. But whenever she called Jane, all she heard was, *Be patient.*

Jane had been both furious and thrilled at the potential new suspect Chase had found. When the lawyer demanded answers from the DA's office, the prosecutor had claimed they were still investigating and would have turned the info over. Apparently, they were examining the towel Chase and Shelby had found for DNA. Anything that might tie it to Mickey's murder. There had been no news yet.

Ruby had to keep being patient.

Her eyes followed Chase as he walked across the room. She'd been doing that a lot lately.

"You're glaring at me. You didn't have to come."

"I'm not glaring."

"Then what're you doing?"

"Just wondering how much of this stuff you need. I don't have room for all of it."

"I'm going to pack up a lot of it and store it in the garage. In case my cousin wants to sublease the house while I'm gone. Then I can cover more of your rent."

"That's thoughtful. Thanks."

He'd brought along some collapsed cardboard boxes. He popped them into shape and started taping the sides. "You know me, Mr. Selfless."

And he had to go and ruin the moment. "Mr. Sarcasm is more like it."

"I thought you loved sarcasm. It's your primary form of expression."

"I thought you hadn't noticed. Because avoidance is *your* primary form of expression."

"I'm not avoiding you. I just don't want to get yelled at again."

"I didn't yell. I never yell."

He tilted his head and arched his eyebrow at her, and for some reason, her next comeback got stuck in her throat. She was too busy noticing his Adam's apple and the cords in his neck.

And now she was staring at him again.

What was with that?

It might've started out as glaring. The man was so stubborn. Almost as stubborn as she was. But then, sometime in the last few days, she'd forgotten to glare and had just been…watching.

He was nice looking. She'd always known that, but lately, those handsome features kept drawing her eye. Probably because she had so little else to look at.

Ruby spun and marched into the kitchen. "You have a pressure cooker? I've always wanted one of those."

"It was a gift from an aunt or something. Don't think I've ever used it, but you can have it if you want."

"How generous. So your little wifey can make dinner before you get home?"

"Not so selfless now, am I?" He gave her a smirk. She rolled her eyes.

But this was better. They were talking.

"Didn't Devon and Aurora hole up here when she was in danger last year?" Ruby asked.

"Yep. And they practically destroyed the place. The front windows were all shot up. Technically not their fault. In the bathroom, though, the curtain rod in the shower was pulled out of the wall. But there was no other sign of a fight in that part of the house."

Ruby laughed. "Then how did they manage to mess up the bathroom?"

"I didn't ask. Max Bennett paid for everything to get fixed. My cousin was thrilled about the new windows."

Chase's phone rang, and he groaned when he saw the name on the screen. "Fuck."

"Hey, no grumpy allowed," she said.

A smile flickered over his lips before vanishing. "It's my dad. I need to take this."

"Do you want some privacy?"

Chase nodded. "That would be good. Could you grab some more shirts and the rest of my shoes from my closet? I'll go through the other stuff in my bedroom later and box it up for the garage."

"No problem." Ruby went into Chase's room, and he answered the phone.

"Dad?"

Ruby closed the door most of the way, though she could hear the tension in his voice as he spoke to his father.

She remembered what he'd told her before—that his mom had left and his dad was an asshole. Except for the day he'd proposed, he'd rarely spoken about his family.

I should have asked, she thought. Because even if they were fighting, Chase mattered to her. They were friends.

She missed joking around with him. The fun, easy banter they'd used to have.

She'd been too hard on him. Chase had done nothing but help her.

You could just say you're sorry.

Grumbling, she went into Chase's closet. After searching his shelves, she found an empty duffle bag to hold his shoes. There were only a few pairs. Some sneakers, loafers. Beach sandals with sand still on the soles.

One shoebox held comic books instead of shoes, and Ruby snorted as she flipped through them.

Spiderman, X-Men, The Incredible Hulk. Chase was a closet nerd like Devon. She was going to give him so much shit later. Not because comic books weren't cool, because anything could be cool if you owned it. But he'd hidden these away in here like a dirty secret.

Maybe it interfered with his perfect white-knight image, and he didn't want his dates to know.

Ruby carried the box of comics and the duffle of shoes to his bed. She looked at the two pillows. The quilt and white sheets.

How many women had slept in this bed with him?

Her brain suddenly conjured an image of Chase with a pretty, giggly blond. Heat raced through her veins, but it was not a good feeling.

Wait.

Oh, hell no.

She was not getting jealous over *Chase*. That would just be… strange.

But the images kept coming. All the things she'd been

noticing about Chase the last several days, now in a very different context.

His lips kissing someone else.

His heavy body pressing another woman into the mattress.

Someone's tongue licking droplets of sweat from his neck.

His back muscles flexing as he fucked someone and *oh god she was visualizing Chase having sex.*

What was going on in her brain?

Ruby had had a few random sexual thoughts about Chase before. He was a man, and he'd been sleeping in her bed. It was only natural.

But this was *his* bed, and he'd definitely had sex here. Probably a lot. Lots of athletic, naked sex.

Ruby sat on the floor, holding her head in her hands. She had to stop this. Right now.

A deep breath.

Okay. The moment was gone. Thank goodness.

She was supposed to be packing up shoes, not having fantasies about his naked body. Or wondering how big he was or what he tasted like.

No.

"Stop being weird," she whispered to herself.

When she opened her eyes, Ruby saw another shoebox tucked under his bed. Without stopping to think, Ruby grabbed the box and dragged it along the floor toward her. Lifted the lid.

There were no shoes inside.

At first, she thought this was just more cop stuff. Spare handcuffs. But these cuffs had a soft lining on the interior. And there were other things in this box, too.

Thick strips of black leather. Silky looking ropes.

She gasped as she realized what this was.

A sex box. Chase had a sex box under his bed, and she'd opened it.

Footsteps crossed the house, and the bedroom door pushed wide. "Hey, sorry about—Oh, fuck."

"I'm, um—" Ruby stammered.

She tried to hold out the box, and Chase lunged for it at the same time. Their hands collided, and the thing tipped over, contents spilling out all over Ruby's lap and the floor.

They both leaned forward and their heads bumped with a smack. "Ow!"

"Shit!" Chase rubbed his forehead. His voice was about an octave higher than normal. "Could you wait for me in the living room? *Please?*"

Ruby stood up. "Let's just be adults about this."

"*Living room,*" he said again, not looking at her.

She left his bedroom and paced until he came out. Chase was holding the duffle bag she'd packed full of shoes. The sex box was nowhere in sight.

And the tips of his ears were bright red.

He walked toward the door. "We've probably done enough for today. I'll pack up the car."

Ruby followed him outside. "I thought it was a pair of shoes."

"Under my bed? I said to get stuff from the closet."

"But it was a shoebox!"

The trunk popped open. He threw the duffle inside.

"Lots of people like to get tied up during sex," she said. "I mean, if that's what you're into. With the ropes. And the handcuffs."

Ruby heard a small intake of breath. An elderly woman with a cane was shuffling by on the sidewalk.

Chase raised his hand. "Hi, Mrs. Thompson." He glared at Ruby and dropped his voice. "Can you stop telling all my neighbors my business?"

"Oops."

"Just get in the car. I'll deal with everything else later."

"Then give me my keys." They'd taken her car because she'd wanted to drive. Probably to annoy him, if she was being honest.

"No. I'm driving back."

"But it's *my car.*"

"But you did something you shouldn't have, so I get to call dibs on driving."

"You're punishing me? That's...slightly kinky."

"Jesus, Ruby." He went back to the house and locked up.

Then they were both in the front seat. Ruby clicked her seatbelt into place. He put the car into gear and reversed out of the driveway.

Cue the awkward silence, despite the road noise and the low hum of the radio.

She tapped her fingers against the passenger door.

Do I say something? Do I pretend it didn't happen?

Do I admit that I'm really intrigued right now?

Should she confess something about herself? That she'd been fantasizing about him?

No. Not that. *Not* that.

"I'm sorry," she blurted out.

"It's fine." His teeth were clenched.

"Not just about...the box under your bed. I'm sorry I got mad at you the other day. You were only trying to help."

"It's okay," he said quietly. "I'm sorry too. I said stupid things."

"We both did."

Then, more silence. Which was still awkward. Cars and trees whooshed by as Chase drove.

Ruby jumped a little when he cleared his throat and spoke again. "For the record, I don't like to get tied up."

She glanced over. "What *do* you like?"

What the hell? Why had she just asked that? She'd joked about his sexual tastes before, but that had been different. That conversation hadn't been turning up her internal temperature.

Was he going to answer?

She wanted him to answer.

Because thinking of Chase naked, of his dick getting hard and the noises he would make as he came, was *really turning her on.*

Chase had one hand clenched on the steering wheel, the

other on his forehead. His tongue licked at his lower lip, and she followed the movement.

His tongue was pink. It was sexy.

Which was not a thing she'd ever realized before.

"I like to be the one doing the tying."

"How tied up are we talking?" Ruby asked, her tone light.

"Depends."

There was a heck of a lot of possibility in that word. Ruby had done the necktie thing with a guy in college. Wrists tied loosely above her head. But Chase's sex box had held much more than that.

"And you do that a lot? Tie women up?"

Was there air-conditioning in this car? She was overheating.

"I haven't done it in a while." His voice was husky. "Haven't been with anyone."

"It's been a while for me, too." She swallowed. "I mean having sex. Or getting tied up. Either one."

And now she was so aroused that the vibration of the car alone might be enough to set her off. Her skin tingled and ached to be touched. Ruby kept shifting against the seat, which felt really good against her clit. Like, deliriously good. She wasn't thinking straight.

She kept on rambling. "I haven't been with anyone since Mickey. I've wanted to, but it just, you know, I don't have many opportunities."

"That's a long time. To not have opportunities."

"No kidding."

For a while, Chase's eyes stayed glued to the road. They stopped at a red light. His thumb tapped the steering wheel. "I don't plan to see anyone else while we're married. I realize you and I didn't talk about that, but…just in case you were wondering."

"Me neither. Not like I'm going to bars or creeping around apps looking for hookups, anyway." Ruby clamped her mouth shut before something else ridiculous could come out.

"Glad that's cleared up," Chase said.

"Me too."

Even though it wasn't clear in the slightest.

Chapter Eighteen

What the hell am I talking about? Chase thought. Things were very much *not* cleared up.

She'd found the box under his bed. He shouldn't have said anything about it. Just pretended it hadn't happened. But then she'd suggested *he* liked being tied up, and he hadn't liked feeling mislabeled as something he wasn't.

So he'd told her.

Which he probably shouldn't have done.

But then she'd seemed…interested.

And now, he had no idea what Ruby was thinking.

They picked up Haley from Megan's on the way home, and he and Ruby both sounded too cheerful. Totally overcompensating.

Haley babbled on the drive home, but Chase and Ruby were silent.

I should say something, he thought.

But what? How could he talk about this without seeming either way too eager, or too dismissive?

He'd never gotten so tongue-tied with other women. Probably because no one else had ever mattered this much.

I won't risk it, he decided.

Because she was Devon's sister.

Because Chase had feelings for her, and she was never going to feel that way back. She viewed him as nothing more than a friend.

He relaxed. It was decided, and that was that. He was fine now. He wasn't going to obsess about what Ruby had said and whether or not she was up for trading orgasms.

Not. Thinking. About. It.

Chase focused on the road. It was a busy Sunday afternoon in West Oaks, and lots of other cars were out. But something bumped his instincts as they pulled into the parking lot for the apartment building.

He'd just driven past a blue Kia Rio. It had been idling at the curb right near the dumpsters, which had seemed like an odd place to wait. And the guy behind the wheel was almost comically oversized for the tiny sedan.

Then Chase got a better look at the guy.

Massive shoulders. A trunk-like neck. Shaved head.

Like the guy that Phyllis from Cakes 'N' More had described. The one who'd run through the alley on the day of Mickey's murder.

Chase drove through the lot and exited immediately on the other side.

He didn't want to scare Ruby. Maybe he was just being paranoid. But he wasn't taking any chances.

"What are you doing?" Ruby asked. "Why didn't you park?"

"I forgot we're out of milk."

"No, we're not."

"I think we are."

"Chase, I have nothing better to do every day than stare at the contents of my fridge. We have plenty of milk. What is going on?"

He glanced at the rearview mirror. The blue Kia had pulled out behind them.

The guy was following.

Shit.

Now, he was officially worried.

"We may have a problem," he said. "I think someone was waiting for us outside the apartment. And now he's following us."

"*What?*"

"Don't turn around. I don't want him to realize we noticed."

Ruby looked at the side mirror. "Who is he?"

"I think he's our alternate suspect. The guy the witness saw behind the cake shop. Ever seen him before?"

"He's wearing sunglasses, but he seems familiar. Like…"

"Like?"

"Like one of the fighters from the circuit." She turned to him, eyes widening. "Haley's in the car. What are we going to do?"

"I'm already heading for the police station." He had to get Ruby and Haley somewhere safe. If the guy got aggressive, Chase would have to think fast.

He accelerated through a stale yellow light. The guy behind him blew past the red.

Chase turned at the next right, and the Kia did too.

"Call 911," he said.

Ruby's hands were shaking as she took out her phone. He heard her speaking into it. At the same time, Haley kept talking in a sing-song voice in her car seat.

He was almost to the station.

Chase's entire body was a knot of tension. He was holding his breath.

He ran a stop sign, and other cars blared their horns. Ruby screamed. Chase's foot pressed the accelerator. They raced forward, going way too fast, and the tires squealed as he pulled into the West Oaks PD parking lot and zoomed up to the gate.

Chase turned around in his seat, looking behind them.

The blue Kia wasn't there. He didn't see it anywhere.

Ruby was shaking in the passenger seat, and Haley had started to cry.

~

"I'M SORRY I SCARED YOU," Chase said.

They were sitting in the kitchen after eating leftovers for dinner. Haley was in her crib for the night.

"Don't be sorry. I think you were right. The guy was following us."

"Maybe. But I might have overreacted."

The patrol officers who'd responded to Ruby's 911 call had certainly thought so. Chase had seen the skepticism on his coworkers' faces. And the recognition when Ruby had given her name.

Chase was trying to calm himself down after the stress of their afternoon. He'd been ready to do something drastic to protect Haley and Ruby, and now he wondered if the threat had been real at all.

To be safe, Chase had contacted Bennett Security to request that a car keep an eye outside. Just for the night. Of course, Noah had insisted that they'd watch the building around the clock for as long as needed. Devon would hear about it, but Chase could explain tomorrow. Tonight he was wiped.

"If that guy killed Mickey," Ruby said, "he'd know who I am. I'm sure he'd be following the news, and it wouldn't be too hard to figure out where I live or what car I drive. But why come here? Why follow us?"

"I don't know." Chase didn't want to think about the reasons. It couldn't possibly have been good.

He'd made an official report about the incident, for whatever that was worth. He'd given the Kia's license plate. But unless the man was driving his own car around and they could find his name that way, Chase doubted West Oaks PD would identify him.

They're going to think you're a head case, Shelby had said.

Chase groaned and rubbed a hand over his face. "I'm pretty tired. I'm going to bed."

"Already? We could watch TV."

He would've preferred to put an end to this frustrating day, but instead he said, "All right. Sure."

They sat on the couch and pulled up a show they'd been streaming. Chase struggled to concentrate.

At first, he was running through scenarios related to the suspect in the Kia Rio. What the guy might have wanted, how Chase could track the guy down.

But then, once that subject had exhausted itself, his mind started to wander…to what had happened earlier.

To Ruby finding the box under his bed. And their conversation in the car afterward.

Then he felt Ruby's eyes on him.

"You're glaring," he said.

She turned back to face the screen. "I'm not glaring."

But pretty soon, he felt it again. Ruby was watching him. Staring.

He'd noticed her looking at him a few times in the last week, too. But he'd assumed she was just getting used to his presence. It hadn't been like this.

Like she was scrutinizing him. Trying to see into his head.

Finally, Chase asked, "*What?*"

The word had come out more sharply than he'd intended.

"What do you mean, *what*?"

"You've been staring at me. I thought you wanted to watch TV, not watch me."

She switched off the screen and set down the remote. "I'm curious."

"About what?"

He knew. Of course he knew.

"About the handcuffs and ropes."

His pulse kicked. "Why?"

"Just because. What do you like about it? I want to know."

He adjusted his weight on the couch. "It's sex. People like different things."

"Yes, but I'm asking about *you*."

"Why?" he asked again.

Ruby's eyes trailed over him, and he saw the same interest

she'd shown in the car. So he hadn't been imagining it. "I like knowing things about you."

His heart rate immediately jumped into overdrive.

Did she want…?

Could she? Was that actually a possibility?

He knew he shouldn't have this conversation. He'd already decided.

But then he thought of how he hadn't gotten laid in a while. And she'd volunteered that she hadn't either.

And he wanted her. More than any other woman in the world, Chase wanted her.

"I enjoy setting the pace," he said. "Being the one in charge."

She smiled coyly. "Being dominant?"

"Yeah."

He could've sworn he saw a shiver run through her. A good shiver or a bad one, he didn't know.

"I guess it's not surprising," she said. "That you like to be in charge."

"Are we starting that fight again? About me being controlling?"

"No. But…Destiny called it."

"Destiny?"

"The friend I met in jail. She said she could tell you liked to get freaky. And it does fit with the cop stereotype. A sadist who gets off on power?" Her eyes danced with amusement.

He smiled in spite of himself, shaking his head. "I'm not a sadist. I don't like causing pain. I like being gentle."

Ruby's throat moved as she swallowed. "*That* doesn't surprise me in the least."

Damn, did that sexy little grin of hers get him going. His stomach swirled with arousal.

Was she flirting with him? Were they joking?

"Sometimes, going slow can be its own kind of torture," he said. "Or so I'm told."

"I had no clue you were hiding an inner sex fiend. I'm wondering what else I don't know about you."

"I'm hardly a sex fiend."

"You tie women up and torture them."

"Only if they want me to."

"Maybe *I* want you to."

His heart almost stopped.

Oh. Fuck.

Was this actually happening right now?

She blinked slowly at him. "Have you ever thought about me…like that?"

An image flashed into his mind: Ruby naked on her bed, wrists tied, legs spread.

"All the damn time."

Had he said that out loud?

"What about you?" he heard himself ask. "What do you like?"

She bit into her lower lip, head tilting. A lock of hair fell across her cheek. "I like…adrenaline."

He lifted his eyebrows.

"If I wanted you to tie me up, how would it go?"

Stay. Calm. He wasn't exactly sure what she meant, and he was *very* sure he shouldn't answer that. "I wouldn't do it our first time. Maybe not even the second. I'd want to be careful with you. See how far you were willing to go."

Ruby made a small whimper. Her hands fisted against the couch. His heart was throbbing, and his dick ached.

She glanced down at his lap. "You're hard."

There wasn't much use trying to hide it. "Yep."

"I make you hard?"

"I think that's obvious." His voice was low, coming from deep in his chest.

She was staring at his crotch. "When I was in your room today at your house, I started thinking about you in your bed, and I wondered what it would be like. Being naked with you. Watching you come. And when I opened that box? I wanted to find out even more."

He hadn't thought it was possible for his cock to get any

stiffer. But all the blood had rushed out of his head and gone south. He was lightheaded.

"Fuck, Ruby. You're killing me. I can't believe you're saying these things."

"Neither can I. I've never thought of you this way before. But now, I can't stop."

His brain had disconnected. That had to explain what he did next.

Chase leaned over, crossing that invisible barrier between them.

And his lips brushed over hers.

"*Chase.*" She sounded breathless.

Mayday. Turn back.

She was his friend. Devon's little sister.

Devon might be able to forgive him, but Chase had said nothing like this would ever happen. His word meant something.

And he was betraying his own heart, too. Because he loved her. And she didn't love him.

"Please tell me to stop." He was begging her. Begging himself.

"I don't want to."

Chase rubbed his cheek against hers. She closed her eyes like she was relishing the sensations.

"Do you like that?" he asked.

"*Yes.*" He was close enough that she breathed the word straight into his mouth.

Chase pulled back and looked at her. "Are you feeling it now? Adrenaline?"

She nodded. "My heart won't slow down."

"Mine won't either."

"My heart was beating hard in the car earlier, when I was scared, but this is different. Because I know I'm safe. Because it's you. I know you'd take care of me."

His fingers touched her chin. Different impulses warred in his mind. Desire and indecision. Need and hesitation.

Electricity arced between them. Pheromones filled the air.

"But I thought you didn't like when I'm protective."

"Right now it's getting me hot," she whispered. "That's *my* dirty secret."

Chase pulled her closer and crashed his mouth onto hers. His tongue licked the seam of her lips and swept inside. Tasting her.

She was everything he'd been craving. Sweetness and hunger and heat.

Ruby put her arms around his waist and gripped his T-shirt in her fists. Her tongue pushed back, battling with his. But he wanted to direct this moment. Wanted to show her exactly how this would go.

He lifted her into his lap and grabbed hold of her wrists, bending her arms so they'd cross behind her back. Ruby broke their kiss, eyes flaring with surprise.

"You okay with this?"

Ruby nodded.

Chase held her arms tightly at her lower back. He licked her throat, and Ruby tipped her head back, moaning. He felt the vibration against his mouth.

Chase did have a wild side. And he was so damn tired of holding it back.

Chapter Nineteen

I want this, Ruby thought. *I want Chase.*

This moment was so unexpected, this side of him was unexpected, and that just made her want him more.

Ruby straddled his lap. She felt the hot, thick ridge of his cock lining up against her clit between their layers of clothing. She hissed at the sensation. His mouth swallowed her moan.

His scent was familiar in this comforting, homey way, yet also in a completely new context that made her nerve endings sing. She felt like she was melting against him everywhere they touched. The soft light in the room added to that cozy feeling. She was warm and safe, and that knowledge made her all the more ready to push her comfort zone.

Chase kept upping the pace and the pressure of his kisses, owning her mouth. He ground his dick against her, and he bound her wrists with his strong hands so she couldn't touch him back. It was infuriating. But it also felt wildly, recklessly good.

She had no idea what he would do next, where this would lead.

The ache between her legs was building, and the hard length of his dick was hitting her at just the right angle.

She just *wanted*, and that alone felt so good. To be in this moment with another person. With *Chase*.

He panted and thrust against her. "Should we…did you want me to…"

"I don't want to stop."

"Neither do I. But if we don't, I'm going to come in my pants like a teenager."

"Would that be so awful?"

He kissed her again. "I have something better in mind."

Chase picked her up and carried her over to the kitchen table. He set her down on the tabletop. "Can I undress you?"

Ruby nodded. Yes. This was a very good idea. "I want you naked too. I want to see all of you."

Chase grinned. "We'll get there. Lift your arms."

She did as he asked, and he pulled her top over her head. Then he tugged the waistband of her leggings. Ruby shifted from side to side so he could get them off.

Her bra and panties were black cotton, and she thanked the beauty gods that she'd gotten her regular wax a couple of weeks ago. She was still smooth and good to go. Not that she ever would've expected to be getting naked with any man, much less Chase.

From the way his waistband clung to his hips, showing off the V of muscle and a glimpse of happy trail below the edge of his shirt, she guessed he was going commando under those shorts.

When they'd been sitting on the couch and she'd seen his erection tenting the fabric, that was the moment she'd known for sure—she needed to get off with him. It hadn't just sounded pleasant or fun. She'd been desperate for it.

She'd wanted to tug down his shorts. Touch him, taste him. She'd felt dizzy, she'd wanted it so much.

Just as needy as she was right now.

Ruby slid her fingers along his short hair, pulling him closer. He smiled and shook his head. "Nope, not gonna let you rush me."

He pushed her down onto the table, holding her hands above her head. His grip on her was gentle, but she still couldn't move.

Chase was in complete control. And she liked it. Liked it so much.

His gaze ate her up, pure lust in his expression. "Look at you. You're so gorgeous laid out on that table for me." His hands moved down along her sides, then to her legs. He pushed his nose into the crotch of her panties. Inhaled. "Fuck, that's sweet."

Who *was* this man?

This wasn't the Chase she'd known for the past year. The guy who was her friend and nothing more.

The man in front of her was pure sex. How the hell had she not seen it?

"Chase, I…I want…"

"Ask for what you want."

"I want your mouth."

"To do what?"

"Lick me." Her skin was on fire. "Suck my clit."

His eyes flared, and his tongue moved over his lower lip. "Who are you asking to lick you? I want to hear my name."

Ruby's fists clenched and unclenched above her head. She couldn't take this much wanting. Her heart was shaking her entire body.

"Chase, please lick me. I need your tongue on me. Inside me. Please, Chase. Please."

"Be a good girl, and I will."

He flicked her bra straps past her shoulders, pulling until her breasts were uncovered. His tongue lashed over one nipple, then the other, making her gasp.

Chase kissed his way down her stomach. When he reached her panties, he used his teeth to grab hold of the fabric and tug them down. Ruby lifted her hips, helping, and the cotton slid down her legs and off.

He stood up, resting his hands on her bent knees, looking down at her. "You have a tattoo." It was a line of stars along her right hip bone, something hardly anyone had ever seen. Even her swimsuit usually covered it. He ran a finger from star to star. "Pretty."

Ruby was glad when he didn't ask her to explain the why or when. She was too wound up to talk about her ink.

"Open your legs for me?" he asked. He smiled when she obeyed.

Chase brought two fingers to her center. Swirled them around her opening. She made a needy whimper.

She felt totally shameless, letting him see her this way. But Ruby had never been shy during sex. It was like she was remembering a part of herself that she'd lost since becoming a mom. A part she desperately wanted back.

He rubbed his face along the insides of her thighs. His stubble was rough against her skin.

"Chase, *please.*"

His grin turned wicked. "Don't worry. I'll give you what you need."

His two fingers widened her even more. Slowly, he bent forward. She felt his breath on her bare skin. One of his knees rested on a chair.

Finally, his tongue slid up and down her sensitive folds. Ruby tipped her head back. She bit her lower lip to quiet her moans.

"You taste incredible. I could eat you all fucking day."

Chase worked his mouth over her. He sucked and licked and savored. The sensations were unreal. Nothing had ever felt this good. Like she was going out of her mind with it. She had to force her eyes open to look down at him, just to make sure this was really happening.

Chase's mouth buried between her legs was the hottest thing she'd ever seen. Maybe because it was kind of wrong. And even more than that—because she felt like she had no control over what she was feeling. She wanted the very thing she'd thought she *didn't* want.

Ruby was writhing and whimpering against the table. "I'm so close."

Chase pulled back, taking a breath. "Should I slow down?"

"*No*. I need to come."

"How bad do you want it?"

"*Please*, Chase. Make me come."

He flicked his tongue rapidly over her clit and pushed two fingers inside of her. Ruby stuck her knuckle into her mouth and bit down.

Her orgasm slammed into her, back arching off the table, legs shaking. But she kept her gaze on Chase. He looked back at her as his tongue worked, and damn if that eye contact didn't rocket the intensity to an even higher degree. Knowing it was him making her feel this way.

Wave after wave of aftershocks flooded her body with pleasure until they finally ebbed away.

Her head lolled back against the table. "I can't move." She felt like he'd put some sort of spell on her. Maybe it was just having an orgasm with another person for the first time in two years.

Right. More like she'd never been eaten out so thoroughly in her entire damned life.

Chase put his arms around her, lifting her upright. She melted against him as he kissed her, his tongue licking into her mouth. But this kiss didn't feel demanding. It was comforting. Like he was kissing away any doubt she might be having.

"What do you need now?" he asked.

"To see you naked. Please?"

"Since you asked nicely. You going to fall over when I let you go?"

"I'm not *that* helpless." Ruby braced her hands on the table.

He pulled off his shirt, his movements languid. Like he was in no hurry.

She'd seen Chase without a shirt plenty of times before, and she hadn't paid much attention. But this was different. Like she was seeing him with new eyes.

Then Chase tugged down his shorts, and his cock bounced back up.

Getting to see *all* of him… She sucked in a breath.

He was thick everywhere. He looked like he'd been sculpted from stone. But she felt the heat radiating from him.

"Can I taste you?" Ruby's voice betrayed the neediness she still felt. To have her lips wrapped around him, to feel the weight of him on her tongue.

Grinning, Chase grabbed a cushion from the couch and threw it the floor at his feet. "Get on your knees." It was a gentle command. But she was more than willing. This was exactly what she had in mind.

Ruby got up from the table and kneeled in front of him on the pillow. His cock pointed straight at her face, glistening at the tip.

She ran her hands up the backs of his legs. Chase didn't have much hair on his body. His legs and chest were mostly smooth. His shaft was long and thick, roped with veins, and his balls were heavy, the skin a darker shade.

She felt wanton. Like a purely sexual being.

"Feed me your cock?" she asked.

His dick jerked. "Oh, fuck." Chase caressed her cheek, then his fingers slid into her hair. "I might not want your mouth on me."

She frowned. "Why?"

"Because you're ruining me. Fucking destroying me for anyone else."

He rubbed the head of his cock across her lips, and her tongue flicked out, tasting the salty precum. Then he held the back of her head as he slowly pushed the tip forward past her lips. "Do you like that?"

She nodded, mouth too full of him to speak. She was just feeling, experiencing, in a way she hadn't done in so long. Maybe in a way she'd never done before.

"Then open up wider so you can take more of me." He touched her chin, guiding her. "Good girl. Just like that."

Chase fucked her mouth with slow, deep strokes. He was careful not to go to the back of her throat. Ruby could have taken it. But she was getting the sense that Chase *liked* keeping himself reined in. And that meant she could relax completely into this, knowing he wouldn't take it too far.

"Ruby, your mouth is perfect." He started to pant faster, his hips thrusting at a quicker rate.

She brought a hand up to cup his balls. They'd drawn tight against his body.

His cock kept pushing into her mouth, dragging against her tongue. Edging deeper toward her throat.

Chase was using her like she was made for sex, for pleasure. His moans satisfied some deeper need that even her orgasm hadn't reached. It was like she'd gone outside of her everyday worries and responsibilities—like he'd set her free.

She already knew she'd crave having this again. This incredible freedom to do nothing but *feel*.

Then he withdrew and gripped his shaft. He fucked into his fist. Cried out. His other hand tightened in her hair.

Cum spurted from his tip onto her chest. His cock pulsed again. Another shot hit her skin. A third. His hips kept pumping his dick into his hand. Finally he stilled.

Chase took a step back, looking down at her. "You all right?"

His cum dripped down between her breasts, and Ruby had never experienced anything so erotic.

"Never better." It made little sense, given everything else going on in her life, but she meant it. Her daughter was safe and asleep, and Ruby had just had the best orgasm of her life with a close friend.

A *hot* close friend.

She wanted to do it again.

Ruby stood up. Chase grabbed his shirt and used it to wipe her off.

"I can clean myself up," she said.

"Nope. This is my job. And I'll do the laundry tomorrow, too."

"Trying to earn bonus points? You've done enough."

He brought his lips to her ear. "Don't argue with me," he whispered.

Part of her wanted to, just to be contrarian. Staying quiet had never been Ruby's style. But tonight, for this moment, she decided not to fight.

Then crying came from Haley's bedroom, and it was like a bucket of ice water had splashed over her.

Ruby grabbed for her clothes, pulling them on as she ran for her daughter's room. "Damn it," she said, realizing she hadn't washed her hands.

When she got to Haley's room, the baby was standing in her crib. Ruby picked her up. "What's wrong, bug? Did you have a bad dream?"

What if they'd been too loud? Had they woken her? This was mortifying.

Of course, there was no way Haley could have any clue what her mom had been doing. But guilt still flooded Ruby's body.

She'd only been thinking of herself in the living room. Not of her daughter.

"Hey," Chase said softly. "Everything okay?" He'd thrown on fresh clothes.

"Sometimes she just wakes up."

Haley had hidden her face against her mom's chest, but when she heard Chase's voice, she looked up. Her chubby arms reached out for him.

"Can I?" he asked.

"Of course. She loves you."

Ruby handed him the baby. Haley put her cheek on his shoulder. Chase bounced her gently and rocked back and forth.

"I don't know if we woke her," Ruby said, "or if she's stressed because of what happened earlier..."

"Or maybe she just wanted to be held. We all need that sometimes."

They hadn't switched on the overhead, but Haley's nightlight reflected his pale eyes. He was holding the baby, but he was watching Ruby.

They'd been sharing a very hot fantasy in the living room. But that bubble had popped.

She'd enjoyed it. A lot. Now that she'd seen Chase in this new way, Ruby wasn't sure she could go back. Or that she wanted to.

But what about Haley, who loved Chase like an uncle? Ruby would never do anything to jeopardize that.

It took a while to get Haley back down. But finally, she was lying calmly in the crib and ready to fall back asleep.

They went out to the main room.

Chase was standing by the front door, staring at the carpet. Like he felt the same guilt she did. "How are you feeling?" he asked.

"I have no regrets. But I'm not sure what to think. I didn't expect any of that to happen."

"Me neither."

"I don't want this to affect Haley."

"It doesn't have to." He rubbed a hand over his jaw. "But…I need to tell you something." He sounded so serious. Like it was something *bad.*

He had a secret girlfriend? An STD?

"What is it?"

"I have a thing for you. It's been going on awhile."

She almost laughed. Of all the things he could've confessed, this was it? "Oh. Really? Like, a crush?"

He nodded, still not looking at her.

"An I-want-to-have-sex-with-you crush?"

Chase finally met her gaze. "Pretty much."

"For how long?"

"A…few months. At least. But it's been a lot worse since I moved in."

"Why didn't you say anything?"

"Because we're friends. You're Devon's sister."

She laughed out loud as she remembered who'd predicted this. "Wait, Destiny called it! She said you were into me. I guess she was psychic."

"We could use her on the force. She'd be great in interrogations."

Ruby walked over to him and slid her arms around his waist. "I'm flattered."

"It doesn't bother you?"

"I mean, it's not like you're in love with me."

He laughed nervously. "*No*. It's not like that."

"So why would I mind? It's nice to feel desirable."

He ran his hands along her sides. "You're extremely desirable. I'm desiring you right now."

She almost felt shy, which made no sense given the shameless position they'd been in a few minutes ago. "You said we all need to be held sometimes. I think I've *really* needed that. To be kissed and touched. And fucked." Even before her life had been thrown into turmoil, she'd been lonely, though she hadn't even realized it until now.

"You want to do this again?" he asked.

How could she not? "As long as nothing changes as far as Haley's concerned."

"Same." Chase touched his forehead to hers. "If you need to be kissed and touched and fucked, I can definitely help you out."

"Always so selfless."

"I'd like to cuddle you, too. If you're into that."

"Who knew Chase Collins could get so kinky?"

She let him pick her up and cradle her in his arms. Chase carried her to their bed and laid her down. Snuggled in beside her.

He kissed her forehead and caressed her face and arms until she drifted into dreamless sleep.

Chapter Twenty

Chase woke up in bed and rolled over to look at Ruby. Her dark hair fell across her cheek, and her eyelashes were splayed. Her pink mouth looked soft and pouty and kissable.

Usually in the mornings, he'd resisted the urge to watch her sleeping. It had seemed creepy. But after what they'd done last night?

Unless that had been a dream. The best, most vivid sex dream of his life.

Chase moved onto his back, staring at the ceiling.

His dick was achingly hard inside his pajama pants. And his memories of last night weren't doing anything to remedy that situation.

If she really wanted to do the friends-with-benefits thing, he was game. And he sure as hell hoped she hadn't changed her mind. Their chemistry last night had been explosive. He'd come so hard he was surprised his balls had anything left.

He'd tried to hint at his true feelings, and that hadn't gone so well. He'd chickened out before confessing the true extent of it. And it was probably a good thing, because Ruby had made it clear she still viewed him as a friend.

But now, he was a friend she wanted to fuck. It was more than he'd ever hoped for.

Ruby was the strongest, bravest, most beautiful woman he'd ever known. But she'd been willing to submit to him, and he couldn't imagine anything hotter. Then being able to cuddle her and take care of her afterward had almost been better than the rest of it.

Almost.

No way could he turn down more of that. His cock was far too greedy. Even if it meant the rest of him could get hurt. But *he* was the one who risked getting his heart broken. That was his problem, not Ruby's.

Speaking of his greedy cock, he needed to deal with this hard-on before he could do anything else.

Chase went to the bathroom, stripped off his pajamas, and jumped under the cold spray of the shower. He could've jerked off. But going solo didn't sound nearly so appealing when Ruby might help him out with that later. He figured he should be optimistic.

After he'd cleaned up and dressed, Ruby was still sound asleep. He wanted her to get all the rest she needed. She probably thought he hadn't noticed how poorly she slept most nights, but he had.

Chase heard Haley babbling in her room. He opened the door and went inside. "What do you think you're doing, huh?"

Haley had one leg over the side of her crib, trying to climb out. She looked at him and smiled ear to ear. "Chay-Chay."

"You're in the middle of a jailbreak, and that's all you have to say for yourself?"

She was all bright eyed, like she hadn't been up in the night at all. Maybe she didn't even remember it. Chase was pretty sure the good stuff sunk in a lot more with Haley than the bad.

He picked her up, and Haley patted his cheek, giggling at how his whiskers felt against her hand. At least, he was pretty sure that was what she was giggling about. That, or she thought he looked funny.

He set her down on the floor, and she ran over to her cubby of books. Chase sat, back against the wall, and watched her play.

She brought a book over to him. "Dis one."

"Can you use the magic word?"

"Peas read dis one."

His eyebrows shot up. "Four-word sentence? Harvard, here we come." Haley plopped down into his lap, and Chase read to her about dinosaurs having a tea party. After a while, she lost interest and went to push the buttons on a noisy plastic toy instead.

"I really like your mom, princess," he murmured. "A lot. More than a lot."

Haley looked at him, big brown eyes blinking.

"But nothing that happens between me and your mom will ever change how I feel about you. I'll always be your Uncle Chase. I'm going to take care of you, and I'm going to keep my promises. No matter what. Okay? Got it?"

He held up his hand for a high five. Sometimes Haley understood, and sometimes she didn't. Or just chose to ignore him.

But today, she toddled over and rested her tiny hand against his.

The door opened. Ruby stood there yawning, hair a wild halo around her head. "You started the fun without me?"

"We were just getting some reading in. She's almost ready to ace her SATs."

"I expect nothing less."

"Coffee?" he asked.

"Dying for some."

"Didn't you sleep well?"

"I slept great. Did you?"

"Never better."

They smiled at one another. Chase's blood pumped like he'd already had his caffeine.

He could feel the changed energy between them as they made breakfast, like there was an electrical charge in the air. It was in Ruby's coy smiles, the way their eyes kept meeting.

But he'd decided to play it cool. He wasn't going to mention last night until Ruby did.

They sat down with mugs of brewed coffee and plates of toast. Chase put peanut butter on his for some protein. Haley smeared grape jam all over her mouth and nose, which made Ruby laugh. That sound fed him even more than his breakfast. He felt so damn lucky to be a part of their lives.

Chase set down his coffee. "I thought we'd get out of the apartment today. Take Haley to the beach."

Ruby perked up. "Yeah? I haven't been to the beach in ages."

"Then let's do it."

"What about the car from Bennett Security?"

"They can come too."

He couldn't imagine a better way to spend the rest of his weekend. And he knew Ruby had been feeling stuck lately. She deserved a day of fun without any worries. No lawyers, no fears about anyone following her.

Chase wanted to give that to her.

They changed into bathing suits, packed up toys and towels, and slathered on sunscreen. He took a moment to check in with the Bennett Security guys, who hadn't seen any sign of the man with the shaved head or the blue Kia.

They headed out, and their extra security followed and found a parking spot with a view of the water. The beach was quiet, which made sense because it was a Monday. His patrol schedule changed about every month, but at the moment he had Sundays and Mondays off, no graveyard or swing shifts. The ideal combination.

Ruby staked out a spot where parents and kids had already gathered. Mostly there were moms, but some dads too. Other toddlers were already playing in the sand. Haley dug right in, squatting down with her pink plastic shovel.

Chase put out beach towels for them to sit. His eyes traced Ruby's curves as she took off her cover-up. She'd worn a dark green bikini and looked so good his mouth watered.

At ease, Marine, he told himself. He didn't even know yet what she wanted.

But after he pulled his shirt off, he found her checking him out, too. Chase took that as a sign of encouragement.

"So," he said. "The stars on your hip."

She rested her hands behind her on the towel. "We all have secrets, don't we?"

"Not so secret anymore."

Ruby looked him up and down, her tongue at the corner of her mouth. Her gaze was so heated that he had to look away.

"Careful," he said. "You're going to get me worked up again. Tell me about your tattoo. Is there a story behind it?"

"I got it done after I had Haley. I wasn't feeling very beautiful, and I wanted to have that back. But it was something just for me."

He was surprised at her explanation, but not her honesty. "There's no way you were ever not beautiful."

Ruby rolled her eyes. "I said I didn't *feel* beautiful. And you didn't know me then. Maybe I was gross."

"Not possible. But I understand your point. Did the tattoo help?"

"It did, yeah. I chose a trail of stars because it reminded me that I was on a path, even if I didn't know where I was going yet." She stretched out her legs, dipping her toes into the sand. "Except for the artist and my doctor, you're the only other person who's seen it."

The sun was beating down on them, but there was a warm glow inside of Chase too.

"I have a tattoo," he confessed.

She glanced over. "You? I didn't see any ink on you last night."

That warm glow turned to fire at the reminder of being naked with her. Of Ruby on her knees for him. "That's because I didn't turn around."

Her eyes narrowed. She leaned so she could see his back, though of course he'd had his shirt off around her before.

"It's not there," he said.

"Wait. Is it on your *butt*?"

He nodded. "I was nineteen, right before my first deployment. Got drunk off my ass with my buddies, which is fitting, since my ass is where the tattoo ended up."

"Chase has a secret butt tattoo. This is too good." She cackled, kicking her legs. "What's it of?"

"Maybe I'll let you see it. If you really want to."

"Are you kidding? Of course I want to."

"You sure about that?"

Ruby's expression changed, the humor disappearing. When she spoke, her voice had lowered. "I want to. I thought we agreed."

He knew they weren't just talking about the tattoo. "I didn't want to assume. But last night was…fuck, I don't think I've come that hard in my life."

A shudder ran through her. "Me neither. Once wasn't enough."

"Nowhere near enough. There's a lot more I want to do with you."

Her smile slowly reappeared. "Like getting out that naughty shoebox of yours?"

"Maybe." Though he'd left the box of bondage gear at his house. If Ruby wanted to try that, he'd order new supplies just for her. "We can work up to that. First, I want to explore every part of you. Find out everything you like."

Her chest was moving fast, as if she were trying to catch her breath. "If we're doing this, we need to set some boundaries."

"Boundaries are good. Such as?"

"We can't tell anyone else. This stays between us. That includes not kissing or getting frisky in front of Haley."

They both glanced over at the little girl, who was studying the grains of sand that had stuck to her hand.

"I don't know how much she understands," Ruby said. "I don't want to confuse her."

"Yeah. Of course."

"And I need for us both to be sure this won't screw up our friendship. Even when the arrangement ends."

His chest clenched with longing. "It won't change anything."

"Good." Ruby sat up, crossing her legs. "If either one of us wants to stop, we stop. No hard feelings."

"Got it. But if we're setting ground rules, I get to make one too."

"And that is?"

"You let me help with the investigation into Mickey's murder."

Ruby frowned. "I don't want to have that fight with you again."

"Then don't fight me. I'm insisting. Maybe I'm not ex-special forces like Max or Noah, and I wasn't a Ranger like Devon. But I've been on patrol with major crimes at West Oaks PD for three years. I've worked on dozens of investigations, and I know how these things work."

"It's not about me doubting your abilities to—"

"Isn't it? You don't think I can toe the line at work. But I can. I'll walk right up to that line and look over. But I won't go past it. And I need you to trust that I know what I'm doing."

"I just don't want you hurt. Or in trouble."

"Ruby, do you trust me or not?" If she didn't, then he couldn't sleep with her. To have the kind of sex he craved with her—that she seemed to want just as much—he had to know that she had complete faith in him.

She watched Haley playing before she answered. "I trust you."

Chase touched her chin. "You sure about that?"

"I *do*," she said emphatically. "But there are things you don't know yet. And I'm not sure I want you to know."

He tried not to show how much that hurt. "Why not?"

"I don't want to change how you see me."

"That would be hard to do. I think you're pretty great."

She sighed. "Okay. I'll tell you what you need to know. But not here. Later."

"Then we agree? I can help?"

"Yeah. But don't get used to me caving." She smiled sardonically. "I'm not always this compliant."

He knew that already. Ruby was no pushover, and he didn't ever want that to change. That spark of defiance in her eyes was one of the things he loved most about her. "Too bad we can't kiss in front of Haley," he said. "Because I really want to kiss that smile off your face."

"And what was it you were *just saying* about not crossing the line?"

But she was leaning in. Chase wondered if he could sneak a quick kiss if Haley wasn't looking.

Then a familiar voice rang out, and Ruby jerked away from him.

"There you are." Devon dumped a beach bag next to them. "Chase, what the heck, dude? You don't answer your texts anymore?"

Aurora waved from behind him. "We were hoping to catch up with you. Mrs. Murtree said she saw you leaving in your beach wear."

Ruby held up her hands. "And here we are. Ta-da."

"Guess my phone was on silent," Chase said. "Sorry." Though he might not have answered Devon's message right away. Not after what he and Ruby had been up to last night.

They were two grown adults. They were *married*. What they did alone wasn't anyone's business.

Or maybe those were just excuses to soothe Chase's guilty conscience. Because even if Ruby hadn't asked to keep their arrangement a secret, there was no way Chase wanted to fess up to her brother.

You're cool with me and Ruby fucking around, right?

Ha. Not likely. That was not a conversation Chase ever wanted to have.

Chapter Twenty-One

Ruby walked down to the water with Aurora. They'd left Haley with the guys. "How are you feeling?" Ruby asked. "When I was pregnant with Haley, I spent my entire first trimester over the toilet."

"I feel all right. Not much nausea so far. Except for Max being a butthead, but that's typical."

They hadn't had much chance to catch up since the post-wedding gathering. Ruby hadn't been avoiding Aurora. Not consciously. There'd been so much going on. But now, Ruby regretted that they hadn't talked.

She didn't want to share what had happened yesterday with that car following them. That had been too stressful. Devon was bound to find out about it, and he'd notice those guys from Bennett Security outside the building. Assuming they hadn't given him a courtesy call already. But for the moment, Ruby just wanted to have a conversation that didn't relate to Mickey's murder or her arrest.

Aurora glanced back at the men. "You and Chase looked pretty cozy when we walked up."

Ruby dipped her toes into the surf. "Did we?"

"Yep. You did." Aurora was squinting at her. "How do you like being married?"

"It's…" *Hot? Because we gave each other monster orgasms last night?* "I like having Chase around. Haley loves it, obviously. He's great for lifting heavy boxes and taking out the trash."

"And that's it?"

"Yep. That's it."

"No other benefits to having a tall, charming Marine around?"

Ruby laughed. "Who said anything about charming?"

Aurora hummed like she'd heard something in Ruby's voice.

Sitting on the beach towel, it had taken a lot of willpower not to kiss him. Even though she'd just made him agree not to kiss in front of Haley.

Now that she'd realized how attractive he was, it was impossible not to notice. But Chase was so sweet, too. Seeing him with Haley did something to the mom part of her brain. Ruby craved being naked with him again, but she also just wanted to touch him and be near him.

Which was an entirely new experience when it came to Chase.

And he'd had a crush on her for months? How had she not noticed?

"Anyway," Ruby said, "what were you saying about Max being a butthead?"

"Just that big brothers can be so annoying. Getting in the way? Interrupting certain moments? If you know what I mean?"

"Not in the slightest." Ruby smiled at her friend. "Quit fishing, Aurora."

She made a show of looking around. "I'm just admiring the ocean views. There's no fishing."

"*Right.*"

They walked along the sand as the waves lapped at their feet. "I've been meaning to apologize," Aurora said. "Devon and I shouldn't have made the baby announcement on your wedding day. It had to be emotional for you, and I should've been more sensitive. I just couldn't hold it in anymore, and—"

Ruby turned around to face her. "No, don't be sorry. Our family needed good news. Really."

Aurora bit her lip. "You sure?"

It did hurt, some. Remembering how hard her own pregnancy had been. That feeling of being abandoned and alone. But it wasn't jealousy. Things would be different for Devon and Aurora, and she was so grateful for that.

"I'm thrilled for you guys. Devon is going to be an amazing dad, and Max will be a wonderful uncle. You're going to be so tired of how sappy and sweet they are."

Aurora wiped tears from her face. "I can't wait. Watching you with Haley, I know that's what I want. To be exactly the kind of mom that you are."

"Ugh, stop. You're going to make me cry too."

They hugged and rocked back and forth.

"I just want you to be okay," Aurora said.

"I will. Don't worry about me, it's annoying."

"Right. You have a husband to take care of that now."

"To take care of annoying me? Yeah, Chase already has that covered." Though she didn't mind his bossiness as much when it led to orgasms.

"He's a good man. A *really* good man. I wouldn't have let you marry him otherwise."

"I know it. On both those counts."

But she hadn't known when they'd gotten married just how sexy he was. How amazing it would feel to give him control during sex, even when she demanded independence in every other aspect of her life.

And now Aurora was grinning at her like she could see these thoughts on Ruby's face. "Just how good a man *is* he?"

"Shush." Ruby kicked water at her. "If you say one word to Devon…"

"About what? I don't have the faintest idea what you're talking about." They kept walking, and Aurora's bright smile could've lit up the sky if the sun wasn't already shining. "I just hope you're having as much fun as Devon and I did when we first got together."

Not taking the bait, she thought.

"I've been meaning to ask you. What happened to the curtain rod in the bathroom at Chase's house?" Ruby asked.

Aurora burst out laughing. "I'll only tell you if you spill the details about what you and Chase have been up to."

Ruby shook her head. "Never mind. I don't want to know."

THEY WENT BACK HOME in time for Haley's nap. Once the baby was in her crib with the door closed, Ruby found Chase grinning at her mischievously.

"What should we do now?" he asked.

"I have a few ideas."

They rushed into the living room, all fumbling limbs as they pushed each other toward the couch. Chase's mouth collided with hers.

They made out for a while, Ruby in his lap. She tugged off his shirt, and he took off her cover-up. They were both in their swimsuits, which was faintly ridiculous, but also kind of hot.

Ruby's hands traced over the curves of his pecs and abs, noticing all the details of him that had done nothing for her before, yet now made her body flush with heat.

Chase was bigger than Mickey had been, not as wiry and lean. She hadn't known bulky muscles could be so sexy. His skin was smooth, and she liked touching it. Kissing it.

Chase's body was like a map of a place she'd been before, yet she'd never really stopped to *see* it. And now that she was seeing it, she wanted to curl up and stay here.

Well, stay for now. Until they'd both gotten what they needed. And then, after it was finished, they'd share this naughty little secret that they could laugh about later.

She sat to one side of him on the couch. "Show me your tattoo."

Chase rolled his eyes, but he stood up. His cock was half-hard in his swim trunks.

He turned around, holding his arms out. "Go ahead."

Ruby stuck her fingers in his waistband and tugged the trunks down.

His left butt cheek had a tattoo of a blue anchor with a red heart around it.

"Oh. My. God. It's so cute. Because you loved the Marines so much?"

"Who knows? I was drunk when I picked it."

"It could've been much worse."

"No doubt."

Another meaning for the tattoo occurred to her. A heart weighed down by something heavy. She hoped it didn't hold that meaning for Chase.

She pinched his cheek, then leaned forward to smack a kiss on the tattoo. "There. You can't say I never kiss your ass." It was a fine ass, too. Round and firm.

Chase tugged up his trunks. "Now I have to kiss yours. Wouldn't be fair otherwise." He grabbed her. They fell back onto the couch, wrestling and laughing. He pinned her down, yanked up her swimsuit over one butt cheek, and planted his lips there.

"Ow! That's not a kiss, that's a hickey!"

But it didn't really hurt. She liked it. Liked the idea that Chase was marking her as his, even if the bruise would fade.

He let her go, and she rolled over. They made out until Ruby started cracking up again.

"What's so funny now?" Chase asked.

"I don't even know. I'm just…happy, I guess. I like this."

The look he gave her was more tenderness than heat. He touched his knuckle to her chin. "I like this, too. A lot."

"I was just thinking that we'll have a naughty secret whenever this ends, but Aurora might've already guessed what we're doing."

"*What?*"

"Don't worry, I didn't confirm anything. She's not going to tell Devon."

"You sure? This is private, and I feel justified keeping it from him, but he's not going to be happy if he finds out. He was already weird about us getting married."

"Then he can keep his opinions to himself. But talking to Aurora reminded me of something else. I really can't afford to get pregnant again. We have to be careful."

Chase's ears were starting to color. "We don't even have to… we can keep doing other things. If you don't want to take the risk."

It was adorable how flustered he was, yet last night his dirty mouth had been shameless. "I want you to fuck me. But we'll need condoms because I don't have any." She was on the pill to regulate her cycle, but she'd been on the pill when she'd gotten pregnant with Haley, too.

"That's easy enough to fix. I didn't bring any with me when I moved in. That would've been presumptuous."

"Neither of us planned for this."

"That's for sure."

But sometimes the best things weren't planned. This was one of her mantras, a truth that had given her hope through her pregnancy. But that didn't mean she should be reckless about having another baby. She couldn't possibly deal with a complication like that at the moment.

Or *ever*, when it came to Chase. This marriage had an end date, even if they didn't know the exact timing yet.

"I do want you to fuck me. Not tonight. But soon."

Chase smiled slowly. "It can be whenever you decide." He kissed her neck. "But you'll have to be good and do what I say."

"And what if I don't?"

"I just might have to make you." Chase rocked his hard-on against her.

A thrill of desire zapped along her spine. Last night with

Chase, she'd enjoyed giving in. But maybe resisting him would be just as much fun.

Ruby's phone rang, and she groaned. "Dang it." She'd kept the volume turned down so it wouldn't wake Haley, but that ring tone was unmistakable. Jane's number had a special notification, so Ruby would always know the call or text was from her lawyer.

Reluctantly, she got out from underneath him and went to pick up.

"Hi, Jane."

"Ruby, I have news. It's not good."

She steeled herself. "What is it? Did something happen in my case?"

Chase walked over and stood beside her, arms crossed as he listened.

"Not the criminal one. My friend who's representing you on the custody matter? She sent me a document that was just filed with the family court. She asked me to prepare you before she gives you a call."

"This is about Haley?"

Chase put his arm around her.

"Yes," Jane said. "Mickey's mother has asked for placement. That means she's requested temporary custody of Haley. If the court grants her request, it would be immediate."

Ruby closed her eyes, lip trembling. "She can do that?"

"As a grandparent in this type of case, yes. She can try. Mrs. Waverley also requested visitation, which the court is highly likely to grant. Obviously, it would be without you present. Your bail conditions prevent you from being anywhere near Mickey's immediate family members."

"They want to see Haley without me there? *No.* No way. They don't even know her. I've never even met them." Panic was rising up like an ocean wave inside her, threatening to drag her under.

"I know, Ruby. But Chase is her step-father now. The court will probably allow him to be there."

Chase rested his cheek against her hair. Having him there helped her to breathe. "When is all this going to happen?"

"Probably soon. My friend will call you to discuss the process. She's the expert in this field. But I wanted you to know I'm here for you, however I can be. Not just as your lawyer but as your friend. Okay? Whatever you need."

"We both know what I need." What if the family court took Haley away from her before her criminal case had even gotten to trial? "What I need is to prove that I'm innocent! So they can't do this to me."

"And I'm working on that. I just need you to be—"

"Jane, don't you *dare* tell me to be patient."

"You're right. I won't. So I'll just say that I'm getting back to work. I'll talk to you soon." She ended the call.

Ruby dropped her phone to her side.

"We're not letting them take Haley." Chase probably hadn't heard every word Jane had said, but clearly he'd heard enough.

"If Mickey's family gets to visit Haley, will you be there? I need you to be there. They're strangers. She might be…scared."

"Absolutely."

"Okay." The panic was receding. "Okay."

Ruby didn't know Mickey's family. Maybe they weren't bad people. They were probably heartbroken over losing him, especially in such a traumatic way.

Maybe they even deserved a role in Haley's life.

But right now, they believed Ruby was a killer.

If she'd been in their place, would she have stopped at anything to get Haley away?

Chapter Twenty-Two

Chase pulled on a West Oaks PD polo shirt over his jeans. Technically, wearing part of his uniform today violated regulations. But he didn't care.

Mickey Waverley's mother was on her way to visit Haley today, and Chase wasn't above using intimidation on Ruby's behalf.

He ran a hand over his jaw and studied himself in the mirror, checking if he'd missed any spots shaving.

Ruby was in the kitchen, stirring a pan of scrambled eggs. Haley rested on her hip. The baby kept whimpering like she knew something was wrong.

"Want me to take her?" Chase asked.

"Sure. Set her in the high chair?"

Chase strapped Haley in, but he didn't sit down at the table. He paced instead, checking the clock.

Ruby poured eggs onto two plates, then scooped some onto Haley's tray. "Chase, sit and eat. You're making me nervous."

"You don't seem nervous." He didn't know how Ruby managed to stay so calm. To smile and laugh, day after day. "I don't want you to be nervous."

"Well, I *am*." Ruby sat down next to Haley and handed her a plastic spoon.

They'd been dreading this day for the past week, ever since the court had set the date. Ruby would be upstairs in Devon and Aurora's apartment. They'd already gone over the details a dozen times, but he understood how difficult this must be for her.

Chase took a seat and stretched his legs under the table, seeking out Ruby's. Her foot inched up his calf.

They'd been a lot more affectionate since becoming friends with benefits. Chase craved that contact with her, and he was glad that Ruby seemed to enjoy it just as much. They'd been giving each other orgasms every night.

Part of him was living in a fantasy world, pretending that Ruby was really his. Getting to touch her like this, cuddling with her in bed. Like this wasn't just a convenient arrangement.

Despite everything that was happening, he'd never been so happy.

Until this morning. The reality of her situation had come roaring back. Ruby was trying so hard to stay upbeat, and Chase wanted to take all her stress onto himself. Too bad it didn't work that way, even if his body was doing its best. His stomach was trying to crawl into his throat.

None of them ate much. The minutes ticked by. Chase cleaned up the dishes, and Ruby wiped the eggs off Haley's face.

"You're going to stay with Uncle Chay-Chay and a nice lady is going to come see you. Everything will be fine." Ruby gave Haley a kiss. "I'll see you soon, bug. Be wise."

She put Haley into Chase's arms. Then Ruby kissed Chase's cheek, which surprised him.

"I thought we weren't supposed to do that in front of her."

"It was a kiss on the cheek. Totally G-rated."

"But the thoughts I'm having right now aren't G-rated," he whispered.

She shook her head at him, trying not to smile. "I just wanted you to know I'm grateful. I'd rather be with Haley during this visit, but since I can't, I'm glad it's you. Out of anyone else, I'm glad it's you."

"Me too." He kissed Ruby on the cheek. She wiped the spot with her thumb.

"Don't leave the room? And call me the minute they're gone?"

"I promise."

"It won't be that bad," she said. Like she was trying to reassure him.

"Hey." He gripped her shoulder. "I will not let anything happen to her."

Ruby nodded, backing toward the door. Her eyes were shining. She spun around and left. Chase heard her footsteps receding down the hall, heading for the stairs to go up to Devon's.

Ten minutes later, there was a knock at the door. Chase picked up Haley and went to answer it.

Two people stood on the welcome mat. One was a CPS case worker who'd visited before. "Officer Collins, good to see you again."

The other woman was tall and slim, her silver hair styled into a sleek shape that reminded Chase of a helmet. She wore a pair of khaki pants and a top with a matching cardigan. "I'm Tessa Waverley."

This was Mickey Waverley's mother. Haley's grandma, who'd never even met Ruby before. Never cared, apparently, until now.

Chase didn't think of himself as a hateful person. He tried to give people the benefit of the doubt.

But he hated this woman.

"Chase Collins. I'm Ruby's husband. Haley's stepdad."

Tessa cringed when he said Ruby's name. "I'd like to see my granddaughter now."

Chase didn't move from the doorway. Haley had hidden her face against his neck.

"May we come in?" the case worker asked, though of course it wasn't really a request. They had a court order.

"Sure. Why not?" Chase stepped aside, and the two women filed in.

Tessa walked around the apartment, face pinched. Like she was judging everything she saw and found it lacking. "It's small, isn't it?"

Sometimes, Chase agreed. But that comment made his hackles raise. "Plenty of room for the three of us."

Jane had instructed him on how to handle this. The case worker was here as a neutral third party. He wasn't supposed to talk about the murder or Ruby's case. But it was hard not to when Tessa was looking at Ruby's home with disdain.

"And how did you meet Ms. Whitestone?" Tessa asked.

"I'm a friend of her brother's."

"You're a police officer?"

"Yes."

"But you only married her recently. After her arrest."

Chase narrowed his eyes.

"Did you think I wouldn't know? My family and I have hired our own lawyers and private investigators. West Oaks PD might be lax enough to allow you to keep your job while being married to a murderer. But I'll make sure justice is done."

"Ruby is a good mom. There's no way she did what they say."

The case worker stood up from the kitchen table, where she'd been sitting quietly. "Mr. Collins, please…"

"She brought up Ruby first," he barked.

Haley grabbed his nose. "Gumpy?"

Shit. He'd been raising his voice. "No, princess. I'm sorry. Why don't you read a book?" He set Haley on the ground. She just stood there by his legs, staring at Tessa.

The woman sat on the living room couch, her back stiff. Tessa bent forward, eyes on Haley. "I'm your grandmother. Would you like me to read to you?"

Haley walked over to get a book. But she brought it to Chase instead. "Chay-Chay?" He sat down on the floor, and she climbed into his lap.

For a while, he read, and Tessa watched. Sitting with Haley made his anger fade away.

This was a terrible situation. But it wasn't truly Tessa Waverley's fault, was it? That was probably what Ruby would say right now. She was a better person than he was.

He wasn't going to convince Tessa through words that Ruby was innocent. That she was a wonderful mom. But maybe he could show her.

"Haley?" he asked. "Can you bring Tessa the book?"

She looked up at him. Then nodded.

The three adults were silent as Haley crossed the rug. When she reached Tessa, she held out the book.

The older woman's chin trembled, eyes glassy with tears. "Would you like me to read it? Would you sit with me?"

Haley held out her arms to be picked up.

Chase tried to swallow the lump in his throat.

The rest of the hour passed with agonizing slowness. Tessa read more books and asked Haley about her favorite toys. Then Haley got restless and watched some videos on Chase's phone.

Finally, the time was up. The CPS case worker stepped out first.

Tessa kneeled to say goodbye to Haley. "I look forward to seeing you again. Maybe for longer next time?" She stood and tilted her head politely at Chase. "Thank you for having me."

"You're welcome." The visit had started out rough, but it hadn't been that bad. Tessa wasn't the villain here, and maybe she could consider the possibility that Ruby wasn't either.

"Do you see how happy Haley is?" Chase asked. "How well she's cared for?"

Tessa's expression hardened. "Your point?"

"That's Ruby. That's all you need to know about her. If you'd give her a chance—"

"Ruby Whitestone's living free while my son is dead. How do you justify that to yourself?"

"I'm sorry for your loss, but I know the kind of person Ruby is. It's why I love her."

"Then I'm sorry for you, Officer Collins, because that woman has fooled you. Just like she fooled my son."

In the hallway, the case worker folded her arms. "Ms. Waverley? We need to keep things civil."

Tessa held up a hand. "You can tell your wife that I'm not going to stop until my granddaughter is safe and where she belongs. With *me.* And if there's any justice in this world, Ms. Whitestone will end up exactly where *she* belongs, too. Rotting in prison."

Chapter Twenty-Three

After putting Haley to bed, Ruby came out to the living room and sat beside Chase on the couch. "Thanks for giving me and Haley some alone time this afternoon. We needed that."

"I like giving you what you need." Chase took her hand, and his kindness floored her once again. What would she have done without him?

Tessa Waverley had left the apartment hours ago, but the visit hadn't left Ruby's mind for a second. During that hour of time, she'd sat upstairs in agony. But she'd known Chase was with Haley, and that knowledge had gotten her through.

After she'd come downstairs, Ruby hadn't wanted to talk about the visit. She and her daughter had taken a nap together and played for hours in Haley's room.

But now, Ruby was ready to hear the worst of it.

"How did she seem?" Ruby asked. "Mickey's mother."

"Upset. Angry. But she was kind to Haley."

Thank goodness for that. "Do you think she might be reasonable? Could we convince her to wait until after my trial before pushing for custody?"

Chase was hesitating.

"Just tell me," Ruby said.

"Tessa said she'll do whatever's necessary to get Haley. I don't think she'll wait a day longer than she has to."

Ruby pressed her lips together and nodded. "Pretty much what we expected." It was almost reassuring, knowing for sure what she was up against. "That means I need proof that I'm innocent *now*, not in six months at the trial. Every lead we find seems to go nowhere."

"I know. I haven't been much help lately. Detective Murphy knows I went with Shelby to investigate that witness tip, and I'm on her shit list."

"It's not your fault. You've done plenty." What Ruby needed was a brilliant idea. An insight. "Do you want to make something?"

"Make something?"

She went to the hall closet and took out a box of craft supplies. "Paint or draw or make a collage. It could be anything." She set the supplies on the kitchen table.

"Um…why?"

"When I'm trying to focus, I like to have my hands busy. Being creative accesses the unconscious mind. We see connections we didn't realize before." When she glanced at him, he was making a skeptical face.

"But I'm not artistic. At all."

"That doesn't matter. It's about the process. Do this with me? Please?"

"Are you going to laugh when I suck?"

"I would never laugh! Not in a mean way."

He nodded. "All right. I'll give it a shot. But only because you asked so nicely."

"Do you want to paint?"

Chase took a seat beside her. "I'll do whatever you're doing."

Ruby spread out charcoal pencils, pots of water-based paints, brushes, and canvas paper. She liked to keep things simple and non-toxic, especially with a toddler around.

"Let's brainstorm everything we know." Ruby dipped her paintbrush into the yellow and dragged it across her paper. "We know that Mickey asked me to meet him to discuss Haley. I went to his apartment and found him wounded. There was someone else there."

"Then the guy with the shaved head ran by the cake shop. Possibly the same guy who came here to your building in the Kia."

"And followed us."

"I'm guessing he recognized your car. He knew what to look for."

"So, who could he be?"

"Aside from the real killer?" Chase fidgeted with his paintbrush. "You thought he could be a fighter, like Mickey was."

"Which would make a lot of sense," Ruby said, "especially if Mickey's death has something to do with the fighting ring. Or Adrian Peele, the man behind it."

Days ago, Ruby had told Chase everything she could about the fighting ring and her connection with it. He'd been understanding, of course, because he was more perfect than the average human. She should've known he wouldn't judge her for being involved in something illegal.

"We need to talk to more people who know about the fighting ring," Chase said. "Maybe they could ID this guy. Or tell us something else that's useful."

"Like Tag or Nora." She switched from yellow to blue, adding water so the colors would bleed together.

Chase made abstract swirls of black on his paper. "We need to interview them. Find out what else they know."

"But Jane hasn't had any luck. She and Max have been to Bailor Fitness, and nobody would say a word to them. Nora said she'd call me if she thought of anything useful, but she hasn't." Ruby dabbed at the blue paint. "Tag was adamant to me that he had nothing to say. But maybe I could convince Nora if I spoke to her again in person. Unfortunately, the last time I went to Los Angeles, Mickey's girlfriend attacked me."

"I could try."

She looked over at him. "Try what?"

"Let me try talking to Nora."

"But there's no way she'll talk to a cop. Look at you, Chase. You think she won't know?"

"There you go again, underestimating me."

"I'm not underestimating you. I'm just being realistic."

"They don't need to know who I really am. It's a gym. I can blend in. A just-discharged Marine, new to town, looking for a place to train. That'll get me in the door. I've already got the haircut."

He turned his head like he was posing, and Ruby couldn't help smiling. "What then?"

"I'll find Nora, tell her you sent me, and see if she'll talk. If she's not there, I'll listen to what other people are saying. See what I can find out."

"Tag said most of his members are off the circuit."

"But Nora's still in it. Others could be, too."

"I don't know…"

"What's the harm in me trying?"

That you'll get hurt? she thought.

But Chase was tough and smart. He'd trained at that cop gym. And he wasn't actually going to fight anybody. She certainly hoped not.

"I can go on my next day off," he said.

"All right. We'll try it." She lowered her voice to a whisper. "But there's something else you need to know…"

Chase leaned in.

She dipped her finger in blue paint and smeared it down his nose.

"Hey!"

"You totally fell for that."

"You think I won't retaliate?" Chase grabbed her and held her still while he painted a mustache above her lips. Then she was in his lap and paint was going everywhere. Smearing on their necks and arms and faces.

Ruby felt paint drying on her cheeks. "I hope you know I don't underestimate you. I think you're basically perfect."

"Why does that sound like a criticism?"

"It's not," she said defensively. "I'm constantly impressed by you."

"Don't you mean annoyed?"

"That's only sometimes." Ruby kissed along his jaw, avoiding the paint, until she reached his mouth. She pressed soft kisses to his lips. Each one grew deeper. More heated.

"I'm nowhere near perfect," he murmured. "And I'm not selfless, either."

"No? That's just your cover story?"

"I'm actually very bad."

"Why don't you show me?"

Chase picked her up by the hips and carried her to the bedroom.

"What are you in the mood for?" He knelt on the mattress and lay down with her, covering her body with his. His erection ground against her through their clothes. He grabbed each of her wrists and held them down.

"Can I suck you? Pretty please?"

Chase rolled onto his back. He'd changed out of his West Oaks PD polo and jeans from earlier. Now he had on shorts and a tee.

Ruby teased her fingers along his waistband. She loved this part, this anticipation. It turned her on like nothing else, seeing how hard he was and knowing she'd done that to him.

But he took over, lifting his hips to push his shorts and underwear down.

"Hey, I was doing that," she complained.

"I wanted to get to the good part."

"What happened to going slow?"

He propped a pillow under his head and grinned at her. She couldn't be too annoyed when he had paint all over his face.

"Hold on, I'll be right back."

She grabbed a washcloth from the bathroom and wet it. "To

wipe our faces. Otherwise I'm going to be laughing the whole time I suck you off."

Chase took the towel and cleaned his face. Ruby did the same.

She tossed the towel on the floor and lifted his shirt to kiss his stomach. When she reached his erection, she licked a stripe along the underside of his shaft.

He groaned. "The view would be even better if you were naked."

"Always so bossy." Ruby stood to strip off her clothes.

She kneeled between his legs and went back to painting his cock with her tongue. Her mouth closed around his crown.

"Mmmm." Chase's fingers slid into her hair.

She could tell he wanted to take charge. But it was fun seeing how long he could last before stealing the control back from her.

It was not very long.

Chase sat up, gently pulling away. "You are very, very good at that, but you need to come before I do."

"Because I'm the woman?"

"Because you deserve it." He tugged his clothes off the rest of the way. Then he reached for her.

"Wait," she said. "There's something else I want."

Ruby had been thinking more about that sex box of his. It didn't seem like he'd brought it to the apartment yet, and she wasn't sure why. Maybe he thought she wasn't ready.

To be fair, she still wasn't ready for him to fuck her. She'd ordered condoms online, but the thought of using them—and of risking getting pregnant—made her feel like she couldn't breathe. It was confusing, wanting something so much yet being afraid to have it.

But tonight, she felt ready to take things a little further. If Chase was into it. Just to show him how much she trusted him, how grateful she was for everything he did.

More importantly, it would be fun. They both needed that.

"I want you to blindfold me," she said.

A slow smile pulled at his lips. "I can do that."

Ruby went to the closet and came back out with a sash from one of her dresses. She sat on the bed, and Chase knelt behind her, placing the fabric over her eyes and tying it behind her head.

"How's that?"

A bit of light bled through the bottom, but not much. She closed her eyes. "Perfect."

Chase rubbed her shoulders and kissed the back of her neck. "I've been wondering. Do you have a vibrator?"

She liked where this was going. "In my nightstand drawer."

"Can I get it?"

"Yes." Ruby felt for the pillows and lay down against them.

She heard the drawer slide. Then a box opening, and a low hum. It sounded like he was testing it out, switching the motor between settings.

Having Chase naked in her bedroom, playing with her vibrator, was not something she'd *ever* thought she would experience.

The mattress shifted as he sat beside her. Chase's lips pressed against hers, their kisses gradually deepening. His taste, his scent—everything was heightened.

Then the low hum started again. She felt gentle vibrations on her inner thigh, moving toward her center.

And this—*this* was even more unexpected.

She'd always thought of Chase as predictable. Yet since they'd gotten married, she was constantly surprised by the things he did.

Chase kissed her again as he moved the toy over her labia. It felt incredible. Ruby moaned into his mouth. He waited until she was writhing and wet before he brought it to her clit. She made a strangled sounding gasp.

"Right there," she panted. "Just like that."

It was so good. And *so* much better than doing this by herself.

Ruby widened her legs. Chase pushed the toy inside her opening. Fucked her with it. The blindfold took away any self-consciousness. She had no idea where he was looking or what expression was on his face, but she felt his erection rubbing against her hip, so clearly he was enjoying this.

Ruby tried wrapping her fingers around his length, but Chase loosened her grasp. "It's not my turn yet. This is just for you."

She grabbed hold of the blankets instead. Pleasure kept building and building inside of her. The stimulation of the vibrator was relentless, and she loved that it was out of her control.

"*Chase*," she gasped, as the orgasm shook her body.

He pulled back the vibrator, then stroked it over her clit again. Another wave of pleasure rocketed through her. He kept up the motion, easing back before coaxing another shudder from her. It went on and on. Finally, her body had nothing left.

He kissed her temple. "Love it when you say my name when you come."

"Ughn." She'd forgotten how to speak. Ruby just breathed for a moment.

Her thumb hooked beneath the blindfold and lifted it. Chase had his head propped against his hand, looking at her. "Did you like that?"

"You lied. You're not bad at all. You're very, very good."

"Funny how those words can mean almost the same thing."

"When it comes to sex, maybe." She took off the blindfold.

Chase set the vibrator on the mattress. "Watching you really does it for me. I'm not going to need much."

"Let me." Her head was fuzzy, like she was drunk, but she wanted to finish him.

Ruby bent over him and sucked his swollen cock into her mouth. She took as much as she could, grunting when his hips snapped, driving him deeper. Her cheeks hollowed around him.

"*Ruby*," he hissed. "Fuck. I can't hold back."

His shaft pulsed and spurted into her throat. She swallowed down every drop of his release, sucking and licking him until he softened against her tongue.

Ruby flopped backward onto the pillows, wiping her lips. He smiled at her with hooded eyes. They snuggled together, and Ruby rested her head over his heart, listening to it beat against her ear.

"Why don't you ever talk about your family?" she asked.

She knew he was from Riverside, a city in the Inland Empire about two hours away. Though it was hard to imagine Chase anywhere but West Oaks.

"Not much I wanted to share. It's a downer."

"But you know almost everything about my family, and I know so little about yours."

He sighed, turning his head to face the ceiling. "My dad still lives in Riverside. He's the principal of the high school I went to, which was *so* much fun whenever I got in trouble."

"You got in trouble?"

"All the time. Told you I'm not perfect."

"Tell me a good memory you have," she said.

"I had a lot of sex in high school. That was pretty good."

Ruby laughed and pushed his shoulder. "Wait a minute, are you saying Chase Collins was a bad boy? *That* kind of bad boy?"

"I skipped class and did stupid things. But I wasn't cool enough to be Ruby Whitestone's friend."

"Oh, I wasn't cool. Don't believe what Devon says. I was artsy and angsty, but I was a virgin until college. You wouldn't have been too interested."

"Virgins were my favorite."

Her eyes bugged. "*Chase.*"

"I'm kidding. Mostly." Chase trailed his fingertips over her skin. "Joining the Marines made me stop dicking around and take responsibility for myself. I realized trying to piss off my dad was just as pointless as trying to impress him. I still see him a few times a year, but I don't let what he says get to me."

"Does your dad know we're married?"

"God, no. He'd just lecture me, like he does about everything. And if I do file to adopt Haley—if that's necessary—I don't want him involved with her anyway. If I'm her dad, I don't want to be anything like mine."

"You won't be. You'd be a great dad. And you're a good man. Even if you're not perfect." The more she discovered his "imperfections," the more she liked him.

"That's what I'm going for." He rolled to his side, holding her closer. "I know you're worried about your case. But we'll find a lead. I'm not going to give up."

"Neither am I. When you go to Bailor Fitness to talk to Nora, I'm driving you. We'll leave Haley with Mrs. Murtree."

"Believe it or not, I can drive myself to Los Angeles."

"But I want to be nearby. You said we're a team. If you're involved in the investigation, then so am I. *Don't* argue with me."

He kissed her forehead. "All right, you win. This time."

Chapter Twenty-Four

Chase pushed through the doors into Bailor Fitness. It was Sunday afternoon, and the place was packed.

He strode up to the front desk. A guy with spiky black hair nodded at him. "Hey, man. What can I do for you?"

Chase glanced at the people lifting weights on one side of the gym. On the other was a sparring area, where a teacher was instructing two guys on a grappling technique. The space was low key, not too fancy or flashy.

He was surprised to find this place so similar to his gym back in West Oaks. Even if the clientele had a different vibe from his fellow officers.

"Yeah, thanks. I was hoping for a temporary pass to try things out. I'm new to the area."

"Good deal. I'm Tag. The owner." He held out his hand.

So this was Mickey Waverley's best friend. The guy Ruby had come to LA to see not long after her arrest.

She'd still insisted on driving Chase here, though they'd taken his truck. Right now, Ruby was supposed to be grabbing drive-through coffee at a nearby Starbucks and staying out of sight. Chase would've preferred that she stay in West Oaks, and he'd even double-checked her bail conditions to ensure she was allowed to leave the county. But he also understood that she needed to feel involved.

They'd decided to have the Bennett Security car stay in West Oaks, guarding Megan's townhome while she cared for Haley. They'd seen no sign of the man with the shaved head. Chase had to assume the guy had given up, or hadn't been a threat at all.

Regardless, he hoped to learn more today to help with Ruby's case.

"Are you military?" Tag asked.

Chase nodded. "Marine. Just got out. Ready for what's next, but not sure what that is." He'd given himself a fresh buzz on the sides, trying to look as military as possible.

"You interested in sparring?" Tag asked.

"Yeah. I heard this was a good place for it. I have experience with boxing, and I've taken some Krav Maga." The style was popular with law enforcement, but with street fighters too. It didn't necessarily peg him as a cop.

But he figured he should be honest, since he didn't know what to expect here.

"Let's grab you a waiver and get your info. What was your name?"

"Jeff Collins." Chase had brought along his cousin's old driver's license from out of state. He and his cousin looked similar. But Tag didn't ask for an ID.

Tag walked Chase to the locker room. He favored his right side so heavily the foot almost dragged. "I run a clean business here. No growth hormones or steroid shit in my locker rooms. If I find out you've got that stuff, you're not welcome." He shrugged. "There are plenty of other places to train if that's your thing."

Chase adjusted the strap of his gym bag on his shoulder. "That won't be a problem."

"My other pet peeve is bothering our female members. Be a gentleman, keep your hands and eyes and comments to yourself. That's basically it."

"Sounds good to me."

Tag left him in the locker room. Chase stowed his bag in a locker and got changed.

Then he went out to the gym floor to get a feel for things. He scanned the faces for Nora, Ruby's friend. But none of the women seemed to match her description, and he didn't want to stare. No point getting kicked out within his first few minutes for acting like a creeper.

Tag seemed like an okay guy, even if he'd been a close friend of Mickey's. But Chase couldn't visualize Ruby here.

He didn't know the members of this gym and didn't want to make assumptions. But at least some of these people were involved in the underground fighting ring, like Mickey. They'd be getting paid under the table. Risking arrest or the possibility that they'd cross the wrong person.

Ruby had deserved so much better than that. She deserved long-term stability. Chase knew she didn't want that from him. They were friends, and she was keeping her heart for some future guy.

But Chase intended to make sure that guy treated her right. Even if it tore him up.

He sat down at a free bench press and warmed up. He was on his first heavy set when another man came up to him.

"Mind if I work in?"

Chase racked the weight and sat up. "No problem. I'm Jeff." He wiped off the bench with his towel and gestured for the guy to go ahead.

"Marco. Could you spot me?"

"Sure thing." Chase got into position, standing behind the rack. Marco had tattoos on his arms and upper chest. He was compact, built like a fighter.

"Are you new here?" Marco asked after his set.

"I am. You like this place?"

They chatted for a while. Chase waited until a natural break in the conversation. "Do you know Nora? I think she works here?"

Marco's gaze seemed to sharpen. "Yeah, I know Nora. Why do you ask?"

Chase had a story ready. "My wife is a friend of hers from a few years back." He held up his ring hand. "She's interested in training."

Marco relaxed. "Nora's a great teacher, yeah. I haven't seen her in a while. But she's bound to show up at some point."

They switched off for another set. Chase decided to press his luck. "Do a lot of women train here? To fight, I mean. That's what my wife is into."

Marco grinned knowingly. "And you're not sure if you like it?"

"I like that she's strong." Ruby wasn't the type of fighter Marco assumed, but Chase loved how fierce she was. Especially when it came to Haley.

"No, strong women are hot," Marco said. "But other guys staring? I'm not as much a fan of that."

Chase shrugged. "If the money's good, it can be worth it."

"I like how you think." Marco laughed and clapped Chase on the shoulder. "The money isn't bad. Especially for the pretty ones."

He definitely knew about the fighting ring. Maybe Marco was a fighter on the circuit himself. He could've known Mickey.

But before Chase could ask another question, Marco got up. "Catch you later, Jeff. Good to meet you."

He walked away. Damn.

Chase was starting to think this undercover mission would last longer than one day. But if he got to know Marco, he might learn something important about the circuit.

Maybe Marco knew the guy with the shaved head.

Chase went over to a cable machine. But when he looked up, Marco was back.

"Hey, Jeff. There's another female fighter here. She works with Nora. I thought you might want to chat with her? For your wife?"

"Um, sure." This seemed promising. Chase grabbed his stuff and followed.

Marco turned down a hallway, then stepped aside. "Right in there." Chase went through the door.

But the room had no one inside.

Suddenly, Marco grabbed him from behind and threw him up against the wall.

"What the hell?" Chase cried. He spun, arms raising to defend himself. Marco had his fists clenched, his mouth a frown. He started to advance.

Chase lunged forward and slammed Marco into a filing cabinet. "What is your problem?"

Then Tag stepped through the doorway and closed the door behind him. "Is Jeff really your name?"

Chase pushed back from Marco, who was scowling. "Let me out of here," Chase said. "Now."

Tag leaned back against the door. He was in no shape to fight, but he clearly wasn't intimidated. "Not until you tell me who you really are and why you're here."

"I don't know what you're talking about."

"You asked Marco about Nora."

"So?"

"Do you know where she is?"

Where she is? That question surprised him.

"How would I know that? I've never even met her."

"But you said your wife knows her."

Marco leaned toward Tag. "He probably made that shit up. Probably doesn't even have a wife. Anybody could put on a wedding ring."

Chase looked from one man to the other. He thought he could hold his own in a fight against Marco, but he wasn't in the mood to get anything bruised up or broken if it wasn't necessary. And he *didn't* think it was necessary.

When he was on duty, he had to assess people's intentions on the street on a daily basis. Whether they needed help, whether they meant harm.

And Tag seemed like a guy who was putting on bravado, but underneath he was worried. Even scared. Scared people could be dangerous, but often, they just wanted someone to relieve their fear.

Chase held up his hands, taking a step away from them. "My name is Chase. Ruby Whitestone is my wife. She's the reason I'm here."

Tag barked a laugh. "*Ruby*? You're her husband? You shitting me?"

"If I can reach into my pocket for my phone, I'll show you a picture of our wedding day." He'd asked Megan to send the photo to him, the only one they took that day. Chase sometimes looked at it while he was at work. Ruby and Haley both with flowers in their hair. The three of them together, posing like a family.

Tag studied the photo. "This is Ruby and Mickey's daughter?"

"Haley. Yeah."

"Pretty as her mom."

Chase took his phone back. "You can see I'm telling the truth."

"I believe you. But Ruby didn't say anything about being married when I saw her."

"It was a recent development. I'm here because you and Nora both refused to talk to Ruby's lawyer. Ruby thought you weren't going to cave, but I hoped I could convince Nora."

Tag put a hand over his chin. "I would've helped Ruby if I could. But the situation is complex. It could turn dangerous if the wrong people find out. I'm already afraid something bad happened to Nora. She hasn't been to work for over a week. Isn't answering her phone or her door."

No wonder the guy was worried. "Who are the wrong people? Is Adrian Peele one of them?"

"If you're still asking, then you don't care about Ruby as much as you seem to."

"What about a big guy with a shaved head?"

"That could be any number of people. Several of whom I want nothing to do with, and neither should you."

Chase was tired of talking to this guy. Tag acted tough and defiant, but the gym owner was terrified of stepping out of line. "I'm going to keep looking for Nora. I'll just have to do it somewhere else. Can I leave now?"

Tag screwed up his mouth like he was thinking.

"Sorry for pushing you," Marco muttered. "Nothing personal."

"Yeah, it's fine. But my wife is waiting for me, so…" Chase gestured at the door, which Tag was still blocking.

"If you can track down Nora," Tag said, "I'll think about talking to Ruby's lawyer."

"You'll *think* about it?"

"That's the best I can promise. But I can point you in the right direction. The next fight on the circuit is scheduled for tomorrow."

"How do you know?"

"Because I make myself aware of things. There's a phone number. You send a text, you get a response with the time and place."

"Not exactly high security."

"And why do you think that is? The people who run these fights have money, power, connections."

"They can get away with murder?" Chase asked.

"I wouldn't put it past them."

Chase looked at the other man in the room. "What about Marco? Why can't he go to the fight to find Nora?"

Marco shook his head. "Hell, no. I got out of that shit. I'm not any more welcome there than Tag would be."

"The members at my club know how I feel about the circuit," Tag said. "Nora's one of the last few who's still in that world."

"What about Mickey's girlfriend? The one who went after Ruby?"

"That's Cami. She hasn't been here lately, either, and I don't care what she does. But Nora's a friend. After seeing what happened to Ruby because of Mickey's messes, I told Nora she was a fool for not getting out. I don't want to see anybody else hurt because of the circuit. But Nora got upset with me. Stormed off. Now, she's missing. If you see her at the fight tomorrow, tell her I'm sorry. And if she needs help, she can come to me."

"Is she in the same kind of trouble Mickey was in?"

"I sure as shit hope she's not. But there's another wrinkle, and it's been bugging me. I'm not sure if it's even important."

"What is it?"

Tag paused, and Chase could see the man considering how much to say. "Mickey hadn't been seeing Cami long. Before that, he'd been hooking up with Nora. It's possible that, whatever Mickey really had going on, he dragged Nora into it."

"NORA'S *MISSING*?" Ruby said.

They were battling LA traffic on the way back to West Oaks. Chase hadn't bothered to change out of his workout clothes. He'd taken down the info Tag had given him and called for Ruby to pick him up.

"Missing might be a strong word. She hasn't shown up to work. Tag said she seemed upset the last time they spoke."

Ruby tapped her fingers against the steering wheel. "What if it has to do with me? She seemed like she might know something, and I asked her to get in touch if she was willing to talk. She programmed my number in her phone. Someone could've found out."

"It's possible. But I think this is something bigger. Tag seemed to think Nora was in the same kind of trouble Mickey was in. Nora and Mickey had been seeing each other before he dated Cami."

"Mickey and Nora? Are you sure?"

"That's what he said."

"It would explain why Nora seemed so upset about Mickey's

death. But it hardly matters. All the more reason to find Nora and ask what's really going on."

"When I get the time and location of the fight, I'll see if Bennett Security can send along some backup."

If Chase ran into that huge guy with the shaved head? An extra bodyguard or two seemed like a wise choice.

"That's a good idea," Ruby said. "Tomorrow night, you can keep an eye out while I talk to Nora. I just hope she's there. I wonder if Sylvie Trousseau could track down Nora's home address. I know Tag said she hasn't answered her door, but maybe we could check there, too."

Chase's mind backed up a few sentences. "Wait a sec, you're not going to the fight tomorrow. Anybody could recognize you."

"I'll wear a wig and change my makeup. With contouring, I can look like a completely different person. That wasn't an option for the gym with all the bright lights, but the fight venue will be dark."

"*No.* There's no way you're going. It could be dangerous. And it would probably violate your bail conditions." They were talking about an illegal fight club. Even if the guy with the shaved head wasn't there, Chase didn't want Ruby anywhere near.

Her knuckles had turned white on the steering wheel. "But you would let your friend Shelby come with you, right? If she asked?"

"Shelby is a cop. She has training."

"And I have specific knowledge. I've been to dozens of these fights. The locations change, but the way they do things doesn't. It's possible something is different after a couple of years, but the fundamentals will be the same. The way people behave, the feel of it. I'll know how to act. And I'm a woman. It'll be much easier for me to approach a female fighter like Nora."

Chase still didn't like it. But what she'd said made sense. "Okay, we'll go together. If we don't see Nora, we leave. No unnecessary risks."

She smirked. "If you don't take any, then I won't."

Chase really hoped this wasn't a mistake.

Chapter Twenty-Five

Ruby slid her hand into Chase's as they walked along the deserted street.

"It's too quiet," he said. "Maybe I should go ahead first. I don't feel right about this."

Ruby grumbled under her breath. "You're just saying that because I'm here."

They kept going, and soon other people started to appear, all of them walking quietly in the same direction. Then more voices. Lights.

Around a corner, a line appeared leading to a doorway. Music pulsed from inside. It was like a night club had suddenly appeared in the middle of an otherwise abandoned block of structures.

"See? What did I tell you." She squeezed Chase's hand.

Tonight's fight would be in an abandoned warehouse in a vast maze of buildings near the Port of Los Angeles. Ruby had been to similar venues. She felt a thrill of excitement and anticipation to be back here.

There was so much about her old life that she never cared to experience again. But this element, that thrill before the fight, still got to her.

She pressed her fingertips along the edge of her wig. It was platinum blond. She'd worn false eyelashes and contoured her cheekbones. Even Chase kept looking over at her like he couldn't believe her transformation.

The only person she was really worried about seeing tonight was Cami, simply because she wanted to avoid another scene like at the gym. But Mickey's new girlfriend wasn't going to recognize her. Even Nora would need convincing that she was Ruby and not someone else.

Assuming Nora was there tonight. Ruby was worried for her.

"Just remember what I said," Chase murmured in her ear. "Don't go anywhere without me."

"My heroic protector." As if she hadn't been to any number of these fights on her own.

A part of her worried that going to see Nora tonight could somehow make her friend's position even worse. But what other choice did they have? They needed to know what was really going on.

Ruby was more sure than ever that the fighting ring had some connection to Mickey's death. And there was no other way to try to prove it. They needed information, and Nora might have it.

But Ruby was glad Chase was here with her. She always felt better with him around. Plus, he looked hot in that tight long-sleeved T-shirt he was wearing, with his baseball cap pulled low over his eyes.

She'd been wrong. He didn't look that much like a cop after all. Looking at him, she could believe he was a fighter himself.

And from the way other women were glancing at Chase, they assumed the same.

Ruby stuck her hand into the back pocket of his track pants.

The line moved quickly. Everyone was searched on the way in, and they had to walk through a metal detector. A bouncer patted down Ruby's clothes, though she couldn't have hidden much in her tank top and mini skirt.

"No phones. No recording equipment." The bouncer's hand lingered a bit too along on her ass, but Ruby only smiled at him.

"I know the rules."

She held her breath until the guy waved them forward.

Noah Vandermeer was supposed to meet them here. He would be posing as a high roller. She'd told him to tip the bouncer a hundred-dollar bill to get access to the VIP area, and she didn't expect Noah would have trouble bringing the necessary cash.

These fights were technically invite only, but if you knew the time and the venue, you could get in. And if you had copious amounts of money to spend gambling, it was even easier.

The minute they stepped inside, the bass of the music vibrated in her bones, and lights flashed like they were in the middle of the hottest LA dance club.

The crowd was densely packed, the heat already building in the massive open room. The ring was at the center under bright lights. The fight going on right now was just a warm-up bout. Nowhere near a headliner.

They made their way around the edge of the room. Chase leaned in. "Do you see anyone you know?" He had to shout over the noise.

Ruby scanned the sea of faces. Some were familiar, but only in a vague way.

Then she spotted someone she remembered too well. A blond with her hair in a high ponytail.

It was Cami, Mickey's girlfriend.

Ruby grabbed Chase's shirt and kissed him. She slid her arms around his strong back. And damned if she didn't get a little lost in that moment. In his scent and the energy of the room, the clashing of these different worlds in her head.

She broke away from him, chest heaving.

"I enjoyed that," Chase said, "but I'm not sure what it was for."

"Saw someone I'd prefer to avoid."

"Mickey's girlfriend?"

"That's her." Ruby saw Cami's ponytail bobbing through the crowd.

Cami reached a couple of bouncers, who unclipped a velvet rope to let her past. "She's going into the VIP area."

"And there's Noah."

Ruby saw him. The Bennett Security bodyguard was already in with the other VIP gamblers, chatting casually like he belonged there. Ruby didn't know him well, but Noah seemed like the kind of guy who could fit in almost anywhere. Or at least do a good job of acting like it. He'd been a Navy SEAL, and according to Devon, those guys had a certain swagger.

Chase had a cockiness about him too, but it was more subdued. Like he was holding most of his energy in reserve. But Ruby knew firsthand how fiery he could be when he let loose.

"How can we reach him?" Ruby asked. "If we don't have our phones?"

"He gave me a communication device to signal him if it's an emergency. Otherwise, it's the old-fashioned way. But this mission is for recon and intel."

"English, please?"

"We're here to talk to Nora. Find out what she knows. Not start trouble."

"Why are you looking at me like that?" Ruby asked. "I don't start trouble."

Chase laughed and shook his head.

The announcer roared into his microphone and the crowd cheered, drowning out Chase's response. A new fight was starting, and this one had ramped up the audience's excitement.

Ruby grabbed Chase's arm. "There's Nora."

She was in the ring. Nora's hair was gelled into a stiff-peaked faux hawk, and she wore heavy eyeliner and blush. Her tiny shorts and sports bra showed off her muscular physique.

She and her opponent didn't waste much time playing to the crowd. The fight began. The two women immediately dove at one another.

"Come on." Ruby pulled Chase closer to the ring, working her way through the crowd.

The other fighter gripped Nora around the waist. She knocked Nora down, but Nora flipped her and put the woman in a headlock. Her face was an angry snarl.

Nora's opponent struggled to regain the upper hand, but Nora didn't give her an inch.

The other woman tapped out. "Nora Rodgers wins!"

Instead of waving or smiling at the screaming audience, Nora left the ring and headed straight for the exit.

Ruby hurried after her.

Nora's faux hawk appeared through a break in the crowd. Ruby pushed forward, letting go of Chase's hand so she could squeeze through the gap. "Nora, wait." She held up a fifty. "Can I get an autograph?"

Nora barely gave her a glance. "No autographs tonight."

"But I have a message for you. From a friend. From Ruby Whitestone."

Nora turned and stared.

Ruby angled her head and pulled back her wig just enough to show her dark hair beneath.

Nora's eyes widened.

"Can we talk? Please?"

The fighter glanced around. "Over here."

She took Ruby into a dark corridor. They passed a bouncer, and Nora nodded at him. "Friend of mine. It's fine."

"I'm with them." Chase had caught up. Ruby felt his hand on her lower back.

Nora led them further down the corridor. There were hardly any lights here. Trash and debris littered the floor, as if the organizers hadn't bothered to clean up this part of the warehouse. A few doors hung off their hinges, leading into abandoned offices.

Nora turned around. "Ruby, what the hell are you doing here?" She narrowed her eyes at Chase. "Who is he?"

"My husband. Long story. Tag's been looking for you. Where have you been?"

"I'm done with Tag, okay? I'm done with a lot of things."

"Does this have something to do with Mickey?"

"Trust me, you don't want to know."

Chase stepped forward. "We *need* to know. Ruby could go to prison. She could lose her daughter over this."

"Please," Ruby said. "I need to know what was going on with Mickey. Did he want to stop fighting? Is that what happened?"

Nora glanced around again, her indecision written across her face. "Mickey did want to get out, but he couldn't. That's not how this works."

"What about Tag?" Ruby asked. "He got out."

"Are you kidding? He didn't leave. Tag was broken after that fight. They only cut him loose because they didn't want him anymore."

Ruby had visited him in the hospital. The doctors had called the police after seeing the way Tag had been beaten. Of course, Tag had refused to say anything about the source of his injuries. It had taken months of recovery, physical therapy. He'd barely managed to walk again.

She didn't want Nora to end up like that. Much less like Mickey.

"If you're in trouble, maybe we can help each other." Ruby put a hand on the other woman's arm, but Nora recoiled.

"There's nothing you could possibly do that would help me. If I were you, I'd take my shot at trial and hope for the best. Because at least that's a chance, and that's more than these people would give you."

"Do you mean Adrian Peele?" Ruby asked. "He's powerful, but if enough brave people testify—"

"*Don't*," Nora hissed. "Don't even think about finishing that sentence. Just get out of LA. Stay away from anyone connected to Mickey. Don't contact me again. Not just for my sake, but for yours."

She went past them and vanished down the hall.

Ruby cursed. "What now? Do we go after her?"

"We leave, like she said. We saw Nora, and we passed on

Tag's message. We held up our end of the deal. If she won't help us, then hopefully he will."

"That's not good enough. She could be in serious danger."

Chase held her by the arms. "We don't even understand what's really going on here."

A large man walked past them, going the opposite direction. He had a shaved head and a determined hardness in his gaze. The man barely glanced at them as he passed.

Every cell in Ruby's body turned cold.

Chase pulled her against him. "Ruby. That was *him*. The guy who followed us outside your apartment last week. You need to get out of here *now*."

But she was still frozen with shock.

She had seen that man before, and not just last week.

When he'd been driving the blue Kia, he'd been wearing sunglasses. But now, she recognized him.

She knew his name.

She'd seen him in the ring with Tag Bailor. In the very last bout that Tag had ever fought. There was no way she'd ever forget that man's face.

The memory of him standing over Tag's bloody, unconscious form was seared into her mind.

"That's Conrad Decker. He's the fighter who nearly killed Tag."

Chapter Twenty-Six

Chase watched Conrad Decker turn the corner and disappear into the bowels of the warehouse.

It was *him*. The man that the witness at the cake shop—Phyllis—had seen the day of the murder. The man who'd terrified Ruby and Haley when he'd followed them.

Conrad Decker had to be Mickey's real killer.

Thank goodness Ruby was in disguise, and Chase had his ball cap pulled low. The guy hadn't known who they were.

Ruby's hands flew to her chest. "He went in the same direction as Nora. What if he hurts her?"

Chase hadn't wanted to face the guy without Noah Vandermeer's help, but Decker was getting away. He debated for a moment before he made up his mind. "I'm going after him."

Ruby grabbed his wrist, tugging him back. "We should go for help. I saw what Decker did to Tag."

And they both knew what Decker had done to Mickey. Stabbed him seventeen times.

Chase didn't want Decker to hurt Nora, either. But his main concern was still Ruby. Decker had gone after her, and he might choose to do it again. Chase didn't intend to let that go.

He fished into his pocket and took out the plastic device

Noah had given him. His thumb pressed the button. "You go back to the main room. I just signaled Noah, so he knows something's up. This has a tracker he can follow, but it'll be quicker if you tell him where I went."

Chase started down the hall.

"Wait." Her footsteps ran after him. "You said we'd stay together. I don't want you going after Decker alone."

"I have to follow him *now*." And Chase intended to get her as far from Decker as possible. "I'm serious, Ruby. Go."

She scowled at him, but this time, she turned and ran toward the noise of the crowd.

Chase hurried down the hallway, trying to keep his footfalls as quiet as possible.

He peered into open doorways as he passed. Some rooms were empty, others littered with overturned furniture and old paper. Night air wafted through broken windows, along with just enough ambient light to allow Chase to see.

The din of the fight had receded to a distant rumble.

He came to an intersection and listened. Footsteps. Voices.

Chase turned the corner and spotted Decker at the far end of the new hallway, opening a door. Decker glanced over his shoulder. Chase ducked out of sight, his back pressed against the brick wall.

He waited a moment, then looked again.

The door at the end of the hall was almost closed, but yellow light spilled from the gap.

What was the guy doing?

Was Nora in there?

Chase inched forward. Water dripped somewhere nearby. Voices murmured.

The door at the end of the hall was barely cracked open.

"You're testing my patience, Decker," a rough voice said.

"With respect, sir, I've done all I can."

"As you should. You follow orders. You don't give them."

The man stepped forward, his face becoming visible through the crack.

It was Adrian Peele, the owner of the fighting circuit. Chase recognized him from a picture Ruby had shown him. Decker towered over Peele, yet the fighter's shoulders were slumped in a subservient posture.

Chase wished he had something to record this conversation. But he hadn't been able to bring his phone into the venue.

"A lawyer and investigator have been poking around," Decker said, "asking questions. They've been to Bailor Fitness."

"Tag Bailor is irrelevant."

"But these people aren't dumb. Some private security company is working with them. This could still lead back to me. I just want to get the fuck out of LA before they come knocking on my door. Give me the money, and I will."

"And what about the woman? Ruby Whitestone?"

Chase's entire body tensed.

"I can't get near her. I hear she's married to a cop, and now there's bodyguards hanging outside her building."

"Sounds like your problem. Not mine."

"I could decide to start talking. I only went to West Oaks that day on your orders."

"Is that *really* the direction you want to take this, Decker? I could destroy you if I wanted. Like I did to Tag Bailor."

"You mean, like *I* did?" Decker's massive fists were opening and closing. He stepped closer. And Peele's gaze sharpened like he was seeing Decker for the first time.

Chase was surprised the man hadn't brought a bodyguard to this meeting. But maybe he hadn't expected Decker to ever go against him.

"Or I could show mercy." Peele shrugged one shoulder of his pin-striped suit. "If you intend to leave town, what do you need?"

"Funds wired to a bank account in Mexico. I already set it up. I'll cross the border, get the money, disappear."

"And if these friends of Ruby Whitestone still come bothering me?"

"They can't if I'm not here. I'm the only tie. I was careful."

"As you usually are, Decker. I know. This situation has become a nuisance through no fault of your own. So you're right, I owe it to you to help."

"Thank you, sir. I won't forget this."

"I'm sure you won't." Peele walked toward the door.

Chase reared back. *Shit.* He dashed into an open doorway just before Peele stepped out into the hall.

Chase retreated further into the shadows of the office. Peele walked by, his heavy shoes thumping against the concrete floor.

Seconds later, Decker followed, lumbering past. He could barely put his arms down at his sides, they were so overly muscled.

When Decker had gone, Chase exhaled.

Peele had ordered Mickey's death, and Decker had carried it out. Chase was going to write an affidavit with what he'd heard, and it would probably be enough to support a wiretap and search warrants. And now that they knew their suspect was Decker, their witness from the cake shop could identify him in a photo lineup.

Tag Bailor might also be more willing to share what he knew.

This was the biggest break they'd had in Ruby's case.

Now Chase had to get back to Ruby and Noah before they drew too much attention. Only a few minutes had passed. Thank goodness Noah hadn't caught up to him yet.

Chase left the office and crept down the hall. He turned at the intersection, listening for the roar of the crowd watching the fight. He saw the same offices as before, the same shadows.

Then a different shape loomed into his path.

Conrad Decker had just stepped out of a doorway, glowering.

"I thought I heard someone. Who the fuck are you?"

All he could do was play dumb. "Sorry, what? I was just looking for the bathroom."

"You're that cop, aren't you?" Decker's huge hand closed on Chase's shoulder. The fighter threw Chase into the doorway he'd stepped out of.

Chase stumbled into the room. It had rows of desks inside. He pivoted to face the other man.

"You've got the wrong guy. Let's just talk this—"

Decker's fist caught Chase in the stomach. He stumbled backward into a desk.

Fuck, that hurt.

The giant's fist pulled back again, this time aiming for Chase's head. Chase ducked beneath the guy's arm. He heard the whistle of that massive fist passing by him in the air.

Decker let out a bellow and turned, charging for him again.

Chase grabbed for anything he could find. His hand landed on a rusty stapler. He chucked it. Decker batted it away. Then the same with a three-ring binder. Papers scattered.

Chase heaved a chair in Decker's path, but the guy just kept coming. *I could really use a taser or my baton right now*, he thought. Or his gun. He'd never discharged his weapon before—that paperwork was a nightmare—but this occasion would've been worth the headache.

Another blow caught Chase in the side, knocking the wind out of him. And this whole scenario wasn't remotely cute anymore. He was getting pissed. He wheezed, trying to get his lungs going again.

Decker took a few more swings. Chase bobbed out of the way, gasping for breath. But his eyes tracked his opponent's movements.

Decker wasn't a technical fighter. He relied on his own brute strength.

Chase was never going to match this guy's size, which meant he had to be faster, smarter.

Or maybe just a hell of a lot more vicious.

Chase lunged. He drove his fist into Decker's solar plexus. But Decker barely seemed to feel it, even though that hit would've put a regular sized person on the ground.

Okay. So that hadn't worked. Plan B.

Suddenly, there was movement behind Decker. Someone brought a metal waste can up and smacked Decker in the head.

Fucking hell. It was Ruby.

"Come and get me, asshole!" she screamed.

The guy had barely flinched. Decker looked behind him, slowly turning his massive shoulders.

He was about to go after Ruby.

Chase leaped onto his back, forearm barring across Decker's throat in a chokehold.

Decker fell to his knees. He reached back, trying to grab hold of Chase. But Chase kicked against the ground, throwing his weight forward. Decker toppled like a tree. Crashed to the floor. Chase lay on the man's back, trying to keep Decker pinned. His forearm tightened against the man's windpipe.

Decker bucked beneath him and roared and clawed.

Chase could barely hold on.

Ruby was screaming something, but he couldn't make out the words. It took every ounce of energy and will to keep Decker down.

This man had made Ruby's life hell. Chase wasn't going to let him hurt her anymore.

Decker's movements slowed. The fight was going out of him.

Then suddenly, there were a lot more people in the room. Flashlight beams and shouts and gleams of metal.

"LAPD! Get down on the ground!"

Police were swarming, pointing guns, yelling. Chase held up his hands, panting to catch his breath.

Decker slumped forward, coughing and retching.

Then Noah Vandermeer strode through the door. "He's a cop, so everyone chill. He's with me."

Chapter Twenty-Seven

Ruby kneeled on the ground. Her mind spun from the chaos of the last few minutes. Paramedics and police had flooded the room, and Decker moaned on the floor.

But Chase was okay. Thank goodness. He lowered his arms, standing up.

She couldn't even put into words how frightened she'd been for him.

"You must be Ruby." An LAPD officer walked toward her, holding out his hand. He wore a windbreaker and a necklace badge. "I'm Detective Sean Holt, LAPD Gang and Narcotics."

"Noah called you?" Ruby took his hand, and he helped her up.

"Yeah, I'm a friend of his. Though I'm starting to regret that decision."

"Nah, you love me." Noah clapped him on the back. "I bet you were having a boring night until this."

"Are you hurt?" she asked Chase.

"I'm okay." He pulled Ruby into a hug. "What were you *thinking*? I can't believe you hit Decker over the head with a trash can."

"What about you? I knew you'd do something risky. That's why I had to come back to find you."

"You have to trust me to do my job."

"Last I checked, you weren't on duty tonight." But Ruby knew what he really meant. That he also considered it his job to take care of her and risk his life for her.

In many ways, that protectiveness annoyed her.

But was it twisted that she also found it *really* sexy?

"Well, this is a nice clusterfuck you've got here," Sean said to them. "I've been wanting to bust this fight club for a while, so I guess I should be grateful for the excuse. But it would help if the three of you could tell me what the hell just happened. Who's the guy the paramedics are giving oxygen?"

"Conrad Decker," Chase supplied. "He attacked first."

Ruby hooked her arm around his. "Chase was defending himself."

Sean laughed. "From the size of that guy, I'd believe it." He stepped away, telling some of the officers to hold Decker for questioning. When he returned, he said, "Time to start filling in the details."

The men nodded at Ruby to go first. "I went to find Noah. I knew Chase had signaled him that there was an emergency. But I didn't know that Noah had a different signal that connected to the LAPD."

"You didn't expect me to show up without my own contingency plan, did you?" Noah asked.

"Might have been nice to know that," Chase said.

Noah shrugged. "Wanted to give you some deniability. You're already outside your jurisdiction."

"Keep going," Sean prompted Noah.

"Well, I told Ruby to head outside and stay out of the way until you guys arrived."

Chase's eyes slid to hers. "But she didn't listen?"

"Of course I didn't listen." Ruby hadn't intended to wait around.

She'd run ahead to find Chase. When she'd seen Decker

attacking him, she'd acted without thinking. Ruby had distracted Decker enough to give Chase the upper hand. But then? Chase had turned absolutely vicious.

She'd never seen him like that before.

Sean rubbed his chin. "And that's when I showed up. The picture's a little clearer. Did you get anything useful for all this trouble? Noah told me you're investigating a murder in West Oaks."

"I heard Decker discussing the murder of Mickey Waverley with Adrian Peele," Chase explained. "Decker wanted money to skip town. He knew Ruby's lawyer had been asking questions about the circuit, and Decker was afraid Mickey's murder would get traced back to him and Peele."

"Are you serious?" Ruby whispered.

Holt whistled. "Adrian Peele, huh? Would be nice to get charges to stick against that slippery fucker. Peele has important friends, if you catch my drift."

"Just tell me you can hold Decker," Chase said. "I'm going to talk to West Oaks PD about getting a search warrant based on what I overheard. It's not much, but it could lead to stronger evidence that would nail Decker and maybe even Peele for Waverley's murder."

So the investigation was still up in the air. But this was the biggest lead they'd had. Ruby couldn't wait to tell Jane.

"I think Decker's good for assaulting a police officer, at the very least. We'll hold him, and I'll make sure he doesn't get to ask the court for bail for a few days. But as for this murder, that's West Oaks PD's business. I need to start sorting out the rest of this mess. The moment we stepped in the building, people started panicking and running. I think I already hear the news choppers circling." Sean pointed at them. "None of you go anywhere without giving a statement."

Sean walked a few feet away, conferring with Noah.

Ruby tugged off her wig and shook out her hair. "What about Nora? Peele and Decker didn't mention her name?"

"Not once. I didn't see her."

Hopefully, the LAPD raid had helped deflect attention from Nora, rather than making the situation any worse for her.

Then Ruby realized what this could mean. "If you're testifying against Adrian Peele, he could try to go after you. You'll be in danger."

"Do you know how often I testify as a witness? All the damn time. It's just part of my job."

Her instinct was to argue. But she'd seen tonight that Chase could take care of himself.

Chase studied her. "Nothing to say to that?"

"Nope. I'm going to trust that you can handle it."

He narrowed his eyes. "This is Ruby Whitestone talking?"

She'd watched Mickey fight in the ring dozens of times, and he'd never looked as bloodthirsty as Chase had when he'd taken down Conrad Decker.

Chase would've kicked Mickey's ass.

Which was a very inappropriate and cruel thought to be having, since Mickey had been murdered, but Ruby's rebellious brain didn't always care what was appropriate.

She'd witnessed Chase's gentle side more often than she could count. But *wow*, was he hot when he was dangerous.

They spent the next two hours giving statements and answering questions. Sean and his team had set up a base of operations right there in the warehouse.

Ruby was sitting in a chair in a corner, nodding off, when Chase came over. "Hey, you ready to head back to West Oaks?"

She snapped back to awareness. "Did you hear anything about the search warrants?"

Chase grinned. "Detective Murphy wasn't happy, but she's working on my affidavit now. We're going to present the warrant to a judge first thing in the morning. And LAPD has Decker in custody for assault. He's not going anywhere."

"Peele?"

"It'll take more time to build a case against him, but for the moment he's got his hands full dealing with LAPD and tonight's raid. When West Oaks executes the search warrant, Peele won't even see it coming. With some luck, it's only a matter of time until we have the proof we need that you're innocent."

This was the best news she'd heard in a while. Ruby stood up and hugged him.

"You must be exhausted," he said. "Let's go home and get some rest."

Chapter Twenty-Eight

Chase woke with Ruby snuggled against him. The room was still dim, with the sunrise just peeking through the curtains.

"Hi," she said.

"Morning." Chase sat up to see her better. "How're you feeling?"

"Okay. I didn't sleep much."

He couldn't blame her. With the adrenaline rush of that fight with Decker combined with the LAPD raid, Chase hadn't slept well either.

"You can go back to sleep," he said. "Haley won't be home for a few hours."

Ruby's daughter was still at Megan's, with a Bennett Security car outside the townhouse to keep watch. Later, Chase would have to head in to work.

Until then, they had the apartment all to themselves.

Ruby bit her lip. "I've been awake for a while, thinking. I've been scared about things that *might* happen, but if last night reminded me of anything, it's that we never know what could come next."

His heart lurched. He hated that she was afraid. "It'll be

okay. The police have Decker. Jane's working on your case. Probably as we speak."

"I know, but I don't want to talk about that. I want to make the most of this time with you. While we can."

While we can. Because it wouldn't last forever.

He wanted to be grateful for what he *did* have. Ruby was here with him. She *wanted* to be here with him. Chase's heart longed to read more into what she was saying. As if this closeness could mean as much to her as it did to him.

But maybe this moment, and however many moments they got until the end, could be enough. Chase wanted to memorize every detail of her so he'd always remember.

As if he could ever forget.

Chase pulled her closer and kissed her softly, running his fingers through her hair.

But Ruby pulled back. "I don't want to waste any more time. I want you to fuck me. Right now."

Oh. *Damn.*

He didn't know what the rest of today would hold, but this was a very good start. "Are you sure?"

"Very." She palmed his erection through his pajama pants. "Please fuck me."

He groaned, skin prickling with desire and heat. "I've been dying to sink my cock into you. But don't we need supplies?" Chase tucked her hair behind her ear.

Her smile turned almost shy. "I bought some things online. I've been saving them."

Ruby went into the closet and emerged with a black leather-bound box.

"Is that what I think it is?" he asked.

She sat beside him on the bed. Ruby lifted the lid, waving her hand like the model in a game show. "My very own sex box."

She tilted the box so he could see inside. Condoms. Lube.

And a pair of leather cuffs linked by a long, thin chain.

His dick jumped. "I love that you bought that for yourself."

Ruby picked up the cuffs and set them in his hand, the chain pooling silkily in his palm. "Did I choose well?" she asked.

"You looking for praise?"

Ruby shrugged. "I don't mind it."

I bet you don't. Chase grinned, leaning in to whisper in her ear. "These are perfect. You want to wear them while I fuck you?"

Ruby nodded, tongue moving across her lower lip. "Cuff me to the bed. Do whatever you want to me."

Shit. "If you want to play, then we'll play." Shivers raced down his spine.

"Yes," she whispered. "I want that. I need it."

Ruby had bought these cuffs for herself. She was making her desires clear, and that turned him on like nothing else. He wanted to make this so good for her.

First, they each stopped in the bathroom. Chase brushed his teeth and quickly washed up. They met back in the bedroom, still in their pajamas. The sun was higher now, and daylight spread through the room.

"Is anything off limits?" Chase asked.

"I told you I trust you."

He used one hand to cup the back of her neck and rested his forehead against hers. Chase was afraid of betraying how much he really felt. How his heart was bursting from his chest. But Ruby's openness with him made it difficult to hold back.

"You just tell me if there's anything you don't like. I want to know everything you're feeling."

She nodded.

Chase undressed her, then shucked off his own clothes.

Ruby gasped, her hands flying to her mouth. "*Chase.* Oh, god. You did get hurt."

He looked down at himself. Dark bruises were forming on his torso where Decker had hit him. But the paramedics had checked him out, and he didn't have any broken ribs.

"I'm fine. Don't worry about it." The bruises were mildly painful, and would probably be worse later based on Chase's experience. But he was already blissed out on pleasure chemicals, euphoric from being here with Ruby.

"You sure you're up for this?" she asked.

He leaned in to murmur in her ear. "Nothing is going to stop me from having you exactly the way I want."

He sat Ruby down at the edge of the bed. His eyes took in her naked body. The soft curves of her hips and stomach, her small, perky breasts. Her legs were knocked together, and he resisted the urge to push them apart.

Usually, he didn't mind waiting for gratification, but Ruby challenged his willpower every time.

He bent to kiss her, lingering to stroke his tongue into her mouth.

Then Chase went to his knees in front of her. "Give me your hands?"

She held them out, palms up. He ran his thumbs down the inside of each of her forearms. His eyes caught on her wedding ring.

She always wore it, even when they were alone. Just like he did. He could almost pretend it meant more than it did.

Chase picked up the cuffs and wound the chain loosely around her wrists, letting her feel the tiny links against her skin. The metal was already starting to warm from their body heat.

"How's that?" he asked.

"Nice."

Goosebumps rose all over her, and her dark nipples hardened. He licked each one.

"Oh. Do that again?"

He did, right before he sucked each one of the buds between his lips. She gasped. It made him so hot to watch her get turned on. His balls were full and heavy between his legs.

Chase gave his cock a quick stroke, squeezing the base so he wouldn't get too excited.

He unwound the chain, pushed back onto his heels, and stood.

"Where do you want me?" Ruby asked.

"Center of the bed."

She stretched out atop the blankets, arms above her head, legs long. Chase ran his hands down each of her limbs and back up again. In the bright daylight, he could see every freckle, every tiny hair on her skin.

Ruby closed her eyes, sighing, so he kept touching her. Dragging his fingertips along her shoulders, her waist, her hipbones.

Chase swung his leg over her body to straddle her, resting his weight on his heels. His sac brushed her stomach. She stared down at his erection. Her expression darkened with lust. "So sexy. Friends with benefits is the best thing ever."

Chase smiled, ignoring the sting of that reminder.

Just be glad you have this much, he told himself. *Even if it'll never be more.*

He grabbed the cuffs. "You ready?"

"I've *been* ready."

"Just for that, I'll make you wait longer." Chase draped the chain over his shoulders. The cuffs rested on his pecs. He licked his hand and fisted his dick, giving it a few slow pumps. Ruby whimpered, and the sound made precum pool at his tip.

"*Please*? Enough torturing me. You *are* a sadist."

Chuckling, he took the cuffs in hand again and fit one onto her wrist. He made it snug enough that it wouldn't chafe, but not tight enough to hurt her circulation. He had to get up from the mattress to thread the chain through the bed frame, and then he attached the other cuff.

Ruby tugged on the chain. It rattled.

Chase walked around the bed to her feet. "You look incredible."

All that naked skin, her sweet little tattoo, her hooded eyes watching him. And the cuffs binding her wrists, fixing her to the bed. An image straight from his most wicked daydreams.

He rested one knee on the mattress. "Open your legs."

But Ruby shook her head. "Make me."

Chase's dick jerked. So *that* was how it was going to be.

His pulse sped up, the vein shaking at his throat, and his chest tightened with anticipation.

In Ruby's leather box, he fished out a condom and tore it open. Rolled it onto his shaft.

The cap on the lube bottle flipped open. The liquid drizzled onto his cock.

Ruby was staring as he prepped. She had her knees bent and was rubbing her thighs together, like she craved contact.

When he was nice and slick, he set the lube aside. Chase got onto the mattress, grabbed her around the middle, and flipped her onto her stomach.

"Hey!" Ruby let out a small cry of indignation. The chain had twisted around. He checked quickly to make sure the cuffs weren't pinching and her arms were in a comfortable position.

"If you're gonna be bad, you just might get punished." His open palm swatted her ass, more teasing than painful. Pain wasn't what he was into, and she knew it.

Ruby giggled. But her laughter cut off when he pressed his fingers between her legs, seeking out the center of her wet heat.

"*Oh,*" she moaned.

"Already so wet for me." His fingers slid up to her clit, massaging her until she was bucking against his hand. "Tell me how badly you want this."

"I need it."

"Then open your legs for me."

Ruby's smile was devious when she looked over her shoulder. "Make me."

He crawled on top of her. Using one hand to brace himself against the mattress, he grabbed her thigh and pushed it up, forcing her knee to bend. She was wiggling around, trying to pull her legs back together. Her arms rattled the chain.

Chase easily held her in place with his body weight. The tip of his cock lined up with her opening. Ruby moaned and writhed against the bed even more. Through the condom, he could feel how soaking she was. How hot.

He bent to kiss between her shoulder blades. "You can still tell me to stop."

"If I wanted to, I would."

Holding her thighs apart, Chase pushed himself inside.

They both gasped.

She was tight, her channel snug around him. He snagged a pillow and lifted her up slightly to place it under her hips. His aching shaft pushed in even deeper until his balls were flush against her. Her round ass pressed into his groin.

"Fuck, Ruby. Your body feels like it was made for my cock."

She was looking at him over her shoulder again. He trailed kisses over her cheek. He brushed the hair away from the back of her neck, and his tongue darted out to lick the beads of sweat there.

Then his hips started to pump.

"Chase, *yes*."

He lifted his upper body and pressed Ruby down with his hands on her back. He used gentle but firm pressure, enough that she couldn't move. But he could tell from the look of ecstasy on her face, her steady gasps and sighs, that she loved it.

He couldn't get enough of seeing Ruby this way, cuffed and sprawled on the bed beneath him. She was letting him claim her in exactly the way he wanted. Letting him *own* her.

Last night, he would've killed Conrad Decker if he'd had to. If it had been necessary to protect her.

Everything he'd done the past few weeks had been for Ruby. Out of love. Friendship. And he hadn't expected anything like this.

But getting to fuck her was an excellent benefit.

His hips thrust forward, driving his cock into her. Chase angled his body so he could watch his slicked shaft pistoning in and out. The smooth glide, the contrasting friction, felt so good it made him lightheaded.

He was desperate for her, still needing more, even though she was giving him everything.

Chase pushed her into the mattress and fucked her harder.

Letting his control slip. Giving in to the urge to possess her completely. The feeling of her was driving him wild. His body slapped against hers with every thrust.

Ruby's fists clenched and pulled against the chain. Her pants sped up, the pitch of her voice climbing. She cried out, eyes fluttering closed.

Then her body squeezed around his cock.

She tilted her pelvis to push back against him as she shuddered and moaned.

When she was done, Chase pulled out and rolled her onto her back. Her eyes were half-closed, the way she always looked after an orgasm.

"What're you doing?" she asked.

"I want to see your face." He pushed inside her again. Ruby's legs wrapped around him, and he propped himself on his hands as he fucked into her.

Mine. All mine.

He was already nearly there. He held his breath as he rammed his cock inside her, making the bed thump against the wall.

Chase's balls drew up. His cock pulsed. Spilled into the condom. The release took him out of himself completely for a blissful few seconds as he kept pumping into her.

He dropped his face into her neck and inhaled her sweet coconut-vanilla scent.

She was his. For this moment.

But if his heart could have its way, Chase would protect her and love her and fuck her and never have to stop. He would lock her down forever.

Chase lifted his head, and her expression had shifted. She looked raw and vulnerable, like her usual strength had been stripped away.

"Hey." Chase rested his hand on her cheek. "What is it?"

Ruby blinked, and that uneasy gleam in her eyes was gone. "All good."

"You're sure? Was it too much?"

Her lips slid into a smirk. "I just got thoroughly fucked. Exactly what I needed."

He gave her a peck on the lips. "Stay right there?"

"I'm chained to the bed."

Chase took care of the condom, then removed the leather cuffs, kissing each of her wrists as he did. "I'm here to rescue you."

"So you're the villain *and* Prince Charming in this fantasy?"

"Are you saying you're the princess?"

"Did *not* say that."

But just as Chase lay down next to her, she scooted off the bed. A drawer slid open, and she pulled a clean sleep shirt over her head.

Chase propped himself up on his elbows, watching her and trying to figure out what had just happened.

Maybe it was just the stress of the fight with Decker, the raid, the questions from the LAPD. Everything they'd been through last night.

But every other time they'd given each other orgasms, she'd stayed in bed with him and cuddled. It was especially important after something as intimate as they'd just shared.

"You want some breakfast?" Ruby asked. "I think I need breakfast." The bedroom door flew open, and she'd dashed off to the kitchen before he could respond.

Chapter Twenty-Nine

Ruby poured a glass of orange juice and took a sip, leaning against the counter.

"Are you sure you're okay?"

She jumped. Chase had snuck up behind her. He'd pulled on a pair of sweats, and they hung low on his hips.

Ruby set her glass on the counter with a clink. "Just a lot on my mind."

"Yeah. I bet." Chase opened the cabinet and took out another juice glass. "But it makes a guy a little worried when his girl runs off right after sex. I mean, not *my* girl. A girl. A friend. You know what I mean."

She conjured up a smile. "I'd tell you if I didn't enjoy it. I needed to release some tension, so…thanks for that."

Inwardly, she cringed at how dismissive she sounded. But there was no way she could confess what she'd really just been feeling.

It didn't have anything to do with the murder investigation or Conrad Decker or the rest of what had happened last night.

But it had everything to do with Chase.

Why couldn't she just tell him that had been the best sex of her life? The deepest connection to another adult she'd ever felt?

He was so kind to her and Haley, always there when they needed him. Strong exactly when he needed to be—like at the fight—but achingly gentle when Ruby needed that, too. Chase constantly surprised her. He made her feel so free and so damn alive…

He was more than she'd ever expected.

And she liked him. A lot. More than she'd ever liked a friend.

This was an altogether different kind of liking.

"I had fun. I promise." She ran her fingertips over the stubble on his chin, though she couldn't quite meet his eyes. "It's just hard to quiet my brain about everything else. It's not your fault."

"The exact words every guy longs to hear after sex."

She dropped her head onto his shoulder, just so she didn't have to look into those piercing ice-blue eyes.

No. She was shutting down that train of thought right freaking now.

Chase was the Prince Charming from some fairytale that Ruby didn't believe in. That she couldn't *afford* to believe in.

"Can I cuddle you now?" Chase asked.

"You have my explicit consent. Do you need me to sign something?"

"Very funny." His arm circled her waist, and he kissed her hair. "I just don't ever want to hurt you," he said softly.

"You couldn't."

Chase's body tensed, and she felt like she'd said the wrong thing. Even if she wasn't sure why.

TWO DAYS LATER, Jane asked them to meet her at Bennett Security.

She greeted them in the lobby. "I have news. And it's big." Jane waved for them to follow, heading toward their usual conference room.

Ruby lifted her eyebrows at Chase. "Do you think this is it?"

"Hope so."

She felt his hand brush her lower back as they walked, but he quickly pulled away.

In the past couple of days, they'd been waiting to find out the full implications of the raid on the underground fighting ring. The car from Bennett Security had been sitting outside their apartment building again, keep watch.

Every time Ruby had called Jane to ask for the status on Decker and Peele, Jane had put her off.

Finally, they were going to get some answers.

To her questions about her case, at least. Ruby's other issues…she couldn't deal with thinking about that right now.

They reached the conference room. Sylvie was already there, typing away on her laptop. Noah and Max arrived shortly after.

Once again, Devon wasn't here. Thank goodness. Ruby's brother had been hovering constantly around the apartment, anxious for news. Same with her mother. Whatever Jane and Max had to share, Ruby assumed her family would want a full report after this meeting was over.

Max shut the door to the conference room, then took a seat. "Jane, I'm going to skip the pleasantries because I know you have something significant to share."

"I do. Just got word this morning from the prosecutors assigned to Ruby's case. They anticipate they'll drop the charges against her this afternoon."

Ruby gasped, and Chase's hand went to her leg. The others cheered, and Sylvie clapped her hands.

"Are they charging Conrad Decker?" Ruby asked.

"I'll explain everything. But I wasn't going to bury the lead on *that* bit of news." Jane grinned. "It's too early to break out the champagne, but the moment that dismissal is filed…"

"I'm chilling some bottles of Dom Perignon," Noah said.

Jane pointed at him. "My thoughts exactly, Mr. Vandermeer. A man of taste."

Chase's fingers tightened on Ruby's knee. She looked over at him, and his eyes were full of emotions she couldn't decipher. She couldn't resist kissing his cheek.

"What was that for?" he murmured.

"A thank you. You made this happen."

"Not *just* me."

Ruby wanted to kiss him again, but she restrained herself.

My case is being dismissed, she repeated to herself. Which meant Tessa Waverley had no grounds to take custody of Haley. And CPS would leave Ruby alone, too.

Just days ago, she'd been desperate for a break in her case. She couldn't believe everything had turned around so quickly.

Almost *too* quickly.

She felt like laughing and crying and screaming all at once. And also throwing up. Because it was just too much.

Max quieted the room. "We're not there yet. Back to business. Jane?"

"Decker has been charged in LA County with attacking Chase, and any day now he'll be charged with Mickey's murder in West Oaks. The prosecution is relying on witness testimony from the owner of the cake supply store, who saw Decker discard evidence in the alley behind her shop. A towel. The lab results have come back, and they show both Mickey's blood and Decker's DNA. A clear link to the murder. But that's not all West Oaks PD has discovered."

Jane nodded her head at Chase. "Thanks to Chase's affidavit, a judge granted a search warrant for Decker's home and car. The police found the murder weapon stashed beneath the floor of his car's trunk."

Ruby couldn't believe it. "What about Chase's other testimony?" she asked. "The link to Adrian Peele?"

Jane spread her hands on the conference table. "That decision belongs to the DA's office, not me. I'm not aware of any search warrants issued against Peele. But I think they'd be foolish to charge the man based on Chase's testimony alone. Perhaps Decker will flip and agree to go against his boss. But so far, Decker denies everything. He claims the murder weapon was planted, which is his best hope because the evidence is so damning."

Noah swiveled his chair. "I also heard from Sean Holt at the LAPD that he's getting pushback on charging Peele for anything related to the fighting circuit. The guy's likely to skate."

"And the fights will probably be back in operation by next month?" Chase asked.

Noah looked rueful. "Probably. Sometimes, that's how these things go. At least we tried. And we got Decker."

"I'd like to continue posting a security detail outside your and Chase's apartment building," Max said. "Just to be safe. Though it's probably an overabundance of caution. The murder weapon and the DNA are the evidence that will convict Decker, so there's nothing to gain by going after you now. And if Peele won't be prosecuted anyway, I can't imagine he's got much further interest in you."

Ruby nodded. Some of her elation had dampened. She hated to think that the man truly responsible for Mickey's murder would get away with it.

Nora was another loose end. Ruby had already spoken to Tag Bailor on the phone, and he'd been shocked but not surprised to learn Conrad Decker had killed Mickey. Tag hadn't heard anything from Nora, though. He was still worried, and so was Ruby. But if Nora didn't want their help, what could they do?

"I know it's frustrating," Jane said. "Not having it all wrapped up in a bow. But let's focus on the positive. You'll be able to get back to your life. Back to your career. I'll get your arrest record sealed. With time and some luck, it'll be like this never happened."

Like it had never happened.

Ruby turned those words over in her head.

As they left, Chase leaned over and whispered, "I'm glad you let me be part of your team."

"I am too."

Her heart swooped. And her first thought was, *I don't want things to go back.*

But she couldn't start with that again. Fantasizing that she and Chase could be something *more*. She couldn't go messing up their friendship because of a few stray feelings that probably wouldn't lead anywhere.

Their marriage might be ending sooner than she'd expected, but it had never been real beneath the surface.

All they'd been doing was playing house.

Chapter Thirty

Chase drove them toward home. On the way, Ruby was quiet, but he could almost hear her mind working.

He hadn't known for certain that Ruby's murder charge would be dismissed today. But he'd heard rumors from Shelby.

"Congratulations," he said. "How does it feel?"

"It's amazing. But strange, you know? All this time, it didn't seem real that this could be happening. That Mickey was dead, and the police thought I was responsible. That I could lose Haley over it. But now, it's the good news that doesn't seem real."

"Like you're scared to believe it?"

"Exactly." She pushed out a breath. "I doubt I'll completely relax until Decker's convicted. But that won't be for a while."

It hadn't all been good news today. But Chase didn't want to ruin this moment by telling her.

That morning, the chief had called Chase into his office. A rep for the police union had been there.

You're suspended pending an investigation into your actions. Turn over your badge and your weapon.

Yeah, he didn't feel like sharing that just yet. Chase only wanted Ruby to feel happy today. Relieved. He liked protecting her, and that would be a hard habit to break.

"Do you really think Jane is right?" Ruby asked. "That I could go back to how things were before?"

"If anyone can make that happen, it's you." Chase forced himself to smile.

This was all he'd really wanted. For Ruby to be cleared and for her family to be safe.

"Is it?" he asked. "What you want?"

Ruby glanced over at him, her expression full of uncertainty.

In the last couple days since the raid, things had seemed fine between him and Ruby. At least on the surface. But there'd been an awkwardness he couldn't pinpoint. Like she'd been keeping something from him.

They'd been affectionate. But they hadn't had sex again. Even though he'd *really* wanted it. Maybe she'd seen the end of their marriage coming and had already been thinking about moving on.

Fuck, he didn't want to think about the end.

"You could probably get your job back at the salon," Chase said. "But I bet you could find something better. Even open a place of your own."

"You think so?"

"Absolutely. There's no stopping you."

"That's an idea. We know that Noah is pretty irresponsible with his money." She grinned. "Maybe he'll give me another loan."

"The guy clearly has so much cash he doesn't know what to do with it."

They were laughing together, even though Chase felt like he had a knife buried in the center of his chest.

What kind of an asshole was he that he was thinking of himself right now?

He didn't want Ruby to go back to her old life. He wanted what they had now. Waking up next to her, coming home to her and Haley. Feeling like he belonged to someone.

But he remembered what she'd said the other night. Chase

had told her he never wanted to hurt her, and she'd said, *You couldn't.*

He couldn't hurt her because she didn't feel that much for him.

And he didn't blame her. Ruby had been completely clear about what she expected. He'd always known he was the one at risk of getting hurt.

Ruby was playing with her seatbelt. "Could we go to the beach?"

"The beach? Right now?"

"The minute I get home, Devon and my mom are going to be all over me, wanting to know everything. I just need a few minutes. I'd rather go to the beach. With you. Will you take me?"

"Why not? I'll help you play hooky for a little while."

"Always swooping in when I need rescue."

"You know me."

At the next intersection, he turned toward the ocean. A few minutes later they'd parked and were walking along the sand, their shoes in their hands.

"How have things been at work?" Ruby asked.

"Better. My partner's speaking to me again. Catching the real murder suspect won me back some credibility."

The union rep had claimed the investigation was routine. But Chase had violated orders by continuing to investigate the Waverley murder when he'd been instructed not to. He'd also gone outside West Oaks PD's jurisdiction and gotten mixed up with a Los Angeles police operation. Not to mention going after a suspect with no backup and injuring the guy.

Chase had to admit it didn't look that good.

They'd reached the water. Ruby walked into the surf.

"You probably want to get back to your old life, too," Ruby said. "Your cousin hasn't rented out your house yet, has he?

Chase's heart wrenched again. She was talking about him moving out? "Um, yeah. I mean, no. No, he hasn't rented the place."

"Haley and I really like having you around. But if you want to get back to normal, you don't have to worry about us."

"I don't mind. It's nice having someone to worry about."

"But do you? Want to go back to how things were before?" She looked over at him.

No, he wanted to shout.

But how could he say that to her? Make that kind of demand?

What was he even thinking, anyway? That they'd stay married? Forever? Were either of them remotely ready for a commitment like that?

"I'm sure you'll like having your space again," he said. "I won't take up more than half your mattress anymore. You won't have to hear my snoring."

"You never know. I might miss those things."

"I'll definitely miss the dance parties."

Ruby watched the waves lap at her ankles. "Some things don't have to go back. I like how close we are now. We're better friends."

"We are."

"I don't want to stop hanging out with you."

"We can still hang out," Chase said. "You can call me anytime you want."

"And you can come over for dinner whenever you feel like it. You don't even have to bring takeout. I'll pressure-cook something."

"Looking forward to it."

They resumed their walk, dodging a frisbee game. Neither of them mentioned the friends-with-benefits arrangement. That was clearly over. But Chase did still want to be an active part of her and Haley's lives. He didn't want to lose this bond with her completely.

He didn't think he could bear that.

Chase still considered Devon his best friend. But in many ways, Ruby knew him even better than Devon did, and not just when it came to sex.

She knew he sometimes had a peanut butter cup craving right before bed. She knew about his relationship with his dad. She knew he was bad at painting, but that he was willing to try.

Ruby knew sides of him that nobody else did.

"It won't be that different," he said. "In fact, it'll be better than before." *See? Here's me being an optimist.*

"I like that. It'll be better." Ruby turned and hugged him.

It's going to be okay, Chase thought. He'd get over this ridiculous obsession once and for all. They'd be close friends, and they'd both be able to move forward.

But then Ruby looked up at him, and he could've sworn he saw the same longing he felt.

Was that possible?

If she kisses me, I'll tell her. I'll tell her exactly how I feel, even if it's stupid. Even if it could ruin everything. Because if there's the slightest chance…

"We should head back," Ruby said. "Before Devon sends his bodyguard friends out to find us."

His hope collapsed like a sand castle when the tide came in. "True."

She held onto his hand as they walked back toward the car.

They drove to Ruby's apartment building, and they both waved at the Bennett Security bodyguards keeping watch outside. Upstairs, Haley was waiting with Devon and Aurora.

But when Chase parked, he couldn't get out. "You know, I think I'll head back to my place tonight."

Ruby had already opened the door. She turned back to face him. "What? Why?"

"I want to go to the gym in the morning before I'm on duty. I haven't done that in a while. It's a much shorter drive from my house. It'll save a few minutes."

He didn't have work in the morning. Because he was suspended. But this way, he wouldn't have to tell her that.

He wouldn't have to sleep next to her, knowing they were just counting down until the end.

"Oh." She blinked at him. "You're right. That's totally fine.

But you should tell Max where you'll be. So he can send another security detail for you."

"I will." That was the last thing he wanted to think about.

"Haley will wonder where you are, though."

Chase shrugged. "She should get used to me not being there anymore, right?"

"She should." Ruby looked out the window at the building. "Do you want to come in? Get your things?"

The thought of packing up right now made him want to punch something. All the more reason to hit the gym. "Nah, I've got enough at the house. I'll come by tomorrow. We can have dinner together. You and me and Haley."

"She'd like that." Ruby was hesitating, hand still on the door.

"You'll be okay?" he asked.

"Absolutely. I'll see you tomorrow. Bye, Chase."

"I'll see you."

He watched her go inside and kept sitting there, long after the door to the apartment building had closed.

Chapter Thirty-One

There was a knock at Ruby's apartment door. "It's open, Mom." She was just packing up the last of her hair and makeup supplies in her bedroom.

When she came out to the kitchen, her mom had unpacked several containers on the table, and Haley was clapping her hands. "I brought snacks."

Ruby lifted Haley into the high chair. "Real snacks this time? Not candy?"

"I'll have you know I brought a vegetable." Megan opened a plastic container and handed Haley a piece of celery with peanut butter smeared over it.

"Mom, all she ever does is lick the peanut butter off."

"So what? If she likes it, why not?"

Okay, that was a good point. Ruby grabbed a plain celery stick from the container and bit into it.

"And how are my girls?" Megan asked. "Are you excited for the big day?

"We're all right. I guess."

It had been a week since Ruby's murder charge had been dismissed. One week since Chase had moved out.

And every day, she'd felt his absence. More than she even wanted to admit.

Today was Max and Lana's wedding. It would be held at a fancy house in the West Oaks Hills owned by Noah Vandermeer's girlfriend, Danica Foster-Grant. A billionaire heiress and famous philanthropist. Ruby had never met her, but she was looking forward to it. At least, as much as she looked forward to anything at the moment.

Ruby had to be there early, and her mom would watch Haley in the afternoon. Later, Mrs. Murtree would come take over so Megan could attend the ceremony.

She took another bite of celery. "I'm sure the wedding will be beautiful. Aurora's spent months obsessing over every detail."

"We can only hope she'll get started planning one for her and Devon soon."

Ruby held back an eye roll. "Mom, that's not our business. They're happy just as they are."

Megan waved her hands dismissively. Haley copied her, shaking a half-licked celery piece in the air. "I know, I know. My children are determined to do everything out of order."

"Because I had a kid out of wedlock, and Devon is too?"

"Did I say I was complaining? At least I get to be a grandma again, even if I've never been a proper mother of the bride or groom. There was you and Chase, but a quickie wedding by the county clerk isn't exactly the grand affair I've been dreaming of."

Do not snap. Remain calm. "I promise I'll throw a bigger party for my next marriage of convenience."

"You know I'm just teasing."

Do I? Ruby thought.

Since she'd been a teenager, she and her mom had tested each other's nerves. But they'd also supported one another and survived a lot. Including a year of living together after Haley was born.

Ruby's mom had arthritis, so she hadn't been able to lift the baby in and out of her crib easily. But she was a Whitestone, so of course she'd pushed herself to do too much. Megan had always been there when Ruby had asked.

"I love you, Mom. I'm grateful for you."

Megan eyed her. "Why do you sound like you're repeating yoga mantras?"

Ruby just smiled.

"Has Jane said anything about when that man Decker will go on trial?"

"That's the prosecutor's decision."

The West Oaks DA had now charged Conrad Decker formally with Mickey's murder. He was still refusing to talk. As they'd expected, Decker's boss Adrian Peele hadn't been charged. There wasn't enough evidence to suggest Peele had ordered the hit on Mickey.

Ruby felt like it was out of her hands. She and Chase both had done their best. If Chase's testimony about what he'd overheard wasn't enough, then what else could they do?

And if Peele wasn't going to be charged, then Chase wasn't in danger as a witness. Just as Max had said. Ruby had dismissed the team of Bennett Security bodyguards who'd been watching her apartment in shifts. The poor guys had seemed extremely bored, and there'd been absolutely no sign of any more danger.

She just wished she'd been able to reach Nora. Ruby had been trying to let go of Mickey's murder and his ties to the circuit, but she couldn't erase her worries about her old friend.

"Chase will be at the wedding today, won't he?" Megan asked. "I haven't seen him much lately."

Haley looked over. "Chay-Chay?"

"No, bug. Uncle Chase isn't here." Ruby picked a piece of lint off her jeans. "I assume he'll be there. He's friends with Max and Lana."

"He didn't tell you?"

"He doesn't tell me everything he does."

"But he's your husband."

"Mom, he *isn't*," Ruby snapped. "Not in the ways that

count." *No grumpy allowed*, Ruby told herself. She sighed. "You know Chase moved out."

So far, Chase had been good to his word. He'd come for dinner, and he'd spent quality time with Haley. Reading books, playing silly games. He and Ruby had texted each day. He'd kept every one of his promises. As always.

Her mom raised her eyebrows. "But you *are* still married."

"We haven't started the process of getting divorced yet. But it's going to happen. It was always going to happen." And now, her voice was shaking. Like she was ready to cry. Haley kept looking over at her.

What is wrong with me?

"I know, honey." Megan rested a hand over Ruby's, and when she spoke again, her voice was gentle. "We expected it. But you sound upset about it."

Ruby's throat felt tight. "Why would I be?"

"My point exactly."

"Chase has his own life. He deserves to have that back."

"I agree. If that's what he wants. But I was surprised to see how well he fit into *your* life. It seemed like he enjoyed being there."

I thought so too.

When she and Chase had walked on the beach a week ago, she'd asked him if he wanted things to go back to how they were before.

But in that moment, she'd wanted him to say no. To say he didn't want to leave them.

She'd wanted him to *stay*.

Even if it wasn't possible.

"I was never supposed to end up with Chase," Ruby said.

"Why not?"

"Because…"

Aurora and Lana had asked her the same question before, and Ruby had used to know the reasons. *Because I'm not attracted to him. Because he's too perfect.*

Because he's a cop.

But only the last excuse was still true.

Haley raised her arms. "All done."

Ruby wiped her off, unstrapped her, and set her down. Haley toddled off to play. Megan got up to follow Haley into the living room.

Ruby trailed in after them and sat next to her mom on the couch.

She didn't even know her next question until she heard herself ask it.

"What was it like when Dad died?"

Her mom got the sad, faraway look she still wore whenever someone mentioned Dad. "You were younger then, but I'm sure you remember. All the people who came here to support us, those sleepless nights." Megan cleared her throat. "It was a lot like when we lost Kellen. Awful. But we had each other, didn't we? That got us through." She patted Ruby's shoulder.

"But…what was it like for you?"

A crease appeared between Megan's eyebrows. "For *me*?"

Had Ruby never asked anything like this before? It really sucked if she hadn't. But maybe she hadn't been able to see her mom's experience as separate until now, when she was a mother herself.

"What was it like losing your partner? You don't have to talk about it if it's too hard. But I was just thinking, it must've been different from losing a dad or a brother. I'd think it would be worse."

Megan studied her before answering. "I can't say it was worse than what you went through. That's not for me to judge. Losing Kellen, for me, was harder. Much harder."

Ruby watched Haley play, feeling that instinctual terror she always did when she thought of losing her child.

"But letting go of your dad was still one of the toughest things I've had to go through. I've never met anyone else who could replace him in my heart." She reached for Ruby's hand. "That's always the risk, isn't it? With loving anyone. Getting left behind."

"Dad didn't choose to leave us. I've been left behind, and when the guy isn't that great to begin with? It's not so hard to get over. I think that's why I chose Mickey in the first place. But with a really good man, who's kind and loving and generous…"

"Are you thinking of Chase? Is that what these questions are about?"

Ruby didn't trust herself to respond.

"You're worried about him dying? Because he's a police officer like your dad and Kellen?"

"Maybe."

"Are you in love with him?"

"*No*. Well…I…don't know. I think I *could* fall in love with him." Just saying those words made her stomach dissolve into a million flutters. "But I don't know if I should. When losing Dad and Kellen was already so hard."

"Ruby, I fell in love with a person. Not a job. Your dad's work was important to him, part of who he was. But we can't choose who we fall in love with. We just have to accept that gift when it comes. In fact, I seem to remember someone saying that when she got pregnant. About how the best things aren't planned?"

Ruby smiled sadly. "I remember."

"What if Chase wasn't a police officer? What then? How would you feel about him?"

"I…"

Shit. She had her answer, didn't she?

When she'd met Mickey, she'd seen a man who couldn't have been more different from her brothers. That had drawn her. There was no way she'd ever have fallen in love with him, so it hadn't felt like such a risk.

But Chase wasn't like her brothers, either. As she'd gotten to know him on a deeper level, she'd realized he was just…Chase. He'd given hints about the sadness inside of him. The anchor on his heart. Yet he'd chosen to be that much kinder and more giving as a result. He was so funny and sexy and not like anybody else she'd ever met.

But the thought of taking that risk with Chase, of really *trying*, still terrified her, and it had nothing to do with his job.

"I think I'm afraid of loving *anyone*," Ruby said.

After so many men had disappeared from her life, it was hard to believe she could find happiness with another.

"But if you could fall in love," her mom said, "would it be Chase?"

She thought of his striking eyes. The masculine scent of him that made her knees weak. How she'd felt safe in his arms. Free.

"Maybe," Ruby whispered.

"Then *maybe* you should grow a freaking pair and tell him how you feel."

"Hey! Watch the salty language."

"Just trying to be more like you."

Ruby did want more than friendship with Chase. She could admit that to herself. But she wasn't able to take the risk of admitting that fact to anyone else. Especially him.

"I don't know, Mom. I need to think about it."

Chapter Thirty-Two

Shelby strolled across the gym floor. She did a double take when she saw Chase at the squat rack. "Hey, you're here."

"I'm here."

"I heard Conrad Decker is being transferred to West Oaks custody soon."

Chase loaded another plate onto each end of the barbell. "I wouldn't know."

"Your suspension is such bullshit. So what if you broke a few rules? You found the real murderer. But this can't last long. There's no way."

"I guess we'll see."

"Okay, what's wrong with you? Everyone's saying how you were right all along about Ruby being innocent. They're lining up outside the chief's office to protest your suspension. And you're sitting here looking like somebody pissed in your protein shake. You're ready to give up? Not going to fight for what's yours?"

Chase didn't say anything, but he felt his scowl deepen.

"All right," Shelby said. "Outside. This is an intervention."

Chase grabbed his bag and followed Shelby to the parking lot.

The past few nights that he'd stayed at his house, he'd barely slept. He missed Ruby's presence beside him. Her warmth and her small sighs while she dreamed.

He'd been lying awake instead. Staring into the dark.

And during his days at home, he'd had nothing better to do than sit and think.

Wondering about too many things.

"What's up?" Shelby asked.

Chase sat on the curb. "Some details about the case against Conrad Decker are bothering me."

"What do you mean?"

"Why didn't he get rid of the murder weapon?"

Shelby held out her hands. "Hell if I know."

"But think about it. The guy dumped that towel with Mickey Waverley's blood in the trash can behind Cakes 'N' More. Which turned out to be a bad idea. But then why keep the murder weapon? Why not get rid of that, too?"

Shelby shrugged. "He was worried it would get discovered."

"Really? In the whole LA basin, he couldn't find a place to stash it besides his car?" Which hadn't actually been a Kia. Chase assumed Decker had stolen the Kia and dumped it, but he couldn't prove it.

"Sometimes criminals are stupid. We can't explain everything they do."

"But here's something else. I keep going over what I heard Decker and Peele saying the night of the fight. Decker never actually said he killed Waverley. Or that Peele ordered it."

Shelby squinted at him. "What's your point?"

"Decker said that something about Waverley's death could lead back to him and Peele. But *what*? It doesn't have to be that they killed him."

"So now you've joined the guy's defense team? You think Decker is *innocent*?"

"No. Decker had something to do with Waverley's death. Peele did too, even though we're having trouble tying him to it. But what if somebody else has these same thoughts, and the case against Decker falls apart, and the DA decides to blame Ruby again?"

"The prosecutor dismissed her charges."

"But it was 'without prejudice.' That means if the case against Decker tanks, they could turn around and charge her again. If I can poke these holes in their case, so can someone else."

"Shit. You're spiraling about this. It's all so far-fetched."

He shrugged. "You asked what's wrong with me. There it is."

"So you're still worried about Ruby. I get it." Shelby sat on the curb beside him. "But I doubt those lingering mysteries in the Waverley case fully explain your pissy mood. What else happened?"

"I'm not living with Ruby anymore."

"That explains some things. Why not?"

"Because we caught the real killer, and our marriage doesn't need to keep going."

"Is that why you're coming up with reasons Decker won't be convicted? So she needs to stay married to you? You want to keep playing the hero?"

Chase scowled.

"Okay! I take it back. Calm down." She bumped her foot against his sneaker. "So, Ruby kicked you out? That's a good reason by itself to be upset."

"She didn't kick me out. I…left."

"Oh." Shelby had drawn the word out, layering it with all kinds of judgment. "It was a premature ejection of sorts?"

"Never say that again in my presence."

Shelby snorted. "Men can be so sensitive."

Chase had been second-guessing his decision to move out every day since it had happened. He'd gone to Ruby's apartment for dinner and to play with Haley, and each visit, he'd longed to stay the night.

But that might've given away what he was really feeling. That he wanted to stay a lot longer. Maybe even forever.

"You might've jumped the gun on moving out, but I understand your reasoning. You knew the marriage would end anyway, so you just ripped that bandage clean off."

"Pretty much. Didn't help that we started having sex, and I wanted the marriage thing to be real. Stupid as that sounds."

"That does sound really stupid. You have a masochistic streak I didn't know about?"

She wasn't saying anything that hadn't already passed through his mind.

"I'm sorry," Shelby said. "For what that's worth."

"Thanks."

"But are you completely sure there's no chance? She doesn't feel the same?"

"We were friends with benefits. I admitted I had a crush on her, and she laughed it off. Even if she hadn't, what would we be doing? We can't stay married. We've never even dated each other."

"But you could *try* dating each other, like normal people."

Chase had thought about that, too. But she didn't want to end up with a cop. Didn't want to end up with *him*.

"It wouldn't work out."

"So you're determined to be miserable. That's what I'm hearing."

He shot a finger gun at her. "You solved it."

"Detective, here I come." Shelby rested her elbows on her knees. "I've known you since the academy, and you've never been serious about anyone like you are about Ruby. You married this girl. Nearly sacrificed your career for her."

"Nearly?"

"Shut up, you'll get it back. But after all that, you're not willing to take the risk of just telling her how you feel?"

"Ruby and I are close friends now. I don't want to lose that. If I want even more, if I ask for too much—"

"Since when is loving someone asking too much? If anybody

has earned the right to be happy, it's you. Did somebody break your heart? Someone left you, messed you up, and you can't get over it?"

"And now I'm done talking about this." Chase stood up and grabbed his bag.

"Chase, come on."

"I have a wedding to go to."

"Another wedding?"

He smirked. "For someone else. Not me."

Ruby would be there, and the whole event would remind him that their marriage would be over soon. That it had never been real in the first place, except on paper.

"Fine," Shelby said. "You're so much fun to be around at the moment. You'll have a blast."

"Oh, I will. This is *exactly* how I want to spend my evening."

"Better than pouting by the squat rack."

Chase didn't respond. Instead, he headed for his car.

Did somebody break your heart?

Fuck that. He wasn't some broken kid, waiting for his mom to come back. For one, that would mean he saw some unconscious parallel between Ruby and his mother, and that would be gross.

It was also ridiculous. Ruby wasn't like his mom. Ruby was devoted to her child.

If anything, Chase was afraid to become his dad. Someone who sucked away the life of everyone around him, taking far more than he ever gave back. Chase would never be like that.

He loved Ruby, and that meant setting her free. Letting her go.

Chapter Thirty-Three

Ruby brushed foundation over Lana's face. "Where did Aurora run off to?"

"Who knows? I think there was some sort of crisis over the flower arrangements."

"They have the wrong color roses." A dark-haired woman had just poked her head into the room. "But don't worry, Lana, Aurora's on top of it."

This was Danica Foster-Grant. Ruby had seen her on TV and in magazines. She was Noah's girlfriend, and she was even prettier in person.

Danica was wearing a black jumpsuit and diamond teardrop earrings. She came over, holding out her hand. "You must be Ruby. I'm Dani. Your husband helped me out a few months ago. Chase? I still don't feel like I've given him a proper thank you."

"I remember hearing about that. I know Chase was happy to do it." Ruby set down the jar of foundation so she could take Dani's hand.

She decided not to get into her marriage issues. Ruby wasn't sure how much Noah had reported about her situation. "It's great to meet you. Your house is beautiful."

"Thank you. It's not my house though. It's my father's. Luckily, he owes me about three million favors, so he couldn't refuse to host a wedding for my friends."

"Lucky for me, you mean," Lana said.

Dani laughed. "Exactly. There's also been a mix-up about the fish option? They brought trout instead of sea bass. Or maybe it was sea bass instead of trout?"

Lana made a face. "I don't care about roses or fish. As long as Max and I end up married at the end of today, I'll eat tuna out of a can and carry my old corsage from prom night."

Aurora swept into the room, typing frantically on her phone. "If I can't get this sorted, L, you might get your wish."

"Is she always this dramatic?" Dani whispered in Ruby's ear.

"Only when it comes to the people she loves."

Aurora stood in the middle of the room and announced, "The DJ is stuck in traffic. How can a DJ from LA not account for traffic?"

"Okay, you." Danica took Aurora by the shoulders and made her sit on the cushioned window seat. "I'm relieving you of wedding planner duty. You are now maid of honor only."

"But—" Aurora sputtered. "There's only two hours until the ceremony!"

"Exactly. You should be enjoying this. Send me your list, and I will handle the caterers and florist and whatever else."

"Are you sure?"

"I'm very bossy. Just ask Noah."

Lana clasped her hands together. "Please, Aurora. I need you here and smiling and happy. Not obsessing over DJs and white fish."

Aurora grimaced. "All right. Fine. Danica, I'll text you my final checklist."

"You won't be disappointed. I might just quit the Foster-Grant Foundation and start a wedding rescue business instead."

Aurora pointed a finger at her. "Don't push it."

Danica threw a wink at Ruby. "Have fun wrangling these two." She left the room.

Lana turned her head, studying her complexion in the three-way vanity mirror Ruby had set up. "I happen to be completely calm."

Aurora sprawled out on the window seat. "I'm hungry. I'm going to text Devon to bring snacks."

Ruby chuckled. "Go for it. He has time to spare. Not like the best man has to get his makeup done. I offered, but he said no." She grabbed the shadow palette Lana had picked and started on her eyes. "Are you nervous about getting married?"

"I've been in love with Max since I was nineteen. And we live together. I feel ready. But I do wonder if it'll be different." Lana's eyes met hers in the mirror. "What do you think? What's it like being married?

"Don't ask me. I barely know anything about being married. Chase only lived with me a few weeks, and now he's moved out."

"How do you feel about that?"

"It's great." Ruby's voice had climbed an octave, and Lana must've heard the uncertainty there.

"You sure?"

"I mean, having my murder charge dismissed is great. Are you going to take over the case against Conrad Decker? Am I allowed to ask you about that?"

"The answer's maybe. To both questions." Lana laughed. "I'm going to play an active role, but between the wedding and trying to find time for a honeymoon, I'm not sure if I'll first-chair the trial. But I'd prefer to have Jane present before we discuss the substance of the Decker case."

Ruby nodded. She wondered what it would be like testifying at the trial for Mickey's murder. She couldn't identify Decker specifically as the person who'd been standing inside Mickey's kitchen. His face hadn't been visible. Thankfully, Lana and the other DAs had plenty of physical evidence, like the DNA on that towel and the murder weapon.

But tiny threads of doubt still nagged at her. West Oaks PD had messed up the case against her, hadn't they? What if they did the same with Decker—the actual killer—and failed to get a conviction?

Lana was studying her in the mirror. "You deflected the topic of your marriage to Chase. Did you think I wouldn't notice?"

"Hey, I don't barge into the courtroom with annoying questions when *you're* trying to work."

Ruby's task took far longer than usual because they kept chatting and laughing, but after another hour, Aurora and Lana were sufficiently coiffed and made up. Devon had brought a tray of cheese and crackers, and Aurora had eaten three quarters of it.

"Ready to get dressed?" Ruby asked.

For the first time that day, Lana's eyes misted over. Aurora clapped a hand over her mouth.

Ruby wagged a finger. "Hey, careful with the lipstick."

"Sorry." Aurora dropped the hand. "I just can't believe this day is finally here." She hugged Lana, careful to keep her face turned away. "You and my big brother are getting married! This is happening!"

Ruby's eyes stung. She wondered if she'd ever get a day like this. The dress, the DJ, the fish selection…

But when she tried to picture it, all her mind would conjure up was Chase.

Aurora and Ruby both helped Lana into her gown. It was simple and elegant, a long column with beaded capped sleeves and a train. A row of fabric-covered buttons concealed the back zipper.

"Don't cry," Ruby whispered to Aurora.

"Trying. Failing." She grabbed a tissue to dab her eyes.

Someone knocked on the door, and Max popped his head in. "Hey, gorgeous." He leaned against the door frame, looking dapper in his shiny tux. Very GQ model.

"You're not supposed to see me before the ceremony," Lana scolded.

"Since when is anyone around here traditional?" Aurora popped another square of cheese into her mouth. She'd already changed into her maid of honor dress. It was strapless, empire-waisted, blush pink.

"Good point." Lana crossed the room, holding up her train with one hand. "Hey, handsome."

"Can I kiss you?" Max asked.

Ruby fixed him with a withering gaze. "Don't even think about it."

Max took Lana's hand and helped her with her train. "Could I at least get a few minutes with my fiancé? Is that allowed?"

They were looking at each other like they were both made of chocolate and were about to melt. Or eat each other up. "Please, go," Ruby said. "Make eyes at each other somewhere else."

Max and Lana dashed off.

"But the ceremony starts in half an hour," Aurora shouted after them. "They're going to be late."

"The ceremony can't start until they get there." Ruby wondered if Chase had arrived. Was he outside in the audience?

She flicked back the curtain on one of the windows. This sitting room was at the back of the house, and it looked out onto the patio, where the ceremony would be held.

White chairs were lined up facing the ocean view, where the sun would soon begin to set. Ruby recognized at least a dozen people from Bennett Security. Sylvie and her boyfriend Nic—a former crime boss who'd gone straight. Devon's fellow bodyguard Tanner, who sat with his girlfriend Faith. Jane was out there too, chatting with Ruby's mom.

But not Chase. Where was he?

"Your mind is a million miles away."

Ruby looked over her shoulder, letting the curtain fall. Aurora was watching her from the window seat.

"You're still here?"

"Danica took over my wedding planner list. Max and Lana are probably getting busy in a bathroom somewhere. And Devon is doing who knows what. I have a few minutes." Aurora got up and sat in the makeup chair. "So, how are you really feeling about Chase moving out?"

Ruby worked on packing her supplies. "Like I said. It's fine."

"But what about…you know." Aurora pumped her eyebrows. "You two were getting *close*, weren't you? Is that still a thing?"

"Not anymore. It was just convenient. We were living together, and we weren't getting action anywhere else. That's all it was."

"I don't believe that for a second. I saw you two together. I know chemistry, and you and Chase have chemistry."

"Okay, we do. But honestly? It's confusing."

"What's confusing? You're both single. You like each other. The sex was good, right?"

Ruby paused, a pouch of makeup brushes in hand. "The sex was incredible. Like, mind-blowing. I haven't been able to stop thinking about it."

"Details?" Aurora asked. "You can't drop hints like that and not give details."

Ruby couldn't suppress her smile. "Let's just say he gave me exactly what I needed."

"Hopefully over and over?"

Ruby laughed, though the sound was tinged with a hint of bitterness. "Maybe. Though I could've used a few more rounds. He made me feel like I was back inside my body."

Aurora looked confused.

Ruby sat against the vanity. "You'll find out soon enough what it's like having a child. It's the most wonderful, astonishing miracle in the world, and it's also like giving your body away to someone else. There's the pregnancy and the birth, which changes you. Then this little helpless person is latched to you twenty-four-seven, whether or not you're breast feeding. I love being a mom. But I also felt like I'd lost the other parts of my identity. Especially the parts that felt sexy."

"And Chase gave that back to you?"

Tingles ran across Ruby's skin as she remembered his hands on her. His mouth. "In every way. He made me feel like a full person again. A mom, but also a woman who enjoyed sex." And plenty of other things, too. "But when it came time, Chase went back to being just friends so easily. Like it didn't mean all that much. Which is fine, because neither of us promised it would be anything more."

Aurora cocked her head. "But now you want it to be more?"

"Maybe?" She groaned. "Okay, *yes*. I do. But I'm…scared. I don't want to get hurt."

"Except you seem like you're hurting right now."

Ruby squeezed her eyes shut. "Is it that obvious?"

"Only because I know you so well. You had something with Chase. I saw how happy you were. And now, that's gone. But you're still wearing your wedding ring."

"I wasn't ready to take it off." Ruby hugged her arms around her middle, fighting back tears.

With her mom, Ruby always felt like she had to be stoic. Strong. But Aurora was different. She was a friend, someone who was open and sincere.

And she was right.

Ruby missed her conversations with Chase. His affection. Holding him and kissing him and seeing him smile just for her.

She missed how he'd boss her around and get on her nerves. Even his snoring and how he sometimes left his sweaty clothes in his gym bag—which was eye-watering the next day. Ew.

And then, there was the sex. Such hot sex. The best sex of her life.

She wanted his dirty mouth and his passion. His strong, beautiful body and wicked tongue and that secret tattoo on his ass. The way he could be so intense and so gentle at the same time.

Chase's friendship meant a lot, but Ruby wanted all of him. Every part.

And seeing Lana and Max together just now? The way they'd looked at one another? Seeing that connection?

It had made Ruby realize how close she'd come to having the same thing. But she'd been too scared to try.

"I *am* hurting. Either way, it hurts." *Which means you have to do something about it*, she told herself. A tear streaked down her face as she opened her eyes.

And her gaze met her brother's in the mirror. He was standing in the open doorway in his tux.

She spun around. "Devon?"

His expression told her he'd heard what she'd said to Aurora. But how much of it?

"Chase slept with you?"

Crap.

Devon's hands balled into fists. "He *hurt you*?"

Aurora stood up. "Dev, please don't—"

He stormed into the hall and slammed the door.

"Overreact," Aurora finished. "Ugh. I'm having serious big brother flashbacks right now, and I'm not liking it. I need to go talk to him."

"No, it should be me." Ruby had to knock some sense into Devon because he was being ridiculous. In all of this, Chase was the least to blame.

"Why are brothers such buttheads?" Aurora asked.

"The age-old question."

Chapter Thirty-Four

Chase ducked down a hallway and rested his back against the fancy wallpaper. The Foster-Grant residence was possibly the biggest house he'd ever been inside. It felt more like a hotel than a private home. There were paintings and thick rugs and vases that probably belonged in a museum.

But it had plenty of places to hide, which was exactly what he needed right now.

There were only a few minutes left before Max and Lana's ceremony would begin. But Chase had already had enough of this event. There was wedding stuff everywhere. Flowers, champagne, music being played by a string quartet. And people asking him nonstop about Ruby.

Any minute Ruby herself would appear. Probably looking stunning, maybe with her hair braided around her head like it had been on *their* wedding day…

There was no rational reason today's event should be so much harder than seeing her anywhere else. But it was. Chase's thumb pushed at the wedding band on his finger.

Footsteps approached. Devon passed by, and he stopped and backtracked when he saw Chase.

"I've been looking all over for you."

"Almost time for the ceremony," Chase said. "Aren't you supposed to be outside? They can't start without the best—" He stopped when he saw the look on Devon's face.

"You had sex with Ruby."

It was not a question. *Fuck.*

This was not a conversation he wanted to have right now. But he wasn't going to deny it.

"I did."

"Unbelievable." Devon closed his eyes, and the muscle in his jaw twitched.

"Can we talk about this later? Please?"

"No. I want to know why my best friend lied to me."

"I didn't lie."

Devon paced back and forth across the hall, hands on his hips. "You said there was nothing between you and Ruby. And that there never would be."

"At the time I said that, I thought it was true."

"But then you conveniently changed your mind?"

Chase shrugged. What could he say? *I didn't think anything would happen, but I really, really wanted it to.*

"I didn't expect anything to happen between us. When it did, Ruby asked me not to tell you, but I wouldn't have anyway. Because it's not your business. I'm sorry, Dev, but it's not."

"But you *hurt her*. That makes it my business."

"I didn't hurt her."

"Then why does she *say* you did?"

Those words knocked the breath out of him.

Ruby had said he'd hurt her?

"When did she say that?"

Devon pointed down the opposite hall. "Just now. Five minutes ago. She was talking to Aurora, but I overheard her. Ruby said she felt confused and hurt after what happened between you."

"I didn't know," he choked out.

Why would she have said that?

Every time he'd seen Ruby the past few days, she'd seemed

fine. She'd acted so easygoing that it had made Chase all the more convinced their relationship—if you could even call it that—hadn't meant anything to her.

Had there been something wrong, and she'd been hiding it? Was it possible he just hadn't seen it?

It killed Chase to think she was hurting because of him.

Devon shoved his hand through his hair. "Just tell me you weren't a dick to her. Please tell me, whatever happened between you, that she got hurt because of some misunderstanding and not you treating her like shit like her ex did."

"I would never treat her that way." Chase was pissed Devon would think him capable of that. Pissed at his friend for a lot of reasons, in fact. "But don't act like you'd be okay with it if I'd asked your permission, or if I'd done anything differently. You've never thought I would be good enough for Ruby. And I get it. You went to West Point. You were a Ranger. You're a bodyguard for a company that serves billionaire clients. And I'm…not."

Devon stared at him, shaking his head. "You think I look down on you? Are you kidding?"

"I'm not jealous or any kind of nonsense like that. But I know I'm right."

Chase was happy with his career. He was proud of what he'd accomplished, despite never being enough in his father's eyes. Unlike Chase's dad, Devon had never overtly put Chase down. But the hints were there.

"I'm good enough to be your best friend, but not when it comes to your sister."

Devon leaned against the wall opposite him. "When I moved to West Oaks, I'd just lost my twin brother. I'd lost my career because my mom asked me to leave the army. And Ruby had just given birth, which meant I needed to support her and Haley plus my mom. The stress was eating me alive. And that's when I met you. Sparring that day at the gym."

"I remember. You practically knocked me out."

A smile pulled at the corner of Devon's mouth. "I had a little pent-up aggression. But after that, your friendship got me through. And when I was protecting Aurora, you were there backing me up. When I say you're my brother, that means something. You're my family."

"You're family to me, too. I'd never want to mess that up."

"Neither do I. That's why I was so shocked by what I just heard from Ruby. But if you say it's a misunderstanding, then I believe you. There's nobody I trust more than you."

Chase nodded, looking down at the ornate pattern on the carpet. "But would you be okay with Ruby and me being together?"

"If that's what you both want, and you're serious about it, then of course. It still seems weird to me, but I can get over it. You have feelings for her?"

Chase's throat tried to close on the confession, but he pushed out the words. "I'm in love with her. I've been in love with her for almost a year." He took a breath, then let it out.

"You've been holding that in for a year?"

"Yep." It had felt good to say. Also terrible. But mostly good. "I don't know what Ruby wants, though. I thought we were just friends, but now I have no idea."

She'd said she felt hurt. But Chase didn't know what that meant.

"You could ask her."

"That would probably be the mature thing to do. Instead of torturing myself over it."

"No, I mean you could *ask her*. Right now." Devon tipped his head, and Chase turned.

Ruby was standing in the mouth of the hallway. "Devon, they're looking for you. It's time for the ceremony."

Her brother looked at his watch. "Crap, I'm late. Is Aurora out there?"

"Yep, and she's getting pissed."

"I'm gonna go." Devon ran down the hall, then turned around. "Could the two of you talk? Please?"

Chase was holding his breath. When his best friend had gone, he faced her.

Ruby did look stunning, though her hair was loose instead of braided. She'd worn a pale blue sundress. It hugged her curves. He wanted to kiss every inch of exposed skin.

"Hi," Chase said.

"You're in love with me?"

So she was diving right in. Of course she was. "You heard."

"Let me guess. My brother came running after he overheard my private conversation with Aurora? I'm sorry about that. I would never have told him about us."

"That doesn't matter." Chase rubbed his eyes, then dropped his hand. "Ruby, I'm so sorry for hurting you."

"Is that what Devon said?"

"That's what he heard you say."

"He's an idiot."

"You're not hurt?"

"Well…I am."

His stomach twisted a little more.

After Chase's mom had left, his father had blamed everybody else. Chase refused to be that kind of man.

But in some ways, he *had* been acting like his father. Not mean or bitter. But underneath his dad's cruel exterior, there was probably fear.

Chase had been scared of telling Ruby how he felt, and he hadn't even admitted that to himself until right now.

"I'm in love with you," he said. "I'm sorry I was afraid to tell you. You've called me selfless, but I'm not. I want to protect you and Haley because I'd stop breathing if anything ever happened to either of you."

Ruby opened and closed her mouth a few times. "Wow. Anything else?"

"That's not enough?"

"You have some momentum going. If you have anything else to confess, this is the moment."

He started walking toward her. "Okay. I think you're the most beautiful woman I've ever seen."

"And?"

"Coming home to you and Haley every day made me the happiest I've ever been."

"Then why did you leave?"

Chase stopped walking when she was a foot away. "I thought you wanted it to be over. Didn't you?"

"I didn't know what I wanted. I was scared, too. I'm scared right now."

"How can I make it better?"

"If you kiss me."

"Really?"

She grabbed the lapels of his jacket. "Please, Chase. Don't make me beg. Just kiss me."

His mouth collided with hers. And it felt so right. It felt like *home*.

Chapter Thirty-Five

Ruby grabbed Chase's hands and pulled him down the hallway. Which was slightly awkward, because her tongue was in his mouth and she had to walk backward.

Chase broke the kiss. "Where are we going?"

"The room where I did Lana's makeup."

She spotted the doorway and tugged him through. Locked the door behind them.

Chase pulled her against him and kissed her. He'd clearly shaved that morning. His face was smooth, and his lips were soft and perfect.

Ruby brushed her fingers over the short bristles of his hair and shivered.

She'd missed that sensation. Missed everything about him.

He'd said he loved her. Ruby wasn't ready to say that back. But she wanted him, *needed* him, and kissing Chase made the fear and uncertainty fade away. She'd always felt safe with him. Which was probably all she needed to know about her feelings for the man in front of her.

She pushed his jacket off his shoulders. Loosened his tie as she sucked his neck. Chase bunched her dress in his hands, lifting it up around her hips.

"I don't think we can both undress each other at the exact same time," Chase said.

She giggled. "It'll be faster if we do ourselves."

"Agreed."

They separated, frantically pulling off their clothes and grinning at each other. Ruby tugged her dress over her head and kicked off her panties. She hadn't been wearing a bra. Chase took longer with all his buttons, but when he shoved his pants and briefs down, his cock bounced back up, long and thick and so enticing.

She dropped to her knees and sucked his tip into her mouth. Salty precum spread over her taste buds.

"Ruby," he moaned, hands going to her hair. His pants were still pooled around his ankles.

She looked up at him. "I missed you. Missed this."

Chase's lips were parted, eyes a shade darker than usual. "Stand up," he murmured. "Let me look at you. I need a second for my brain to catch up, because this doesn't feel like it's really happening."

His dick dragged along her skin as she stood. His length pressed against her stomach when she put her arms around him.

The wedding march played outside. Lana was probably walking down the aisle. Ruby felt a little guilty for missing the ceremony, but she also figured Lana would forgive her. If she even noticed.

Chase toed off his shoes, stepped out of his pants, and dropped his dress shirt onto the floor. Now they were both naked, chests moving as they breathed.

He took Ruby's hand. "You're still wearing your ring."

She nodded. "I haven't taken it off."

He held up his left hand. "Me neither."

Her lungs were already working in overdrive, but they squeezed even more. "I did say I felt hurt. But you didn't hurt me. Not in any way you should feel sorry for."

"Why did you feel hurt?"

"I made a place for you in my life. And when you were gone,

it felt like something was missing. *You* were missing. I just wanted that back."

Chase cradled her face and stroked her cheeks with his thumbs. He leaned forward to whisper in her ear. "Tell me what you need right now."

"You inside of me. I've been dying to feel that again."

The music swelled on the patio, and the curtains shifted in a light breeze.

Her fingers closed around his shaft and stroked. His skin was velvety soft, his dick hard and corded beneath. "Do you have a condom?" If he didn't, it would have to be his fingers or his tongue.

But he smiled. "My wallet. I put one in there the other day, hoping we might need it. Didn't have the heart to take it out." He bent and grabbed his pants, fishing into the pocket.

Ruby looked around the room. "Here." She knelt on the window seat, spreading his undershirt on the cushion. "I want you right here."

Condom in hand, he strode over to her, his erection bobbing in front of him. "Beneath the window?"

"We can be quiet."

"I can. But you're pretty loud."

"You can make me be quiet," she whispered with a smile.

Chase put on the condom and sat next to her. He was a work of art, bathed in diffused light, muscles swooping beneath his skin. She knelt to either side of him, positioning herself over his cock.

The curtain fluttered. Outside, the officiant spoke.

She ran her fingers over Chase's forehead, then down to his jaw. He was really here with her. He'd shared so much in the hallway, and Ruby knew she owed him more of an explanation.

"I wish I could tell you exactly how I feel or what I want beyond this moment. But I don't know. I only know I care about you. And I miss you."

His hands grazed her hips. "Then you can have me. I'm yours. This whole time, I've been yours."

Her stomach flipped. There was the fear again, but it just made her want to hold on to him tighter.

Ruby lowered herself onto the tip of his cock, gasping as he pushed inside.

"Look," he whispered.

Ruby followed his gaze. He'd nodded toward the other side of the room, where the three-way mirror on the vanity had caught them squarely in its center. She saw herself, thighs spread over Chase's lap, ass pushed out. He ran his hands over her bare skin as she watched in the mirror.

"We're beautiful together." Ruby moved her hips, sinking even deeper onto his shaft, and she saw the motion in the reflection. Felt him within her, splitting her open.

"We are."

She'd enjoyed sex with Chase before, but this was sweeter. More tender. Neither one of them was in control. They just moved together, giving and taking in perfect sync.

Ruby heard Lana's voice carrying from outside. Then Max's. They were saying their vows.

Chase's eyes held hers. His arms were tight around her, hips thrusting himself into her. She wanted to be like this with him, over and over. She wanted all the time in the world. To explore one another, make each other come. Make each other happy.

Pleasure bloomed at her core, racing outward. She leaned forward so she could murmur in his ear. "I'm almost there."

He fit his hand over her mouth to muffle her cry. Ruby looked over her shoulder at the mirror, and that was all it took to send her over the edge.

Chase grabbed Ruby's hand and sucked her fingers into his mouth. He grunted as he thrust his hips against her. She felt his dick pulse inside her.

They rode out their orgasms together.

The officiant raised her voice. "Max and Lana, I'm honored to pronounce you husband and wife." Wild clapping followed.

Chase started laughing first. Ruby caught the giggles like it was contagious.

"We'd better get dressed," he said, "before anyone comes looking for us."

"We're okay. I locked the door." She got up so he could get rid of the condom, then curled against his side. Ruby laid her head on Chase's shoulder while his fingertips grazed her bare back.

"Will you come home with me tonight?" she asked.

"I'd love to. I will. But I'm not sure I should go back to living with you."

She lifted her head. "Why?"

"I want to take you out on a date. Lots of dates. I know you don't love me yet, and that's okay. I'd like the chance to win you over."

"So traditional of you."

"You going to argue with me?"

"No. Dating could be good." It would give her the distance to sort out what she was feeling. And deal with this fear she'd been holding inside for so long. "But I want to stay married to you. I don't want to put pressure on either one of us, and I can't promise 'til death do us part, but the thought of getting a divorce just feels…"

"Wrong?"

"Like cutting my heart out."

Chase put his palm to her chest. She felt her pulse shaking her body, heart pumping against him. *For* him.

"It's the health insurance, right?"

She snorted. "Exactly. Just the health insurance."

Chapter Thirty-Six

Chase looked down at the incredible, still-naked woman next to him. He didn't think his body could contain this much happiness. He couldn't stop touching her. Kissing her.

Of all the things that had happened to him lately, this was possibly the most unbelievable.

But he heard voices outside, and doors opening and closing. "We'd better get dressed and make an appearance." They'd already missed the ceremony, and he did want to give Max and Lana his congratulations.

They got up and started getting dressed.

"So what are the rules now?" Chase asked. "Am I allowed to kiss you in front of Haley?"

"Let's just do what feels natural. I don't want to have to hide how I feel about you."

And there was that spark of euphoria inside him again. To hear her say things like that. Things he'd never thought were possible.

Chase buttoned up his shirt, but he didn't put on his tie. "Before we go back out there, there's a few other things I need to say. "

Ruby still didn't know about his suspension. He didn't want to keep anything from her. Not anymore.

"The chief suspended me pending an investigation. He's not happy about what went down in LA at the underground fight."

The smile vanished from Ruby's face. "When did that happen?"

"The same day your charges were dismissed."

"And you didn't tell me?"

Chase sat back down on the window seat. Ruby came over and sat beside him. "I didn't want you to blame yourself," he said. "I always knew what I was risking. It was worth it."

"But how serious is this? Is there anything I can do?"

"I have a union lawyer representing me. Most of the department is on my side. Even Detective Murphy has been speaking up for me."

But now that he and Ruby were really trying this, trying to be together, he was willing to sacrifice even more to make it work.

"Ruby, you said in the past that losing your dad and brother made you feel like you could never be with a cop. If you need me to, I could quit the force."

She was quiet for a moment. "Is that what you want?"

Devon had made it clear that Chase had a standing job offer from Bennett Security. Being a bodyguard would be dangerous too, but there were other positions. He could sell security systems to rich people. And the pay would be good. He could provide all the stability that Ruby and Haley needed.

But she'd asked what *he* wanted. And he owed it to her to be honest. Hiding his true feelings hadn't been going all that well. "I want to stay with the department. I love what I do, and I feel like it matters. That's important to me. But I want to be with you more."

Now that he knew he had a real shot at a future with her, Chase was willing to do anything to make it a reality.

She caressed his cheek. "I'd never ask you to give up what's important to you. My fears are my issue to overcome, not yours. You deserve to be loved just as you are."

"Even if I'm not perfect? I'm annoying and reckless sometimes?"

"Your not-perfect parts are the ones I like most."

They kissed, getting lost in each other until there was a knock on the door.

"Ruby?" a voice said. "Are you in there? Is everything okay?"

"That's Danica." Ruby got up from the window seat. "Yes, everything is fine. I'll be out in a moment."

"Take your time. Just wanted to check."

"Is Chase in there with you?" a deeper voice asked.

Chase groaned. So their absence hadn't gone unnoticed. "Go away, Noah. We'll be right there."

There was muffled laughter, which receded down the hall.

"I think our secret's out." Chase grabbed his tie and tucked it under his collar.

Ruby went to the vanity mirror to fix her hair. "It's a faster way to tell everyone, don't you think? They'll see us kissing at the reception and figure it out pretty quick."

"So I can kiss you at the reception?"

"I was planning to kiss *you*. It would be awkward if you don't kiss back."

Chase walked over and slid his arms around her waist. Their eyes met in the mirror. Damn, they looked good together. "People are going to ask. What should I tell them? That we're staying married, but not living together, while also dating each other?" He was really asking for himself. Chase didn't want to push, but he was still unclear on their status.

"Let's just say we're a couple, and we're figuring the rest out."

He kissed her temple. "That works for me."

Ruby spun around in his arms to face him. "You said you've been mine this whole time. I want to be yours."

That was the best thing in the world she could've said.

He almost stopped and told her about the one last topic that had been bothering him—the possible holes in the evidence against Conrad Decker.

But Shelby had been right. He'd been overthinking, searching for some reason that Ruby still needed him. She *did* need him, but not to defend her against invented problems. It was Jane Simon's job to be Ruby's lawyer, not his.

Conrad Decker was guilty, and it was up to Detective Murphy and the prosecutors to prove it. Chase wasn't going to let Decker or Mickey Waverley's murder take up any more space in his head.

AURORA HAD outdone herself with the reception. A white tent covered an open expanse of grass overlooking the ocean. Fairy lights were strung all over the garden and under the tent, and garlands of flowers hung everywhere. Chase didn't know much about decorating or wedding style. But even he thought the setting was romantic.

He kept hold of Ruby's hand as they chatted with the other guests.

Every once in a while, he would lean over to kiss her neck, or she'd put her arm around his waist beneath his suit jacket. Not as many eyebrows raised as Chase might've expected. They were already married, after all. But he noticed Ruby's lawyer Jane and her mother staring, whispering to one another.

"Ladies and gentlemen, may I have your attention?" The DJ had arrived not long before and hurriedly set up his equipment. "May I present the bride and groom, Lana Marchetti and Max Bennett!"

Everyone cheered and clinked utensils against champagne glasses. Max and Lana walked into the reception, both of them laughing, stopping for Max to tip her backward into a kiss.

An aura of happiness glowed around them. Or maybe it was just the twinkling of candles and fairy lights. But Chase felt their joy like it was in the air.

It was the same thing he felt every time he looked at Ruby and thought, *She's mine.*

She's actually mine.

Ruby squeezed his hand. “I left Aurora hanging earlier. I’d better give her an update before she runs me down and demands one.”

Chase nodded. There was someone he needed to talk to as well.

He crossed the reception area and found Ruby’s mom at the open bar, getting a refill of her champagne glass. “Hi, Megan.”

“Chase.” She opened her arms for a hug. “It’s wonderful to see you. Ruby wasn’t sure you’d be here tonight.”

“I wouldn’t miss it. But I was hoping to talk to you. About Ruby, actually.”

Megan’s smile told him she already suspected what he would say. “Did she finally take my advice?”

“I’m not sure about that. I can only speak for myself.” Chase stuck his hands in his pockets. He’d never done anything like this before. “I’m in love with Ruby. And I’d like your blessing to date her.”

Megan leaned in. “Sweetheart, you’re already married to her. It’s a bit late to ask permission.” But she laughed. “Of course you have my blessing. I was hoping something like this would happen. I always suspected you felt more for her than just friendship.”

“You did?”

“Mothers know these things. And I couldn’t imagine a better son-in-law than you.”

Chase’s heart expanded that much more. “That means everything to me. Thank you.”

“And even though Ruby’s dad and Kellen aren’t here with us, I know they would give their blessing too. They’d heartily approve.”

Chase couldn’t have hoped for more than this.

Megan sipped her champagne. “But I certainly wouldn’t say no to another wedding, this time with a little more fanfare for the two of you. Hint, hint. Don’t tell Ruby I said that. But keep it in mind.”

Chase winked at her. “I’ll see what I can do.” He didn’t want to keep any secrets from Ruby, but he figured he could let this one slide.

He and Ruby were nowhere near ready to renew any vows. But Chase liked the idea. If they were getting married today, he would've made different promises to her. His vows would've had a lot more words like "love" and "adore" and "forever."

"And you could invite your family, too," Megan said.

Chase felt his smile turn brittle. "Not sure they'd want to come. Or that I'd want them there."

"It's clear you don't get along well with them. But the gesture is still meaningful, even if it's just for you. And you never know."

"I'll consider it."

The rest of dinner passed in a blur of laughter and kissing. Some of it from Max and Lana, but after a while, Chase stopped paying attention to anything but Ruby. He couldn't even have said what they ate. Ruby mentioned something about the fish, but it went right over his head.

After Haley's bedtime, Ruby called Mrs. Murtree, who confirmed the baby was sound asleep.

Then they danced to a slow song with their arms around one another, foreheads touching. The way he would've wanted to dance with her at *their* wedding, showing Ruby and everyone else how much he felt for her.

The fairy lights caught in Ruby's eyes, and Chase had never seen her so beautiful.

Devon appeared and patted them both on the shoulders. "I'm sorry I slightly overreacted earlier." He held up his fingers and put them an inch apart. "Very slightly overreacted."

Chase was pretty sure his best friend was drunk.

Ruby frowned at her brother. "It was more than slight. It's like you were taking lessons from Max."

"Max was a thousand times worse. Do not compare me to Max. You have no idea how scary he can be."

She snorted. "Say that a little louder. I don't think the people at the back heard." Besides, Max hadn't seemed all that scary when he'd given Devon a huge hug after the toasts.

"Hey! If I hadn't gone to Chase, *this* might not be happening right now." Devon pointed between the two of them. "So I'm forgiven, right?"

"Yeah, man," Chase said, trying to keep a straight face. "We're good."

"Except we were having a romantic moment," Ruby added. "And you're interrupting."

"I was just leaving." Devon backed up, bumping into another couple. "I'm supposed to be getting Aurora some cake."

Ruby and Chase laughed as he walked away. "He'd better not be driving home," Chase said.

"We took an Uber here."

Aurora came over, holding out Ruby's phone. She'd left it on their table. "Hey, your phone just rang. Have you seen Devon?"

"He's getting cake." Ruby accepted her device.

Aurora wandered off in search of her boyfriend, while Chase watched Ruby check her voicemail. As she listened, her smile disappeared.

Immediately, Chase's stomach burned with anxiety. Something was wrong. "What's going on?"

"That was Mrs. Murtree. She said something about a noise? It didn't make much sense. But I heard Haley screaming in the background." Ruby clutched her phone in her fist. "Haley's been having a lot of trouble sleeping the past few days."

"Since I moved out?"

Ruby nodded sheepishly. "I thought maybe she was picking up on my bad mood. I should get home."

"Then I'll take you." Chase wanted to see Haley and comfort her. He wanted to hold onto both his girls and not let go.

Chapter Thirty-Seven

Ruby watched through the passenger window as Chase's truck wound its way out of the hilltop neighborhood.

Mrs. Murtree hadn't called again. Ruby thought about checking in, but the poor woman probably had her hands full with Haley.

Ruby had just switched off her screen when the phone rang. But this wasn't Mrs. Murtree's number.

It had a Los Angeles area code.

"Hello?"

"Ruby? It's Nora."

Finally. "Where have you been? I've been really worried since the fight. Are you okay?"

"Adrian Peele is dead."

"*What*?" Ruby shared a glance with Chase. "Okay, hold on a second. I'm with Chase. My husband. I'm putting you on speaker." She pressed the button. "Peele is dead? What happened?"

"I don't know yet. It just went down, and the minute I got word, I packed up and left. I've been sleeping on friends' couches. But I can't stay in LA. Not now."

Ruby was trying to think through what Nora was saying, but

she couldn't begin to puzzle out the few hints her friend had given her. "I want to understand. Why would Adrian Peele's death make you have to leave LA? You didn't…you didn't have something to do with it, did you?"

"No way," Nora said adamantly. "I've been trying to keep my head down since the fight venue got busted. This is the last thing I wanted."

"But *why*?" Ruby didn't wish anyone dead, but Adrian Peele had probably deserved this. How many enemies had the guy made over the years? "If Peele's gone, he can't bother you anymore."

"I can't explain it all now. There's so much shit happening, and I swear I don't want anything to do with it. I just want *out*." She sounded like she was panicking. "I need a place to stay."

"Where are you?"

"West Oaks. Parked in a public lot at the beach."

Ruby looked over at Chase again. What was Nora doing in West Oaks? What in the world was going on?

The truck was still turning back and forth, making its way out of the hills. Ruby felt like those same twists were inside her mind as she tried to make sense of the little Nora had told her.

"Are you in danger? Did anyone follow you?"

"Nobody knows where I am. Except you." Nora exhaled into the phone. Ruby could hear the woman's exhaustion.

"If you're afraid of someone coming after you," Chase said, "you need to call the police."

"That's not an option. You both think you know what's going on, but you *don't*."

"Then tell us."

"Ruby, you're the only person I can trust. I'm begging here. It's just for tonight, and I'll be gone in the morning. Then I won't bother you again."

Nora wasn't going to explain, at least not over the phone. "Hold on. I need to talk to Chase. Don't hang up, okay? I'm going to put you on mute." Ruby set down her phone.

Chase gripped the steering wheel. The lights of the main

boulevard appeared ahead. "Maybe we should call Sean Holt at the LAPD. If Adrian Peele is dead, and Nora could be a witness—"

"Then that's her business for the moment. It sounds like she's terrified and running, and I know how that feels. I want to help."

"You've always thought Mickey could've been into more than just the circuit. Nora could be, too."

"But I can't turn my back on her." How could she blame Nora for getting too close to Mickey when Ruby had made the same mistake? "Please, Chase. Do this for me."

He was shaking his head. But she could already tell he wouldn't say no. "She can stay at my house. There's a key hidden beneath the grill on the back patio." Then he held up his hand. "But *only* if she explains what's really going on."

Ruby leaned over to kiss his cheek. "Thank you." She unmuted the call. "Nora? We have a place for you to stay. But there's a condition."

"Which is?"

"I'm going to meet you there, and you'll tell me the whole truth. Everything that I don't know."

"Whoa, hold on," Chase whispered. "*You're* going?"

Ruby ignored him. "Nora? What do you say?"

There was quiet on the line. Ocean waves crashed faintly in the background.

"You're not going to like it," Nora said. "I'm scared you'll hate me."

Chase kept glaring over at her, switching back and forth between watching the road.

"I've made bad decisions too. I believe in second chances. But you have to earn it, Nora. Be honest with me."

Nora paused again. "Okay. I'll tell you. But *only* you. Not your cop husband. And don't tell anyone else where I am. That includes Tag."

So she knew Chase was a police officer. "Fine. Just me." Ruby gave her the address and explained where Nora would find the key. "Meet you there in about an hour." She ended the call.

The traffic light turned red, and Chase punched the brakes. "You're not going there alone. No way."

"Nora's been hesitant to talk this entire time. She trusts me more than you."

"Yes, but that doesn't automatically mean you should trust her back. I'm the one who should go talk to her."

"But she just said she didn't want to talk to a cop."

"Then I'll tell her I'm not a cop at the moment. I'm suspended."

Ruby breathed through her annoyance. Chase was protective, and that wasn't going to change. But she also had to make him understand the nature of their relationship.

They were a real couple now, but that didn't mean Chase got to call all the shots. Ruby was as opinionated and stubborn as she'd always been.

"One of us has to go home to Haley right now," Ruby said, "and one of us needs to talk to Nora. I've made my decision on who's going where. Don't argue with me."

Chase was frowning. Biting back his protests. "Okay. You'll go talk to Nora. But at least take someone with you. Call Bennett Security."

"You mean the guys who are drinking at Max's wedding right now, like Devon? What about Officer Shelborne? You always say how much you trust her." And Shelby might seem less intimidating to Nora.

"I'll call her. But if she can't come with you, I'm going over there to meet Nora myself."

WHEN THEY REACHED Ruby's apartment building, Shelby was already waiting by the curb. She was dressed in jeans and a dark blue West Oaks PD sweatshirt. Not too subtle. They'd have to make sure Nora didn't see.

"Where's the Bennett Security guys who were watching the building?" Chase asked.

"I assume at the wedding with everyone else. I told them we didn't need them anymore. They were camped out here for weeks, and they had better things to do. Max agreed with me."

"But you should have told me. I thought you had protection the past week while I was gone."

"Chase, it's fine. I need to get going." Ruby didn't want to leave Shelby or Nora waiting. "Give Haley a kiss for me."

He parked the car, and they both got out. "Be careful."

"I've made it this many years figuring things out on my own. Without a husband *or* bodyguards."

Ruby waved at Shelby and started toward her. But Chase grabbed her hand. He cupped the back of her neck and kissed her. Shelby wolf whistled.

"I know you can survive without me," Chase said. "But I can't survive without you. So hurry home."

"I will." She didn't trust herself to say much more. But on the inside, she was getting all mushy. "You're being too perfect. It's annoying me."

"I'll keep working on that."

"You'd better."

Ruby got into Shelby's hatchback. Shelby hopped in the driver's seat and started the car. "From the looks of that kiss, I'd guess you two worked out your issues?"

"Most of them. We're together. Officially, not just on paper." Ruby couldn't hold back her grin.

"It's about time. But he's my friend, so I have to do the obligatory 'don't break his heart' speech. Chase can act tough, but he's squishy underneath that armor."

"I promise I'll take care of him."

Shelby held up her fist, and Ruby bumped it.

Chapter Thirty-Eight

Chase went into the apartment building, but he didn't go upstairs yet. Instead, he watched Shelby's car drive away with Ruby inside.

When it came to Ruby's safety, he really hated being out of control.

But the biggest remaining threat against her—Adrian Peele—was now dead. Shelby would have Ruby's back, just like she'd had Chase's in the past.

And if they learned Nora had information about Adrian Peele's death, Shelby could place the call to LAPD. Chase didn't even need to get involved. No use pissing Ruby off the very first day they were official.

Yet as he stepped into the elevator, he still couldn't quiet that sense of unease.

He settled for sending a text to Shelby, asking her to keep a close eye on Ruby. To keep her safe. It wasn't necessary, because Shelby would be doing that anyway, but he needed to do *something* to soothe his nerves.

The elevator arrived, and Chase stepped out, still typing. He was halfway done composing his message when the hairs on his arms raised.

Chase looked up.

All the apartment doors in the hall were closed—except one.

Ruby's door was cracked open by several inches. He could see that gap even from the elevator. Felt the wrongness of it deep in his bones.

Maybe Mrs. Murtree had left it open, either on purpose or by mistake. But she'd never done anything like that before.

Which meant that someone uninvited was probably in the apartment. With Haley.

Unless they took her already.

His training told him to call for back up. But he had to find Haley, and he couldn't waste a single second.

Fuck. What do I do?

Hands shaking, he added the numbers 459 to the end of his text to Shelby and hit send. Meanwhile, his feet were already carrying him to the apartment door.

His thumbs kept moving over the phone screen, dialing 911.

Chase listened. He heard Haley babbling inside. He wondered if he'd been wrong.

Then his fingertips pushed the door, and it swung open on silent hinges.

Nothing could've prepared him for what he saw inside.

Tag Bailor sat in a kitchen chair facing the door. Haley was in his lap with a book, holding it upside-down. She looked up.

"Chay-Chay." Haley dropped the book and reached out for him.

"*911,*" the phone said. "*What's your emergency?*"

Chase wasn't breathing.

Tag shook his head.

"*Hello?*" the operator said.

Slowly, Chase raised the phone to his ear.

Tag's hands tightened around Haley's middle, and Chase felt like they were tightening around his own throat.

"I'm sorry. False alarm. No emergency." He ended the call.

"Drop the phone on the ground."

"What do you want?"

"Chase, I said to *drop it.*"

He did.

Tag looked down at Haley, but he continued speaking to Chase. "I wasn't expecting to see you. I thought it would be Ruby."

A hundred different impulses battled in Chase's body. He wanted to demand answers. Lunge for Haley and get her away. But he couldn't risk it. Not yet.

"What do you want?" he said again.

"To exchange information. That's all."

Chase struggled to keep his voice calm. "Where's Mrs. Murtree? Is she hurt?"

"The babysitter? She'll be fine."

"Why should I believe you?"

"You can see for yourself." He pointed.

Chase came further into the room.

Mrs. Murtree lay behind the open door. She was unconscious, and she had her hands bound behind her back with a plastic zip-tie. But her chest was moving.

"What did you do to her?"

"As little as possible."

"She needs medical attention. There's a cut on her head."

"Then let's make this quick. Close the door so we can talk."

"Not until I know what you really want." Chase took a step in the man's direction.

Tag's hands tensed, and Haley whimpered. Her eyes watered like she was about to cry.

"You're going to scare her," Tag said.

His tone implied Chase was the intruder here instead of Tag.

Gain his trust. Build a rapport.

Chase closed the door. But he didn't take his eyes off Tag and Haley.

"Do you have a gun on you, Officer Collins?"

So Tag knew he was a cop. "No. I was suspended. They took my weapon."

"Turn out your pockets."

Chase's wallet and keys fell to the floor next to his phone.

"Lift your shirt and turn around in a circle. I want to make sure you're not armed. Last thing Haley needs is a gun going off, don't you think?"

Clenching his jaw, Chase did as Tag had asked. "What about you? Do you have a weapon?"

Tag shook his head. "I didn't come here to hurt anyone."

"What about Mrs. Murtree?"

"I came to the door. She didn't hear me knocking at first, but Haley did. I heard her crying. Then the babysitter opened up, but she wouldn't let me in."

So Tag had pushed his way inside, and none of the neighbors had done a thing?

Chase dismissed that thought. It didn't matter. He had to focus.

He thought of hostage negotiations he'd witnessed. "Look, let's be reasonable. Okay? Neither of us is armed. We don't want anyone else hurt. I'm willing to talk. But I need you to give me Haley first."

Tag's gaze returned to the baby in his lap. "She's not yours. But you love her, don't you? I could tell when you were at the gym. The way you looked at that picture on your phone of the three of you."

Her little body strained against Tag's grip as she reached for Chase.

His blood rushed with fury. "If you do anything to hurt her..."

"I asked if you love her. Just answer the question."

"I love them both," Chase choked out. "Ruby and Haley. I would die for them." *I would kill for them.*

Chapter Thirty-Nine

Shelby turned onto Chase's street. "Which one is his?"

Ruby pointed. "Just up there."

"Do you think your friend's arrived yet?"

"Should have. Nora said she was already in West Oaks, parked at the beach." And the most popular public beaches weren't far from Chase's house.

Shelby pumped the brakes. "Lay down in your seat, and I'll drive by. I want to take a look before you go in."

Ruby scooted down so she wouldn't be visible through the car window.

On the drive, Ruby had told Shelby as much as possible about Nora and the underground fighting circuit. But the officer had already known plenty about the investigation into Mickey Waverley's murder.

Shelby drove forward. "There's a light on inside. Curtains drawn. Not much activity." After about a minute, she stopped again. "How do you want to do this? Does she expect you to unlock the door?"

Ruby sat upright. "I was thinking I'd just go knock."

Shelby tapped her finger against her lips as she thought. "All right. But I want to stay close. What's the layout of the house like?"

Ruby described it. How the front windows looked into the living room, while the back door was straight behind in the kitchen. Chase's bedroom was off to one side.

"You go to the front," Shelby said, "and I'll come around from the back."

"You have to make sure Nora doesn't see you. If she realizes I came with someone, especially a cop, she might take off."

"But what is she so afraid of? Unless she's actively avoiding the authorities because she did something, and she's afraid of getting caught."

Which was exactly the cop mindset. "For someone like Nora, you don't go to the police for help. We have to do this my way."

Shelby grumbled. "I'll stay out of sight. But keep yourself near the back of the house. That's where I'll be. If anyone approaches from the front, don't answer the door."

"Got it." Ruby reached for the passenger door handle.

"Wait, one more thing. From what you've told me, Nora could crush you in an instant if she wanted. I'm assuming you feel safe around her if you're meeting with her alone. But are you completely sure that's wise?"

Ruby opened her mouth to respond, but those words caught in her mind. *Wise.* She was always telling Haley to be wise.

What would be the wisest move of all right now?

She could turn around and go home. But would that be wise? Never finding out what other danger could be coming? Abandoning a friend who needed her?

There had been no way to help Mickey the day of his murder. But if Ruby could somehow help Nora out of the jam she was in, she had to take the chance. She had to assume Nora meant her no harm.

So she was definitely doing this.

But what was the wisest way to go about it?

"What do you suggest?" Ruby asked.

"You need a weapon."

"I'm not taking a gun in there."

Shelby grinned. "Have you ever used a taser?"

RUBY WALKED down the sidewalk until she reached Chase's house. Her knuckles rapped on the door.

Nora answered. She pulled Ruby immediately inside and into a hug. "Thank you for this. I'm not going to forget it. I promise." She closed the door and locked it.

"I'm glad I could help."

Shelby had told her to stay near the back of the house. Ruby eyed the kitchen. "Have you had something to eat?"

"I'm not hungry. My stomach is in knots."

"How about I make some coffee? I could use the caffeine."

"All right. Sure." Nora followed her into the kitchen. "Actually, are there any bagels? Or any kind of bread? Usually I avoid carbs on days I don't train. But I think today's an exception."

Ruby put her purse on the floor by one of the chairs. It had the taser inside.

But bringing the weapon along felt ridiculous now that she was here. Nora seemed so dejected. The poor woman was asking for a bagel.

"You're in luck." Ruby opened the fridge and pulled out a sleeve of English muffins. "Chase is a carb fan."

There were still dishes in the sink from Chase's breakfast that morning. It was strange to think of him sleeping here the last several days. The house smelled like him. Now Chase was at her apartment with Haley, while Ruby was here.

She forced her mind to her present task. The sooner Nora opened up, the sooner Ruby would be able to go home.

To my husband, she thought with a secret thrill. *To my family*.

Ruby popped a couple of English muffins into the toaster. She got two coffee mugs out of the cabinet. "Looks like Chase is out of the real stuff. He only has instant."

"Not ideal, but I can make it work." Nora scooped instant coffee grounds from the can on the counter.

Ruby started the water boiling. "Have you seen Tag lately? He seemed really worried about you."

"I'm staying away from Tag these days."

"Why didn't you want him to know where you are?"

"There's so much I need to explain first. I don't even know where to start."

Ruby remembered what she'd said on the phone. *I'm afraid you'll hate me.* She was pretty sure she knew Nora's reason for anxiety. "Why don't you start with you and Mickey? I know you were seeing him at one point."

Nora's eyes widened. "How did you know?"

"Chase went to Baylor Fitness, and Tag told him. But it doesn't bother me. I never really loved Mickey. And even if I had, he's been gone from my life for so long."

Nora closed her eyes. "I did love him. Still do. I've loved him for years, even before he met you. I would've done anything for him."

Ruby's heart went out to her. "And he must've hurt you. I'm so sorry. But I understand now why you seemed so upset when I came to Bailor Fitness. You were grieving for him."

"It was rough. And I couldn't even show it because Cami was his girlfriend, not me."

"That day, I could tell you were keeping something back."

"I didn't want to. I wanted to tell you, I swear."

"It's all right."

"No, it's *not*. Because that wasn't even the worst of it."

"What was the worst?"

Nora paced across the kitchen. "I didn't want it to happen. Truly. I didn't."

"What? Just say it."

"The worst was…" Silent tears streamed down Nora's face. "Knowing I had killed him."

Chapter Forty

"You love Ruby and Haley. They deserve that after the shit Mickey did to them."

"Is that what this is about?" Chase asked. "Mickey Waverley?"

Haley let out a wail. Tag shushed her, bouncing her on his knee. She pushed at his hands. "Of course it is. But it's not what you think. None of it happened the way you think."

"No!" Haley's little arms reached for Chase. "My Mama!"

She wanted Ruby. She thought he could bring her to her mom.

Chase couldn't take it.

"Please put Haley down," he begged. "Let her come to me. She's scared."

"I can't do that. I need to know you'll listen and give me a chance. That you won't try to do something foolish."

"I'll listen. But only if you put her down."

"Then we're at a stalemate, aren't we?"

Chase thought fast. "What about a compromise? Put Haley in her high chair. Then she's not with either one of us."

Tag screwed up his lips. "All right. I can agree to that. Back up a few feet. Keep your hands where I can see them."

Chase held his arms out, backing up.

Tag stood. He took several lumbering steps, then set Haley in her high chair, seeming to struggle with the buckle. She whined. "No. My Mama!"

Tag didn't move well because of his injuries. If Chase could just get close enough. If Haley wasn't near…

"There's a box of cookies on the counter," Chase said.

Tag looked at the kitchen. Then back at Chase. "Don't do anything foolish," he said again.

Tag limped to the counter. Got the cookies. Chase calculated the distance between himself and the other man. It was too far. Tag was too close to Haley, too close to the knives and heavy objects in the kitchen.

Tag lowered himself into the chair beside Haley and scattered a handful of cookies on her tray.

She glanced back at Chase, who nodded. "It's okay," he said. "You can have a cookie."

She picked one up and nibbled the edge of it.

For a moment, neither man said anything.

Chase walked forward in slow motion, hands still out. Returning to his prior position. Tag didn't protest. He just watched like he was studying Chase. Making strategies of his own.

"Why did you leave Ruby's front door open?" Chase asked.

"I figured she'd be upset no matter what about me being here. I wanted to give her some warning. I don't mean Ruby or Haley any harm."

Chase couldn't tell if the guy meant it. If Tag was delusional or completely rational. And that confusion was unnerving. It made Chase anxious. He hated not knowing what was really going on.

"Why didn't you expect me to show up?"

"I thought you didn't live here," Tag said. "I didn't see any of your things in Ruby's bedroom."

"You went through her bedroom?"

"Just to check my surroundings. I'm a cautious man. Didn't

want you running for a gun you had hidden somewhere. If there is one, I didn't see it. Which suggests it would be hard to reach, anyway."

There wasn't a hidden gun, as much as Chase would've wished one into existence.

"I moved out. Temporarily."

"But you love Ruby. Did she ask for the separation?"

"I'm not discussing my marriage with you."

Tag shrugged. "Didn't mean offense. I've got nothing against you. And certainly nothing against Ruby. It's too bad she got wrapped up in this. But I need information, and I felt I had no other options. Kind of like the way you lied when you came to my gym."

"I lied. I didn't invade your home or threaten your wife's child."

"Which you have every right to be upset about. You have a sense of justice. I might not be a cop, but I'm the same. After you took down Conrad Decker, I almost sent you a thank-you card. You and I have a lot in common. We care about people. When someone violates that trust, we want answers. Right?"

"Can you get to the point?" Chase struggled to keep from raising his voice. Haley picked up another cookie.

"My point is, I know you want to protect Ruby. I'm giving you the opportunity to do exactly that."

"I thought you wanted information."

"I do. But this is part of it. Where is she right now? Ruby?"

"I don't see how that matters."

"Is Ruby with Nora? Is that where she is?"

Chase opened his mouth, but he paused. "How did you know that?"

"Because I figured after what happened with Peele today, she'd run. But she can't go to anyone on the circuit or anyone at Bailor Fitness. So, where else would she go but to Ruby?"

"Why wouldn't Nora go to you?"

"Because I know what she did."

"Did she kill Peele?

"This is important, Chase. Is Ruby with her?"

"Yes," he bit out. "Ruby went to talk to her. Nora said she needed help."

"Then I got here at exactly the right time. Because Nora isn't who Ruby thinks she is."

"What are you talking about?"

"Nora's a liar. She's betrayed Ruby before. She's betrayed *me*. And given the chance, she wouldn't hesitate to do it again."

Chapter Forty-One

"You killed Mickey?"

Ruby glanced down at her purse, where the taser was hidden inside.

"Not literally. But it felt like I had. It was my fault."

Ruby's head rushed with relief. "You freaked me out there."

"I haven't told you the rest of it yet. You'll probably still despise me."

The kettle whistled, and the English muffins popped up from the toaster. Ruby set them on a plate while Nora poured water into the mugs.

Then, they sat.

"Tell me what happened."

Nora took a small bite of English muffin and chewed. "Almost two months ago, Cami found out Mickey had a daughter in West Oaks. He definitely hadn't told her about you or Haley."

Which wasn't the least bit surprising to Ruby.

"Cami was furious. She confronted him at Bailor Fitness in front of everyone. Accused him of cheating, of having a family in another city. Turns out she'd found his apartment lease for his new place in West Oaks. He laughed it off like it was all bullshit.

But later, I asked him about it. He admitted he wanted to quit the circuit and try to connect with Haley." Nora lifted her eyes. "He wasn't as hard as he seemed sometimes. Mickey could be thoughtful. Even kind."

"I know," Ruby said quietly. "I remember." Mickey hadn't shown that side often. But it had been there.

Nora took a gulp from the mug. "But I thought he didn't mean it. Peele wasn't just going to let him leave. Not after..." She glanced at the window. "After certain deals that Mickey had made. I thought Mickey would change his mind, the way he always did about everything. But he was serious. He told me he'd contacted you about wanting custody. He'd set up a date and time to hash out an agreement. And..."

"And?"

"I was so *angry*," she whispered. Nora stared into the murky surface of the coffee. "I'd been patient. I'd waited while he screwed around. First you, then Cami. He always came back to me in the end. But suddenly he was leaving the circuit? Moving to West Oaks? Risking whatever wrath Peele might unleash as a result? I just...I couldn't take it."

Her tears had stopped falling, but the wet streaks remained on her face.

Ruby dreaded hearing the rest. But she had to. "What did you do?"

"I went to Conrad Decker."

And you thought that would end well? Ruby wanted to say. But she kept silent.

"I just thought he'd scare some sense into Mickey. Warn him about what a fool he was being, so Mickey could change his mind before it was too late. I...I told Decker about the apartment in West Oaks. And Mickey's plan to meet with you."

Ruby's stomach churned, and bile rose into her throat. She pushed the coffee away. "So when I saw you at Bailor Fitness, you knew Decker was the killer? *You knew*?"

Nora nodded. "I thought Decker must've decided to tell Peele what Mickey had been planning, and that Peele ordered his death. I was sick over it. I'd never imagined that could happen. *Never.*"

Ruby knew she should stay calm, but outrage roared through her veins. "And you knew the police had blamed me. I'd been charged with Mickey's murder. Were you just going to let me go to prison? Let them take Haley away from me?"

"*No.* I was trying to figure out some way to help you."

"You could've picked up the phone and told the truth. Why didn't you? Maybe you felt responsible, but the police wouldn't have blamed you."

"How do you know that? And what do you think Peele would have done to me? I had to come up with some other plan."

"And what was this brilliant plan of yours? Because the last time I talked to you, at the fight, you gave me nothing. Chase had to go after Decker instead—partly because we were worried about *you*—and Decker could've killed him. The man I love could've died because of you."

Ruby didn't even stop to think about what she'd just said. *The man I love.*

Nora leaped up from her seat and threw her coffee cup against the wall. It shattered with a bang, brown liquid flying across half the room. "I thought Decker *did* kill the man I love! I was going to end him. I was going to make sure he never lived another day." She stood there, chest heaving.

Ruby was frozen with shock. "If you planned to kill Decker, what happened?" The guy was in custody for Mickey's murder. And very much alive.

Nora sank back into her chair. "I stopped going to work so I could watch Decker. He was always going on errands for Peele. One day, I saw him boost a blue Kia and go to your apartment. I think he was going to threaten you to stop investigating and stay quiet. Obviously, that didn't work. But that same afternoon, I went back to Decker's house. I knew I couldn't wait any longer. I had to punish him before he hurt anybody else. Like you or your family."

Ruby wasn't going to thank her for the gesture, so she stayed quiet.

"Decker wasn't back yet. But his regular car was sitting in his driveway." Nora's voice was a steady drone now. Devoid of emotion. "I was hiding out of sight. I heard a car. I'd brought a gun with me, a pistol that had been my grandfather's. I thought it was Decker, so I got ready. But the person who appeared wasn't Decker at all. I saw him approach Decker's car. He was holding a bundle. He crawled underneath the chassis. Left the bundle behind. And when he was gone, I snuck over to look."

Ruby could hardly take a breath. She couldn't believe what she was hearing. "Did you open the bundle? See what it was?"

Nora nodded.

"It was a knife?"

"Yes," she whispered. "I knew it had to be the murder weapon. The knife that killed Mickey. Which meant Decker probably hadn't killed him at all."

"Then who did?"

Suddenly, furious knocking on Chase's back door interrupted them. Ruby nearly screamed, and Nora jumped up from her seat.

Shelby's face was visible through the window, twisted with panic. She banged on the door again.

"Who the hell is that?" Nora cried.

"A friend of Chase's." At least Shelby had thought to take off her West Oaks PD sweatshirt and tie it around her waist.

Ruby ran to the door and opened it.

Shelby had her phone in her hand. "Chase sent me a text on our way here. I glanced at it, but I didn't see what he'd put at the end. Not until just now." She held up the screen. "Code 459."

"Is she a cop?" Nora demanded.

"Wait, what does that code mean?" Ruby asked. As a kid, she'd heard her father use police codes a million times, but that had been years ago. "I thought you didn't even use those for dispatch any more."

"459 is burglary. And we don't. We use CAD, Computer

Aided Dispatch. But I think Chase was trying to tell me something, and he didn't have time for more. Burglary is unlawful entry with the intent to commit a crime."

Had Chase found someone in Ruby's apartment? Someone who didn't belong?

"Haley's there." Ruby grabbed her purse.

"I already called it in," Shelby said. "A few seconds ago."

"Fine, but I'm not staying here. We have to go. *Now*."

Chapter Forty-Two

"Are you saying Ruby's in danger?" Chase asked. "From Nora?"

"It's possible. I thought she was my friend, and I nearly died as a result."

Chase looked down at his phone. It was still on the floor. "I need to call her."

"Not yet. Not until we agree on what's going to happen."

"You haven't even *said* what you really want."

Haley looked over at Chase and held out a cookie. Chase took a step toward her, and Tag shook his head.

Chase's pulse drummed at his neck.

"I want to know where Nora is," Tag said.

"Then what?"

"I'll stop her from hurting anyone else."

Stop her? What did that mean?

"Did Nora kill Mickey?" Chase asked.

"As good as. She's done plenty."

Chase nodded at his phone. "I'll call this in to West Oaks PD. I'll tell them where Nora is, and they'll handle it."

Tag smirked. "The department that arrested Ruby? No,

thanks. You're the only one who got near the truth, and you're already standing here in front of me."

Haley threw a half-eaten cookie on the floor. Her face crumpled, and she whined again. "All done. Mama. Chay-Chay." She tried to climb out of the high chair, but the strap held her in place. He couldn't believe she wasn't screaming already.

"Just tell me where Nora is," Tag said, "and I'll go."

Chase's entire body vibrated with tension. "Tell me exactly what Nora did, and I'll consider it."

Tag crossed his legs, leaning back in his chair. "She slept with Mickey while he was still with Ruby. Which was bad enough. But what Nora did to me was worse."

"And what was that?"

Tag pulled up the sleeve of his shirt. He pointed at the long scar on his forearm. "I had a compound fracture from that fight with Conrad Decker. Bone sticking out of my skin. Before that night, I was undefeated. Did Ruby tell you that?"

"No." Chase was having trouble following the threads of Tag's story. He couldn't understand how that fight related to Nora or Mickey. But in Tag's mind, it clearly did. And it was upsetting him. Distracting him.

Chase continued to listen, but his eyes darted around the room. Searching for something he could use. Some kind of plan to grab Haley and run.

"People look at me now, and they see what's left of me. I hear what they say when they forget I'm around. That I'm broken. I'll never be the same." Tag yanked down his sleeve. "Do you know how Decker beat me so badly?"

Chase's eyes kept moving. Searching. *Be ready*. "How?"

"Adrian Peele had told me I was supposed to throw the fight. I had to lose to Decker. Like I had no say. Like I was his puppet. I refused." Tag laughed bitterly. "I didn't realize Peele was going to *make sure* I lost."

Haley put her head on the tray, whimpering again. She had to be exhausted.

"What happened?"

"Peele had me drugged. Spiked some kind of shit into my Gatorade right before the fight. Peele had told Decker to punish me, to set an example for all the other fighters. Decker made sure I would never fight again. I almost didn't *walk* again."

"That's terrible." But Chase couldn't say he was surprised. Tag had been foolish to ever trust someone like Peele.

"I spent months in the hospital. Months more in physical therapy. I almost lost Bailor Fitness, but my friends banded together to help make ends meet. You know who was right there, front and center? Cheering me on, fundraising, bringing me fucking meals? Mickey Waverley. My *best friend*."

Tag's expression hardened with rage.

"I had no idea that my supposed best friend had sold me out."

Haley let out a piercing wail. Chase tightened his muscles.

Tag took another cookie from the package and set it on Haley's tray, but she threw it down. "*No*."

"Mickey knew what Peele and Decker had been planning," the man continued. "Since I'd been undefeated, the odds favored me to win, and Peele wanted as big a pay-out as possible. Peele told Mickey to bet I'd lose. And he did. Mickey was already rich, but he couldn't resist raking in a bit more off his best friend."

Chase took a small step forward. Tag didn't notice. "Are you sure he knew Peele would drug you?"

"Had to. Because I'd told Mickey that Peele had asked me to throw the fight, and that I'd refused."

"What did you do?" Chase was pretty sure he knew, but he wanted to keep Tag distracted. He took another small step. Haley screamed and reached out.

"For over a year, I had no idea. Until one day that the gym was closed for the evening. I'd forgotten something and went back in. The gym floor was dark, but I heard voices. Nora was saying she felt guilty about what they'd done to me. She thought Mickey should tell me the truth, fess up to how he'd bet on me to lose, which of course he refused to do. Because he never cared about anyone but himself. Not really. But Nora stayed silent, too.

I could tell from her conversation with Mickey that she'd known the whole plan *before* my fight. She could've warned me. And she didn't."

Haley cried and struggled in the high chair. Tag kept talking like he didn't even hear her. Haley's terror was like a knife raking Chase's skin.

"I called in sick for the next week. Asked Nora to cover for me, and she was so concerned. So worried about my wellbeing. Even brought me soup. That week, I almost gave up. But that would mean letting Mickey and Nora skate for what they'd done. So I started to plan instead. Preparing. Watching for exactly the right moment."

Chase shifted his weight forward. Took another step. *Hold on, princess*, he thought. *I'm coming.* "The day Mickey planned to meet Ruby in West Oaks?"

"Here's how treacherous Nora is. She betrayed Mickey, too. Told Decker that Mickey was planning to leave the circuit. Told him where and when Mickey would be alone and least likely to expect the attack. But by then, I was already watching everything she did at work. I knew her phone code, her email. I could've warned Mickey. But I came up with something better instead."

"You followed Decker to West Oaks?"

"I waited nearby, watching the building's exits. Decker arrived, went in, came out. He'd parked several blocks away, so I waited until he was gone and went up. There were people going in and out, moving furniture, but I made sure they didn't notice me. I found Mickey in his new apartment, nursing a bloody nose. Decker had threatened him not to leave the circuit, just like Nora had wanted. He didn't understand why I was suddenly there in West Oaks, but he was *so* glad to see me."

Tag smiled, eyes glassy as he remembered. Haley kept screaming.

"You were there when Ruby arrived," Chase said.

"The whole thing took longer than I'd expected. I'd meant to be gone by the time she was there."

"You wanted her to find Mickey's body? To get blamed by the police?"

"No, I never would've wanted that. The whole point was to blame Decker. I was going to plant the knife in his possession and call in a tip. But when Ruby showed up when she did, my whole plan got a little fucked up and delayed. I just had to get out and lie low for a while."

Chase couldn't understand how Tag had gotten out of the apartment building so quickly. The police had arrived within minutes after the 911 call. But maybe that didn't matter. He'd managed it. And he'd nearly destroyed Ruby's life.

"When Ruby got arrested?" Tag went on. "I wanted to help her. She was a victim in everything that happened, just like I—"

Chase's cell rang. It was like the spell over Tag had broken. He looked over at it.

Chase lunged.

He shoved Tag. The man toppled backward, his chair hitting the tile with a huge smack.

Chase grabbed hold of Haley. He yanked the harness free of the high chair lining. Ran for the door.

A fist hit his side, and Chase collided with the living room wall, shielding Haley with his arm. He swung his elbow and pivoted his body. The elbow connected hard with Tag's face, making the other man stumble back.

Tag was holding a knife. *Shit.* He must've pulled it from the block in the kitchen.

Chase grabbed for the door. Pulled it open. Dashed into the hall. He held Haley tight against his chest.

He was almost to the stairwell. But footsteps thudded behind him. Going fast.

The man was *running.*

What the hell?

Chase pushed himself to speed up. Doors in the hallway opened, curious neighbors peering out. "Call 911!" Chase shouted.

The doors slammed closed.

Chase reached the stairwell. He threw open the heavy fire door, and it collided with Tag. The man bellowed.

Chase practically leaped down the first steps to the landing. Turned. Careened down the next set of stairs.

Tag was still behind them. And his limp had vanished.

Chase would have stopped to hold his ground and fight. But he had Haley with him. Maybe he could take down Tag one-handed—maybe, depending on how strong the guy actually was—but Chase couldn't risk Haley getting caught in the middle.

So he kept running, feet pounding down the steps. He reached the second floor. Haley's screams echoed against the concrete walls.

Tag was a few yards back.

Chase saw the exit to the street at the bottom of the stairs.

He sprinted toward it.

Chapter Forty-Three

Shelby sped through a yellow light. "Dispatch said they'd send a car. But they asked for details, and I had to say I didn't know for sure Chase was in trouble."

Ruby tried calling him, but Chase didn't answer. She punched *End* on her screen.

The car was flying, and they were just a few minutes away. Ruby tried to keep her panic locked down. Chase would do anything to protect Haley. Ruby had faith in him.

But if something had happened to Chase?

"Please drive faster," she said through gritted teeth. Then she turned around. Nora was in the back seat. "Keep explaining. Who really killed Mickey?"

Back at Chase's house, Nora had almost bolted after seeing Shelby. And Ruby had almost let her go. But Nora still had information, and Ruby needed to know who might've gone to her apartment. And why.

But Ruby wasn't prepared for what Nora said next.

"Tag killed Mickey."

"*What*? Mickey was his best friend. Why would he do that?" The car swerved. Ruby grabbed hold of the seat.

"At first, I didn't understand it either," Nora rushed to say. "I saw Tag plant the knife in Decker's car, and I thought there had to be some mistake. Tag had found it somewhere else. Or maybe it wasn't the knife that had killed Mickey at all. For days, I had no idea what to think. And then I just decided I didn't *want* to know. Whatever was happening, I didn't want to be involved. That's when I saw you at the fight, and I tried to tell you to do the same."

"But the police *did* find the murder weapon in Decker's car. You put it back?"

"Of course I did. I hated him. I didn't know what role he'd played in Mickey's death, but I wasn't about to help him. I popped open the trunk and left the knife there. And when the police found the knife, it cleared your name, right? I just..." Nora shook her head. "I decided to forget about all of it. I didn't know whether to trust Tag, so I couldn't go back to Bailor Fitness. But I was just going to pretend I didn't know anything."

The car stopped short, and they all lurched forward. Shelby cursed. Another car honked. "Sorry," Shelby said. "Don't mind me." She steered them around the obstacle and pushed the accelerator.

"Then why did you have to leave LA today?" Ruby asked Nora.

"Because a friend on the circuit texted me that Adrian Peele had been murdered. Stabbed, just like Mickey. And it all clicked. I finally understood, and I knew Tag would come after me next."

"Why?"

"Because he blames me for what happened! The fight where Decker almost killed him. Tag blamed Mickey, so he killed him and tried to frame Decker for it. He killed Peele. The only one left was me. That was why he'd been trying to find me. Tag hadn't been worried about me. He wanted to *kill* me."

"I don't understand," Ruby cried. None of this made any sense, and Nora had been speaking so fast her words had blurred together. "Do you think it's Tag at my apartment?"

"Has to be," Nora said. "He's trying to find me. The only

reason I'm in this car right now is that Tag might try to use Mickey's daughter to get to me. I couldn't live with that."

If anything happens to Haley or Chase, Ruby thought, *then trust me, Nora. I won't let you live with it, either.*

"But I swear," Nora said, "I didn't think Tag would do this. I don't even know how he realized I'd come to West Oaks."

"Like you said. You had nowhere else to go."

Shelby turned onto Ruby's street. Street signs flew past, and her apartment building appeared. Shelby punched the gas.

From somewhere nearby, she heard sirens. But no squad cars were visible yet.

They were less than a minute away. But something poked her mind like a hidden splinter.

"There's something that doesn't fit," Ruby said. "If Tag killed Mickey, he would've had to run from the apartment before the police arrived. With his limp, how could he have moved that fast?"

Nora didn't reply. Ruby glared back. The other woman looked exhausted and pale. "When he planted the knife on Decker's car, I saw Tag walking normally. He's been faking it. I don't know for how long."

Which explained how a skilled fighter like Mickey could be attacked without even defending himself. He'd never expected Tag to move so fast.

And that meant Tag Bailor was an even greater threat than Ruby had imagined.

"There's the entrance!" Ruby shouted. Shelby had almost missed it. The car braked and swerved into the building's parking lot.

At the same moment, Chase burst through the side exit door and charged at full speed across the grassy area beyond the parking lot.

He was clutching Haley.

A second later, Tag emerged. Blood poured from his nose.

Tag had a knife in his hand.

"Don't stop the car." Ruby grabbed the steering wheel and aimed it at Tag.

"You want me to run him over?" Shelby cried. She started to brake. "That is not protocol."

"Shelby, *go*."

"Oh, fuck. Fine. Let's do this."

Shelby drove the car off the concrete. It bucked wildly as it cleared the curb and landed on the grass.

Tag looked over just as the car rammed into him. He flew across the hood. Rolled and fell to the grass.

Ruby didn't waste a moment. She grabbed her purse and threw open the car door. Ran.

Incredibly, Tag was struggling up to standing. A savage snarl had twisted his face.

Ruby dug into her purse.

She held out the taser and pressed the trigger. The prongs hit Tag in the chest. Instantly, he convulsed and fell back to the ground.

Ruby stood over him. "That's what you get for messing with me and my family. You piece of shit."

Chapter Forty-Four

Chase lay on one side of the bed, looking at the two most important people in his life. Ruby was facing him. Haley lay between them, and after many fits and starts, she'd finally gone to sleep.

The past few hours had been surreal. Chase had attended a hundred crime scenes before, but he'd never been one of the parents holding a screaming toddler, trying to comfort his family after the worst had happened. Well, nearly happened.

"You should try to rest," he whispered to Ruby.

"So should you."

"Too wired."

"Same here."

Chase just wanted to watch them and know they were okay.

Ruby rested her hand on Chase's neck, her thumb brushing over his jaw. "Thank you for taking care of Haley." A tear rolled onto her cheek, and she sniffled. "I can't believe how close Tag came to being able to…and he was *holding* her…"

"I know." Chase touched Ruby's face, mirroring her posture. Seeing her cry made his heart feel like it was tearing itself apart. "I know."

He'd heard the revving of the car's engine when it had

roared into the parking lot and jumped the curb. Then the terrible thud as the vehicle had plowed into Tag. Chase had pressed Haley's head against him, keeping her from looking.

Once again, Ruby had risked herself by running toward danger instead of away from it. But he'd also never been so relieved to see her.

Explaining things to the police afterward, Ruby had been calm and poised. Though she'd had plenty of strong language to convey how pissed off she was.

Only now was she showing how terrified she'd been, and Chase wanted to comfort her. Shield her. Take on her pain. Even though he couldn't.

Maybe it was enough that they were here together, sharing it.

"I'd protect Haley with my life," Chase said. "But you're always giving me a hard time about having a hero complex. If that description fits anyone here, I don't think it's me."

Ruby laughed, though she was still crying. "I'll stop giving you a hard time about protecting me if you can return the favor."

"I can try. But we might want to take turns being the hero. Because if one of us does something reckless, the other one needs to be the voice of reason."

"That would be wise." Ruby's eyes were so tired, but she kept forcing them open. "I wish I'd never gone to see Tag in the first place. If I'd stayed away from LA—"

"Then we'd have no idea who the real killer was. You'd still be heading for trial. And Nora would probably be dead."

Though Nora was far from Chase's favorite person at the moment. She could've ended all of this far sooner if she'd come forward.

The West Oaks DA's Office was going to have a hell of a time sorting out this convoluted mess. They were on their third suspect for Mickey Waverley's murder. But Tag had killed Adrian Peele too. He'd assaulted Mrs. Murtree, broken into Ruby's home. Held Haley as a hostage. *Something* was going to stick.

Especially if Lana took over the case. She'd arrived at the

scene tonight, as had half of Bennett Security. Devon had sobered up quick. It had been quite the circus—detectives, paramedics, patrol trying to keep the neighbors and the uninvited bodyguards out of the restricted area.

Mrs. Murtree was now at the hospital, and from the last they'd heard, she was recovering nicely. Devon and Aurora had gone with her so she wouldn't be there by herself.

Shelby was going to have tough questions to answer. A use of force investigation would be coming her way. Chase couldn't imagine Shelby would be disciplined after all the facts were known.

Chase had reported everything Tag had told him, including the man's confession about killing Mickey.

Ruby had been shocked by Nora and Mickey's betrayal of their friend.

To Chase, the most unnerving part of the story was how Tag had believed he was *helping* Ruby. Chase wondered if he'd even intended for Ruby to find Mickey's body, as if she would get some satisfaction out of it.

Maybe there was no way to understand Tag's line of thought.

At some point in the last two years, Tag must have fully recovered from his injuries. But instead of moving forward and living the life he had, he'd sacrificed everything for revenge.

"For a moment when I was talking with Nora," Ruby said, "I thought she'd actually killed Mickey. But she blamed herself for it. I'm still fuzzy on why Decker would come after me, though. Why did he come to the apartment and follow us?"

"He must've really believed *you* had killed Mickey. I think Decker planned to warn you not to drag him or Adrian Peele into it."

Which would also fit with everything Decker and Peele had said to one another at the fight. Decker had been afraid that Bennett Security's investigation would lead back to him because he'd actually been in Mickey's apartment.

This wasn't completely over. Chase and Ruby would probably have to testify in court. But he knew Ruby's biggest worry was about Haley. Whether she was okay.

"Will you stay for a few days?" Ruby asked. "I know we talked about you going back to your house, but Haley needs you. *I* need you."

"I'll stay as long as you like." He brushed at her tears with his thumb. "But I need you, too. I hope you know that. I need you both. I love you." He kept saying those words as Ruby's eyes closed. "I love you."

At some point, they must've fallen asleep. Because Chase woke to Haley patting him on the face. Ruby was still out.

"Chay-Chay. Luvoo."

His heart felt like it was swelling in his chest. "I love you too, princess. So much."

She smiled, showing off her tiny teeth. "Fies?"

"Fries for breakfast?" He laughed. "Why not." Chase grabbed his phone to check on Devon, Aurora, and Mrs. Murtree. They all deserved some comfort food.

~

Two Months Later

CHASE HEARD the front door open. Ruby was home from work.

"Smells good in here."

He'd just been putting their dinner in the oven to stay warm. He jogged to the door and greeted her with a kiss.

She dropped her bag onto the floor with a sigh. "Nice apron. But shouldn't you be naked under there? Isn't that how this scene goes?"

"This is a date, not a porno. Getting naked is for later."

She wrapped her arms around him. "But I want to get to the best part."

"Just gotta be patient."

"You know I hate being told that."

"But it'll be worth it. I promise."

Tonight would be Haley's first time sleeping away from Ruby since the day of Max and Lana's wedding—two months ago. It had taken Ruby a while to feel comfortable letting Haley go overnight. But the little girl was upstairs with Devon and Aurora, close enough that they could call if anything came up.

Chase had plans to take advantage of this alone time with his wife. She'd been stressed lately, and she deserved to relax.

And to be kissed and touched and *fucked*. At least, Chase was hopeful.

The corners of Ruby's mouth turned down. "Haley's had her dinner?"

"Aurora was making curry. I'm sure Haley loved it."

"And she's got her stuffed lamb? And extra diapers?"

Chase smoothed his hands down her arms. "Haley's going to have a blast with her aunt and uncle. I took care of everything."

"Of course you did. What's this date I've been hearing so much about?"

Chase took off the apron. He'd mostly worn it to make her laugh. "I cooked dinner. Well, I warmed it up, because I suck at actual cooking. But first, we're going to make something."

Ruby's eyebrows lifted. "Make something?"

"Not *that* something. Yet." He walked her further into the room and showed her the art supplies he'd set out on the kitchen table. "It's been a stressful couple of months. I thought you might want to do the art thing."

Her eyes shone. "You're the sweetest. And *definitely* getting a blow job later."

"That was my plan."

Chase's life had returned to normal in some ways. He was back on duty for West Oaks PD and getting along with his partner. Detective Murphy had become one of Chase's biggest defenders, and she'd been calling him in to help with some of their most important cases in major crimes.

He'd decided to wait on trying for detective. Chase was rooting for Shelby to make it, but he'd also heard that Sean Holt from the LAPD was interested in moving over to West Oaks.

Given the increase in crime in their town, Chase had to believe Holt's expertise would be welcomed.

The salon on Ocean Lane had begged Ruby to return, and for the time being, she was happy working there again. But Chase had encouraged her to put together a business plan and apply for a loan to get her own place. Whatever she decided, he would support her.

For now, she wanted to pay back Noah for Jane's legal fees, and Chase had been chipping in money each month for that fund as well.

He and Ruby had continued to live apart, getting together almost daily for dinner or just to spend time as a family. But Chase felt like their lives had finally settled back into a comfortable rhythm. He got to show Ruby how much he loved her every day, and even though she hadn't said those words back yet, he knew that they were serious about one another. For the moment, that was all he needed.

Well, that and a night of hot sex with his beautiful wife, being as loud as they liked.

They sat down at the kitchen table. Chase dabbed paint on his paper and watched Ruby add watercolor to her canvas. The tension in her shoulders unwound as her paintbrush moved. She made the different colors bleed together like an abstract sunset. It looked like something from a modern art gallery.

"That's beautiful." Chase held up his. "Mine looks like Haley made it."

"It's better than that. Slightly."

Chase laughed. "I can always count on you for honesty." He'd painted a heart with two smaller ones nested inside it. A yellow sun with a smiley face was in the middle. "The three hearts are for you and me and Haley. And the sun is how you make me feel."

"Aww. That is *cute*."

"I know, right?" He'd totally been trying to score points.

"It's gross how perfect you are. I just threw up in my mouth."

"I might get this heart design tattooed on my other butt cheek."

"You're officially no longer attractive."

"Should I be bad instead?" Chase dragged his finger through yellow, then feinted toward her.

"Hey!"

But instead of smearing the paint onto her nose, he kissed her.

"Mmm," Ruby murmured. "Are we finally getting to the good part?"

"You mean the *bad* part."

The moment quickly escalated into more, so Chase wiped his hand on a towel so he could kiss her properly. His hands dug into her hair, tipping her back as he claimed her mouth.

"What do you have planned?" Ruby's teeth bit into her lower lip, and Chase knew exactly what she wanted.

"Why don't I show you?"

He pushed their painting supplies to the far end of the table. He picked her up and set her on the tabletop. Ruby had on a pair of leggings, so he started there, tugging them down by the waistband along with her panties.

His cock strained against the zipper of his jeans. He couldn't wait to slide his tongue between her legs. Hear her moan.

She still had her dress on, thighs pressed together. He grabbed her knees. Thrust them apart. Pushed her dress up over her hips.

She cried out as his tongue moved over her core. Her hand went to touch him, but he grabbed it and twined their fingers together.

They hadn't had sex for days, so he went faster than he usually might. His teeth nipped at her labia, lips sucking at them. He flexed his tongue just the way she liked. Lapped up her wetness.

He couldn't get enough of the smell of her, the taste. Everything that made her Ruby.

She didn't hold back when she came, crying out and shoving her hips against his face.

Chase's dick was eager to come out and play. He unbuckled his belt. Undid his pants. He pulled a condom from his back pocket and started to unwrap it.

"Wait. You could fuck me without the condom. If you want."

A lightning bolt of desire singed down his spine into his balls. He did want. "Are you sure?"

He knew she was on the pill. But Ruby was usually so worried about the possibility of getting pregnant.

She nodded, expression relaxed after her orgasm. "I'm sure. I want to feel you. Just you."

Chase shucked off the rest of his clothes. Ruby stood up from the table. He thought she might take off her dress, but instead she only removed the fabric sash from her waist. It was a thin strip of silky black material.

"Bind my wrists?"

"I think you're the one with the plans tonight."

Her grin was devious. "I was fantasizing about you all day. I almost gave someone bangs instead of layers. Thank goodness I realized before the scissors closed."

He wound the fabric belt around her arms, tying them loosely together.

"Bend over the chair," he commanded.

Ruby obeyed, resting one knee on the seat, her bound wrists on the back of the chair.

Chase lifted her dress to expose her ass. He ran his hands over her thighs, then up her stomach beneath her clothing. He loved that he was naked, but she wasn't.

The tip of his cock found her opening, and he pushed into her wet heat.

The feeling of having her bare was indulgent. His balls wanted to empty into her, right then and there. Chase reached between his legs to tug on his sac, forcing himself back from the edge.

They both groaned as he started to move. Sliding into her,

pulling back out. Ruby's bound hands gripped the back of the chair.

He held onto her hips and thrust into her.

Sometimes Ruby wanted him demanding and dominant. Sometimes she liked things more equal. Sometimes she wanted a battle. It hardly mattered to Chase, though he did have his own preferences.

More than anything, he loved giving Ruby exactly what she needed. Seeing that look of pure pleasure on her profile made him hotter than anything else.

"Oh, fuck. Ruby. You feel so perfect." He held her tightly against him as his cock throbbed, shooting inside her. Chase laid his head against her shoulder, just relishing this moment.

When he withdrew, she stood up and draped her still-bound hands around his neck. Chase's arms circled her waist. "I love you," she said. "And I want you to move back in with me and Haley. For good."

Chase pressed his forehead to hers. He couldn't contain his smile. It really did feel like the sun was inside of him, shining out. As silly as that was. "I love you, too. And yes. I'd be thrilled to move back in. But we might need a bigger bed. And a bigger apartment."

He'd have to tell his cousin he was finally moving out of the bungalow.

Ruby laughed. "I'll keep working on my business plan and see what I can do."

Epilogue

TWO YEARS LATER

Ruby

"Do not follow me."

Ruby waddled into the hallway, holding her belly. "I want five minutes to myself."

But Chase wasn't listening. "What if something happens?"

"We're in a hospital. Doctors and nurses and midwives are everywhere."

Another contraction came, stealing her breath. Ruby moaned and bent over, bracing against the wall. She pointed a warning finger in Chase's direction when she heard footsteps.

"Don't. Even. Think about it."

She'd forgotten how much labor sucked. And she was sick of people hovering. Even her husband, who was usually one of her top two favorite people in the world.

Ruby breathed through the contraction until the overpowering pain had passed. Then she resumed her slow walk down the hall, keeping hold of the railing on the wall.

Another mom-to-be was coming toward her on the opposite side. The woman kept looking at her. Which was annoying. The entire universe right now was annoying.

Then the other mother said, "Ruby? Is that you?"

Ruby squinted at her. She wasn't sure how anyone would recognize her in her current state, not unless they'd seen her nine months pregnant, dressed in cheap institutional cotton, and looking like a mess before.

But Ruby remembered the face across from her, and it all started to make sense.

"*Destiny*?"

It was her cell mate from that night in West Oaks County Jail over two years ago. Ruby waved a hand at Destiny's huge stomach. "You too?"

"I know." Destiny hooked her thumb at the man with her. "Blame this guy and his strong swimmers."

"Mine's the one back there. Being all supportive. Like *that's* so hard when he doesn't have another human being inside of him that refuses to come out."

"Wait, I remember him. The cop?"

"Yep. We're married."

"So you two ended up together after all." Destiny lowered her voice to a stage whisper. "Happy ending? Or is the jury still out?"

Ruby looked back at Chase. He had his hands in the pockets of his jeans, leaning one shoulder into the wall, wearing a patient smile. Looking handsome and charming as ever.

During their two-plus years of marriage, they'd had fights and tough times. Especially when she'd been starting her salon business. And when Chase had been stressed during his first months as a detective. Or when Haley had broken her arm at preschool.

But she could say with certainty that those had been the happiest years of her life so far.

And now they were about to add to their family. Haley would be a big sister. If Ruby could just get this freaking baby into the world.

"The jury's out," Ruby said, "but they're impressed by what they've seen so far. What about you?"

"Doing a lot better than when I last saw you. I'm working towards a degree in social work. This baby will slow me down, but I'll get there."

"I'm sure you will."

"I feel like you and I only get to see each other for the tough parts." Destiny's face pinched. "Shit. Here comes another one." She held out her hand.

Ruby crossed the hallway and grasped Destiny's fingers, counting as the other woman breathed. The moment Destiny's contraction had finished, it was Ruby's turn.

She squeezed her eyes closed and crushed Destiny's hand with hers.

Maybe they'd only met during the tough parts. But those had also been the moments that they'd needed one another.

Finally they hugged, and Destiny shuffled off with her man. Ruby went back over to Chase.

Some of her friends, like Destiny, had only intersected with her life in brief, intense moments. Others had been with her day after day. Chase was the very best kind. Her closest friend, her partner. The man she loved. The person she'd always want on her team.

"Hi," Ruby said. "Want to walk with me?"

"I'd love to. Am I going to get yelled at?"

"I never yell." They continued down the hallway side by side. "But if you say 'No grumpy allowed,' I can't legally be held responsible for my actions."

Chase

THEY RENEWED THEIR VOWS BAREFOOT, right at the edge of the water. Chase held Haley, while Ruby had baby Kayla in a wrap over her sundress. Ruby had tucked flowers into Haley's braids, though she'd left her own hair loose. The strands moved in the breeze.

"The rings?" the officiant asked.

Chase tickled his daughter's stomach. "Haley, this is your part."

"Oh. I forgot." She pulled the two rings from the pouch she was holding. "Why did you take them off if you want them back on?"

There were a few laughs among their friends and family. People often joked that Haley sounded wise beyond her three and half years.

"It's part of the ceremony." Chase slid the band onto his wife's hand. He recited the vows that he'd crafted carefully, that he'd pondered and agonized over until the words were just right to capture what was inside him.

"Ruby, you know me better than anyone does. You've accepted me exactly as I am, and at the same time you inspire me to be more. I promise to love you and our children with my whole heart. Forever."

Haley held the second ring out. "Here, Mommy."

"Thank you, bug." Ruby smiled and took his hand. "Chase, because of you I know what it's like to feel truly safe and content. Your love has given me the courage to take risks I never would've imagined. I choose you as my partner, as the love of my life, and I can't wait to keep giving you all the love you deserve."

She replaced Chase's ring on his finger.

These were the rings they'd used at the county clerk's office over two years ago. Chase had bought them from the only jewelry store that had been open in West Oaks that Monday morning, a fancy place on Ocean Lane. He'd never told Ruby that they were platinum and had cost half a month of his patrol officer's salary.

Chase had offered to buy her something flashier, like a diamond or sapphire or fire opal. Whatever she wanted within the limits of their current savings, which were depleted after buying a condo and renting a space for Ruby's salon. But he was glad she'd still wanted their original rings. Not because of the expense, but because it was sentimental. Chase was a softy like that.

After the vows, they got to his favorite part—the kiss. He leaned over and pressed his lips to Ruby's. Their audience clapped and cheered.

Haley tapped his shoulder. "That's enough, Daddy." The cheers turned to laughter, and the little girl frowned. "Why are they laughing?"

"Because they're having fun."

Chase had wanted to renew their vows sooner, but time had gotten away from them. There'd been too much everyday stuff to deal with. Not just adult responsibilities but rich, meaningful moments, too. Spontaneous afternoons driving along the coast. Weekends spent camping with Devon and Aurora and their little boy.

"I want to play now," Haley said.

Chase set Haley down and grabbed Ruby's hand, pulling her into another kiss. He longed for a few minutes alone with her. But their guests had surrounded them, eager to offer congratulations.

Megan swooped in for a group hug. "So proud of you both."

"I know this isn't the high-class shindig you were hoping for," Chase said.

"Nonsense. This is perfect. Besides, I got to dress up for Devon and Aurora's."

Bennett Security employees Sylvie and Tanner appeared next, along with their significant others, Nic and Faith. "I've never been to a beach wedding before." Faith elbowed her husband. "We should've had one of these!"

"And my mom would never have forgiven me." Tanner and Faith had gotten married on his family's farm the year before. They'd announced Faith's first pregnancy just a few months ago. Tanner shook Chase's hand. "Good job, man. Happy for you."

"You, too."

"And congrats on baby Kayla!" Sylvie said. "She slept through that ceremony like a champ."

Ruby patted the baby, who continued to snooze inside her wrap. "She'll sleep anywhere and everywhere except at home at night."

Sylvie had become one of Ruby's closest friends, and as far as Chase could tell, the woman practically lived at Bennett Security. She had an army of underlings and must've made serious bank, if you judged by Sylvie and Nic's swanky new home in the West Oaks hills.

Nic owned a contemporary art gallery on Ocean Lane. Chase had been getting to know Nic and learning about photography from him. Chase didn't think he'd ever be artistic, but every dad needed some camera skills, right?

There were friends here from West Oaks PD, too. Angela Murphy, Sean Holt. Shelby, who was Kayla's godmother. Jane Simon was talking to Lana, who'd just been appointed the West Oaks District Attorney after her boss had left unexpectedly. Lana planned to run for the spot in the next election.

Noah and Danica were in New York right now, so they hadn't made it today. They'd sent their love instead. The pair had eloped earlier that year in Hawaii, and Noah had retired from his duties as a bodyguard to work with Danica at the Foster-Grant Foundation full time. But the two had a tendency to show up in magazines, which Ruby loved bringing home whenever she spotted them at the grocery store.

These days, Tanner and Devon shared captain duties at Bennett Security, wrangling their team of two dozen bodyguards to protect the wealthiest citizens of Southern California. But Max still contributed his company's resources for free to law enforcement and to some criminal defendants.

Every once in a while, Chase got to work with Devon on a case. Half the time they bickered, but damn, they got shit done and laughed really hard, too.

Ruby got roped into a conversation, so Chase went to check on Haley. He found her over on the playground, where half their wedding guests had migrated.

Haley ran over to him. "Daddy, I want to play with that girl, but she won't let me." Haley pointed at the three-year-old Max and Lana had recently adopted. The little girl was holding fast to Max's leg.

"Sweetheart, not everybody wants to do the same thing. Why don't you go down the slide? Maybe she'll see how much fun you're having and come join you. But it has to be her choice."

Haley's frown said she didn't appreciate that advice.

"Or you could go swing with Kellen." Haley's cousin was in the baby swing, pushed by Aurora and Devon.

Haley liked that even less. "Kellen's too little. He can't do big-kid things like me. I'm going to build a sand castle with Grandma Tessa."

"Okay, bug. You do that." Chase didn't call her princess anymore. He'd eventually come around to Ruby's side on that issue. He figured Haley could be a princess if she wanted, but she had lots of other options too. Like warrior, firefighter, ballerina, or president. Just to name a few.

Haley ran over to Tessa Waverley, who was chatting with Chase's dad, of all people. But the two of them didn't know many others here. And they both lit up with smiles at seeing Haley. They had that much in common.

Chase's sister hadn't been able to make the trip for the renewal ceremony, but she'd visited California with her family several times in the last couple of years. She, Chase, and their father had been mending their relationship. They probably would never be as close as Ruby's family, but they'd made progress. Chase's dad had been kinder since he'd met his grandkids, as if their influence had softened him.

As for Tessa Waverley, the court-ordered visitations had continued for a while, until they'd no longer been necessary. Chase was proud of Ruby for making such an effort to bring Mickey's family into their daughter's life. When Haley had asked, Chase and Ruby had explained that her biological father had died, but that Chase was her father now.

He'd adopted Haley. Chase loved Kayla every bit as much, but there was a special connection that came with choosing to make Haley his daughter. A bond that wasn't based on blood but purely on love.

Chase saw his wife was alone, and he went over to steal a few moments with her. "Hey, having a good time?"

She smiled up at him. Ruby looked beautiful every day, but today she was especially stunning. Her hair had lightened a bit from Sundays spent outside planting vegetables in the community garden near their condo. Her cheeks were flushed with sun and contentment. "Never better."

Chase bent to kiss Kayla's sleeping head. "We're lucky," he said. "We have so many amazing people in our lives."

"We do."

Together, they watched their guests chatting, laughing, playing.

Ruby put her arm around him. "I've been thinking about something Destiny said when I saw her at the hospital. She asked if you and I have a happy ending. But I don't think it's the ending that makes the story. The best stuff happens along the way, probably when we're not expecting it. And I love getting to share all the in-between stuff with you."

Chase couldn't think of anything better to say than that. He didn't want to think about endings. He just wanted to keep loving Ruby—loving all his girls—as long as forever lasted.

The End.

The world of West Oaks continues with THE SIX NIGHT TRUCE! Jane Simon and Sean Holt go from enemies to lovers in this action-packed, suspenseful love story.
Don't miss it!

More from Hannah Shield

Hart County Series

Starcrossed Colorado (Ashford & Emma)

Moonlit Colorado (Dane & Grace)

Stormswept Colorado (Teller & Ayla)

Sunkissed Colorado (Callum & Zandra)

Homeward Colorado (Grayden & Piper)

~

Last Refuge Protectors

Hard Knock Hero (Aiden & Jessi)

Bent Winged Angel (Trace & Scarlett)

Home Town Knight (Owen & Genevieve)

Second Chance Savior (River & Charlotte)

Iron Willed Warrior (Cole & Brynn)

One Last Shot (Dean & Keira)

~

West Oaks Heroes

The Six Night Truce (Janie & Sean)

The Five Minute Mistake (Madison & Nash)

The Four Day Fakeout (Jake & Harper)

The Three Week Deal (Matteo & Angela)

The Two Last Moments (Danny & Lark)

The One for Forever (Rex & Quinn)

~

Bennett Security

Hands Off (Aurora & Devon)

Head First (Lana & Max)

Hard Wired (Sylvie & Dominic)

Hold Tight (Faith & Tanner)

Hung Up (Danica & Noah)

Have Mercy (Ruby & Chase)

About the Author

Hannah Shield writes spicy, suspenseful romance with pulse-pounding danger, fun & flirty banter, and tons of heart. Both a Californian and a Texan in her past, she now lives in the Colorado mountains with her family.

Visit her website at www.hannahshield.com and join her newsletter to get access to bonus content and never miss a new release.

www.ingramcontent.com/pod-product-compliance
Lightning Source LLC
LaVergne TN
LVHW091106080826
845145LV00008B/1827
* 9 7 8 1 9 5 7 9 8 2 1 1 3 *